The
GΩD STRING

Book 1 of The God String series

By
MONTGOMERY THOMPSON

Copyright ©2020 Montgomery Thompson

All rights reserved

ISBN: 1463736657
ISBN-13: 978-1463736651

DEDICATION

For my Pauline, proof that love wins.

Chapter 1

Babylon Gone

'Yesterday's weirdness is tomorrow's reason why.'
~Hunter S. Thompson

The blank face of the LED clock stared at Rand Carter from across the landscape of the pillow. The power was out.

"Moira?" He reached over, searching the other side of the bed but she wasn't there. He lifted his head and squinted into the bathroom. She wasn't there either. *Odd*, he thought, *it's usually her that sleeps in*. He called out again as he pulled on his robe then went to investigate the other two rooms in the small flat. Steadying himself against the kitchen door, he stared into the empty living room. She had never not been there.

"What the hell?" He grumbled.

He went to the window, pushed aside the heavy curtains and peered down from his second story flat to the street. The city of Omagh glistened as the sun briefly broke through the low clouds, making him wince.

He cranked open the window. "Moira?" He shouted down to the street, but there didn't seem to be anyone around. At the curb was their old green Vauxhall, crushed against a white van. Broken glass was scattered across the road but it wasn't only his car; the carnage continued up the small hill that lead towards the center of town. Empty vehicles lay askew in the streets, abandoned.

"Holy shit."

He flung the door open, ran down the stairs and stumbled into the still-life of chaos. Cars were jammed up against buildings and hung up on bent-over street signs. Oil and other liquids pooled in the street and black smoke rose above the skyline in the distance, but these things took a backseat to a realisation that froze him to the core.

Where the hell is everybody?

Except for his pounding heart, the town was dead quiet.

"Moira!" He yelled up the street. "Hello? Is anybody here?" He cupped his hands, "Hello?"

The only answer was the sound of glass crackling under his feet. He felt fear starting to take hold of him. He struggled to fight it off.

Wait. He thought. *Slow down. Think. Ignore the missing people and just focus on Moira. Where could she be? Down at the store maybe? No, she would have taken the car. Maybe she saw the accident and she went with the cops to make a statement. That doesn't make any sense, she would have me woke up, and this is no fender bender. Okay, okay try another idea… Earthquake?*

There were no cracks in the asphalt or downed power lines. Besides, earthquakes were rare in Ireland. In the middle of the thought he realised he was bare-footed and standing on broken glass in a pool of anti-freeze. Carefully he picked his way back through the hazards, his heart racing. When he reached the stairs he brushed the glass shards from his feet and went back up to the apartment. As soon as he got back inside he grabbed his cell phone and tried everyone he could think of, but no one was answering. Out of options, he stood for a long moment. Then, as if something gently shoved him forward, he got moving again.

He rifled through the closet and put on some rugged clothes. Searching the town looked like it was going to be hazardous so he tossed a few tools into a daypack and headed for the door. Outside, the sun had been covered by a blanket of high, grey clouds. He decided to start by investigating the mess in the street.

When you get into an accident you get out of the car and go see if anyone is hurt. He circled the damaged car. *You don't just close the door, walk off and leave the keys in the ignition.* He eyed the sky and the pillars of smoke in the distance. *Maybe it was a nuke?*

It was a stretch. He knew an EMP burst would have disabled anything electrical, but it couldn't explain what happened to all of the people. He continued up the hill to John's Street, the sense of dread grew stronger with each step. The street was typical of an Irish town; a curving, narrow, one-way lane flanked on either side by unbroken rows of buildings. On the corner was Sally's Pub, his regular gig. As an American musician, Rand was treated warmly, especially since he showed an interest in Trad music. But the bar, so full of patrons and music the night before, was now silent, cold and empty.

Farther up, a line of cars blocked the street. He climbed over them reluctantly. The sound of his work boots on the buckling sheet metal echoed through the quiet street, making him feel small and alien. At the end of the pile up, he slid down the trunk of a black sedan, but stumbled when his foot landed on something in the road. He quickly recovered and realised that he had stepped on a motorcycle.

The bike lay on its side with the front wheel stuffed half underneath the car's front passenger door. Wrestling it out from under the car, he stood it up. Aside from some scrapes it was undamaged. Rand had spent a lot of his time growing in Montana on dirt bikes. Though his gut twisted at the thought of taking someone's bike, he knew it was his best option for navigating the tangled streets. The keys were still in the ignition so he hit the starter. As the bike rumbled to life he reassured himself that it would be okay to borrow it considering the circumstances.

Soon he was weaving his way through the town, hoping that he would find an answer, but each curve only revealed the same tangle of fender benders and streets devoid of people. He came out at the end of John's Street at the top of a long hill that started at City Hall and dove straight through the center of the High Street. He stopped and surveyed a route through the maze of cars. From the bottom of the hill the street rose again into another small crest. From there, it descended past the tall glass Omagh Bomb Memorial, across and intersection and into an area known as Campsie. At the crest of the second hill, he could see the red sign of their local grocery store. If Moira had stepped out, the store is where she was most likely to be.

He picked out his route and started to roll forward when he heard a high pitched whine grow as it echoed across the sky. His vision was blocked by the rows of buildings and low clouds but the sound was unmistakable - it was a plane. The shriek ended suddenly and a massive thud shook the ground. Rand ducked instinctively. A mushroom cloud of black smoke rose over the buildings. He judged it at seven to ten miles away, but it was hard to know for sure.

Filled with a renewed sense of urgency he gunned the bike and raced to the store. Skidding to a stop on the sidewalk, he flipped down the kickstand and climbed over the hood of a car that had roosted in the middle of a pair of crumpled sliding doors.

"Moira? Moi! Are you in here?" His boots slid on the broken safety glass. "Is anybody in here?"

He worked his way through the dim aisles clutching his crowbar and watching for looters but the shelves remained undisturbed. Rand quickly explored the back store room with his little flashlight but found no one. On his way toward the front door he grabbed supplies - ibuprofen, a bigger flashlight and batteries from the utility section, a large bottled water and a few packs of apple danish. Back outside he sat on the bike, ate the pastry and considered his next move.

There are no signs of panic or exodus. He thought. *It looks like everyone just stopped in the middle of what they were doing and left or just vanished.* He was beginning to think the evidence pointed to the latter. *But people just don't disappear. There must have been some kind of accident.* He rewound events. He had slept hard last night. He couldn't remember the last time he had slept so deeply. *Probably because of those pints.* There was some dream, it was like he was floating in nothingness and he had to get back. A flash of light, he remembered, it brought him back, that's when he woke up. *Maybe Moira heard the accident or whatever it was. She woke up, looked outside, saw the chaos and panicked. Or she got involved trying to help someone and got injured herself.* The idea seemed feasible. *So she might be at the hospital*, he thought, *or maybe she's back home.* That was enough for him.

He fired up the bike and retraced his way back to the apartment. Somehow, he knew before even opening the door that she wouldn't be there. The place had a different energy about it when she was around. Usually coming home felt like walking into a sanctuary, unassailable and secure. Now it was a broken fortress, a violated space where tragedy had tumbled in and lay heavily, obstructing his every step.

He took a minute to leave a note on the door: *I'm out looking for you. Stay here and I will check back. XO Rand.* He tacked it to the door with duct tape then stuffed the tape back into his daypack. He closed the door with a sourness in his gut. It was a feeling that cut through all the turbulent emotion of the day. He knew it well - the feeling of goodbye. It streamed off his shoulders as he sped away, trying to stretch him back to that place. Five miles later it stretched itself thin and finally broke.

"That was then, this is now." He muttered.

It was his dad's mantra, his solution to every problem. Every time Rand scraped his knee or fell off his bike it was "So it hurts. Walk it off. That was then, this is now." Rand opened the throttle, pressing on to the hospital; his next bastion of hope.

Back past the store and down the hill, the emergency flashers on a double parked truck made him slam on the brakes. The door was open. It was the first vehicle he had seen with signs of life. Climbing off the bike, he looked inside the cab. Everything was normal. There was a cell phone and a clipboard with papers on the passenger seat. He found the CB radio and keyed the mic.

"Hello is anyone there? Can anyone hear me?"

Channel by channel he broadcasted the same thing, but there was no response. Turning on the stereo he was rewarded with only static, but the radio gave him an idea. *Maybe I should go to the radio station and broadcast a message,* he thought, *kind of like what Will Smith did in that zombie movie...* the thought made him stop short. *Zombies? Don't be ridiculous.*

"Focus." He scolded himself aloud. Throwing the CB mic onto the floor he jumped out of the truck. "Get to the hospital, that's my mission." He started the bike and accelerated down the street.

The rest of the ride to the hospital was a blur. As he pulled into the parking lot, the scene was hauntingly familiar; an ambulance parked out front with the doors open, a stretcher haphazardly lay against the curb with bloodstains on the sheets and of course, cars everywhere. He drove the bike right through the automatic doors and into the lobby. The power was on. *Must be back up generators.* At the reception desk, he found the mic for the PA system.

"Hello?" he said hesitantly. "Is anyone here?"

He listened for a second. Down the corridors a symphony of alarms beeped and whistled like a flock of electric birds. He keyed the mic again and spoke loudly.

"Anyone in the hospital please come to the reception area immediately."

A sudden thud shook the floor and he heard a crash from far off inside the building. Rand took off at a run, checking rooms as he went. Through waiting rooms with phones dangling off the hook, surgery with IV's hanging loose, dripping anaesthesia, calling out as he worked his way towards the sound. The smell of smoke reached him just before he rounded a corner and found the source of the explosion.

Flames and smoke poured out of a pair of double doors that lead into the cafeteria. He pulled a fire extinguisher off the wall mount and edged through the doors. The heat poured through the doors but the fire was still over fifty feet away. He crouched and shielded his face with one hand as he inched closer, pulsing the extinguisher. The CO_2 cooled the air in front of him as he crept down the hall searching for the source of the blaze.

Through the smoke he spied a stack of oxygen bottles in a cart parked next to a flaming doorway that lead to the kitchen. One had already blown through the suspended ceiling and embedded into the concrete. The rest of the rack was ready to go any moment.

He dove for a door on his left. Crashing through it, he found himself tumbling down a flight of stairs. Above him the oxygen bottles went critical in a deafening machine-gun series of hard pops followed by the shrill white noise of the gas escaping. A bottle shot through the door, ricocheting off the wall in a fiery arc. It glanced off the railing just above Rand's head then tumbled down to the landing below where it spun, hissing and clanging in a tantrum until it finally rattled to a stop. Rand, shaken and bruised, cursed and looked up to see if any more projectiles were coming his way.

The metal door at the top of the stairs was still closed but the top corner was bent inward where the gas cylinder has burst through. Flames flicked through the opening and smoke started to fill the stairwell. Rand quickly descended the rest of the stairs to the bottom and took the only door out. He quickly closed it behind him and peered down a wide hallway. Fluorescent lamps on the ceiling came to life, triggered by a motion detector. The flickering tubes lit the pale green walls of the long, tiled corridor in a yellowish light. It gave the place a toxic feel. A slender arrow on a plastic sign pointed the way: *Morgue*.

He worked his way down the hall, his heart rate rising with each step. Slinging off his backpack he rummaged around and retrieved the big flashlight and his headlamp, the elastic band fit snugly and the bright LED beam cut through the insipid light. Still, the tight beams made the hallway seem smaller, giving him a claustrophobic feeling. He was underground with fire above him, no windows and only the dead to greet him. By the time he reached the stainless steel door fear was steaming through his pores. With every sinew strung tight he peered through the wire laced window of the stainless steel doors.

Swallowing hard he raised the heavy aluminium flashlight and shuffled cautiously into the room. He was greeted by the smell of rubbing alcohol and rotten onions. The room was larger that he would have thought. Like some kind of macabre kitchen, every surface was either was white tile or stainless steel. Two examination tables stood clean and, much to Rand's relief, unoccupied. But then he saw the little refrigerator doors lined up in neat little squares on the wall. He held the flashlight like a baseball player ready to swing. His hands slick on the grip of the torch, he approached the wall of little doors. *There's no such thing as zombies.* He repeated to himself. He wiped his sweaty hands and approached the first door.

A paper label had been slipped into a small holder, a sure sign of occupancy. With one hand he reached out slowly, clinched his teeth and lunged at the handle. He jumped back as the door swung open, banging against the wall. For a moment he stood, eyes wide, breathing heavily, poised to strike. Sweat rolled down his forehead as he summoned the courage to look inside. The bulging, thick black plastic bag confirmed the presence of a body. Rand quickly said a blessing over them and slid it back into the freezer. Feeling like an idiot, he breathed sigh of relief. There were no zombies in here. After looking at all the labels on the doors he confirmed that none of them was anyone he knew and left to continue his search.

He opened the door back into the stairwell cautiously, keeping an eye on the bent door at the top of the stairs. He made his way up and carefully cracked open the door. The fire alarm continued to bray out its nasally warning. The area was clogged with smoke and dripping water from the sprinkler systems, but the fire hadn't spread. He held his breath and ran to the exit of the cafeteria and into the clear air. Pausing to take a few gulps of water he considered his next move. *There's no way the whole place is empty.* He thought. *I can't be the only person left in the world.* It made absolutely no sense. He continued on through the hospital, searching, but the more he looked, the more he suspected that he wouldn't find anyone.

It took him over an hour to go through the place room by room. With the exception of the dead, the rooms were bare. Standing at the end of the last hallway he quietly closed the door to a cleaning closet and stood dumbly. He had been fighting with every ounce of creative problem solving he could muster, but the facts remained.

"Everyone is gone." The statement hung in the sterile air.

Not knowing what to do he worked his way back to the lobby, numb and exhausted. He knew there was one more place he had to check just to be sure he had tried every possibility. Moira's brother Niall lived on the outskirts of Omagh. Fifteen minutes later he was standing at Niall's door. He knocked first but when no one answered he broke the glass pane on the door, reached in and opened the latch.

"Moira? Niall? You guys okay? It's Rand."

Silence, but he searched anyway to no avail. As he came back downstairs he spotted a picture of Moira and Niall hanging by the front door. He stared at her face, then slumped to the floor as tears reddened his eyes. He was going to marry her. He remembered her smile while he played music at the pub; the firelight dancing in red flickers among the strands of her dark hair. How could she just be gone? No sickness, no car accident, no reason, just gone. And her brother... Niall was a wonderful, smiling man, just gone. What about his two boys and his wife? What about their lives? Was everything they lived for; all the kindness they did, all the effort, struggle, pain and joy for nothing?

He was filled with confusion, anguish and rage; did God take them? Did aliens take them? Did Jesus come back? Why was he left behind? His mind turned and turned like a trapped animal trying to find its way to freedom. Why didn't he see it happen? Why did he just sleep through the morning? Squeezing his eyes shut he fought anger and tears. Pushing himself away from the wall he took a stand on his knees.

"Lord, what is going on? Why was I left here? Help me find the answers to this, this... what must be one of the greatest mysteries that your creation has ever known. You can't have abandoned your children. I know we were bad, I mean, hell, we made Babylon look like kindergarten! But we have a lot of redeeming qualities as well."

It wasn't working. He was fighting to maintain composure but the unfairness of it all overwhelmed him.

"What is this, some kind of test? You want to see what I can take? Is this some kind of old school, old testament bullshit?"

He flinched at his words and remembered when he once asked his parish priest, 'If God is goodness itself, and God made everything, then what is evil?' The priest looked at him like he was an idiot and replied, 'Evil isn't a thing unto itself, it's the absence of God, it is nothing.' But there wasn't nothing. He was still here and so were the birds and the town and the sky…the world was still here, he just seemed to be the only one in it.

Seemed. He rested on that.

"I'm sorry." He said, getting the upper hand on his rage, "I am sure you have a perfectly good reason for all of this." He cradled his head. "After all, if I'm the only person around then I guess I get special attention don't I?"

He cried quietly, sitting on the stairs looking at the picture of Moira, until he couldn't any longer. Small and spent from the weight of the day; cried out, worn out, bruised and hungry, he got up, wiped his eyes and looked at himself in the hallway mirror.

"Right, I guess that was inevitable. I think you need a beer mister."

Daylight was beginning to fade. He knew he couldn't face a night in Niall's house, and certainly not his and Moira's flat. He needed some place familiar but not personal. Sally's Pub would do. The narrow roadway of John's Street was beginning to get dark as the October sun peeked below the clouds and touched the treetops. Sally's dark green wood columns supported a sign header with elegantly carved gold lettering. The double doors of the main entrance were narrow, about the size of a regular door split in two. They were locked.

That means that everyone must have vanished before they opened this morning. Turning his attention to the door he thought through the problem of gaining entry. *I could go through a window but then it will be impossible to heat the place.* The crowbar wouldn't be of much use as the doors were reinforced against break-ins. Feeling like a bit of a criminal, he sighed and made his decision. He chose a little Ford, it would fit in the door frame and the keys were still in it. He started it up reluctantly. He had always liked those doors, dammit, but there was nothing for it. With apologies to the owners, he aimed the car and stomped on the accelerator.

The violence of the impact surprised him. He wasn't going that fast but the jolt was more than he'd bargained for. The real shock came from the air bag slamming him in the face. It was like being punched by a large boxing glove. He batted the air bag down as the engine knocked, choking on its mangled radiator and belts. Okay, he thought, you're in, maybe not so much bravado next time MacGyver. He got out and surveyed his handiwork.

"Are you kidding me?" He groaned.

The car had broken through the outer doors but the identical inner doors were also locked. There was no way the car would fit into that tiny entryway. In frustration, he pushed the little car back and stomped over to the back of a large SUV parked on the sidewalk. Smashing out the rear window he lifted the mat and fished out a lug wrench. After a few minutes, he had the spare tire off the mounts on the rear door. Lunging, he heaved the tire against the doors. With a dull crack, the bolt gave way a bit, just enough to encourage him. The big tire bounced past him, crunched against the little Ford's windshield then fell and wobbled with a metallic scrape in the street. Exasperated, he attacked with the crowbar. Hacking away chunks of wood until, at last, the lock surrendered. Sweat ran down his face, and his hands hurt from the effort. As he forced the damaged door open he thought, *They make it look so easy in the movies.*

The bar was cold and dim and smelled like stale beer and bleach. Only ten minutes after six and it was already getting dark. Winter was coming. He found some matches behind the bar and lit some table candles. Faux weathered walls gave a homely feel to the room which was large enough to host over a hundred people. Heavy, dark wood furniture was generously upholstered with leather or red velour. The walls were lined with wooden booths, shelves and benches and trimmed with large wooden beams. Next to the corner booth where the musicians sat, was the ample fireplace. A large basket of turf and a bucket of coal were still there, restocked from the night before.

Rand thought about the staff closing up the bar the night before. *I left around ten after two in the morning. They usually open at lunch, around one in the afternoon. So everyone must have disappeared somewhere between half two in the morning and at least an hour before I woke up around half-eleven.* He found the thought unsettling. *That was only this morning.* It seemed like so long ago. To keep himself distracted, he poured himself a pint of Guinness. While it settled he found a newspaper and rolled up sheets for the fire. Soon it was kicking a cheerful, warm heat into the room. It was a small comfort, but a comfort nonetheless.

Just as he began to relax, a loud boom shook the ground. It was too far away to be worried, but close enough to startle him. Darkness had settled in as he went outside to look around. Dogs barked throughout the town. As his eyes adjusted, he could see spots of glowing orange reflecting on the low clouds. The smell of burning buildings drifted down the street in the evening breeze. *Fuel tank maybe?* He wondered at the source of the explosion. *Doesn't seem close enough to spread to me.* He went back inside and settled at the bar.

He wondered if it was world-wide. He might even be the last man on earth. Then again, if he had survived, it was likely that others had too. He wondered how many people had a day like his. *Were they also trying to cozy up in their local pub?* Who were they? Who was the smartest one of them and what were they doing? He became grim.

"They are me and I'm getting my shit together, starting right now."

He grabbed a pen and paper from behind the bar and began to brainstorm aloud. "Okay, what's first? Food, it's everywhere but it will be going bad." He scribbled the list. "The power is gone. Of course, there are canned goods, dehydrated food and military rations. Still, I need to be able to hunt and protect myself. When Katrina hit New Orleans it didn't take long for abandoned pets to become dangerous hunting packs."

He had done a lot of hunting growing up in Montana and was familiar with most types of firearms. He knew he would need a rifle for game, a shotgun for birds and a pistol for protection. He started thinking about all the movies he had seen with similar scenarios to his. It would be difficult to locate firearms in Northern Ireland but it was becoming clear that it was a priority.

He looked at the broken door. *It was harder than it looked getting into this place. I'm going to need a sure fire way to break into to buildings to get what I need.* He continued to add things to the list. It was clear that he would need to make a trip to an outdoor store and a military or police facility. He could not remember ever having seen an army surplus store in the area. He guessed that maybe it only an American thing. *Still, the cops in this part of the world are equipped like an army. I should find a lot of supplies there.* The list grew and he started to form a plan. Suddenly, a noise at the broken door made him freeze. He slowly reached over and picked up the fire poker. Something was definitely coming inside.

At the door, a pair of eyes shone in the firelight. They were big but low to the ground as they peered around the cracked doorframe. He raised the fire poker over his shoulder and said aloud, "If you want a piece of me, you're gonna pay a high price."

The eyes didn't move. He crept slowly toward the door in his best kung-fu stance, muscles tensing. A sharp bark launched him about a foot into the air. A black and white Collie approached sheepishly, tail wagging. Rand lowered the poker and exhaled.

The God String

"Come here, c'mon boy." Rand encouraged with a hand held out. The dog gave him a sniff but refused to come closer. The dog's nose was working overtime but quickly went from Rand to the door leading to the kitchen. Rand put on his headlamp and went to look in the kitchen. A minute later he came back out with a loaf of bread, cold chicken breast and some bananas.

"You're probably wondering why nobody brought you your dinner."

More movement at the door caught his attention as another little dog came cautiously into the bar. Rand watched it curiously. *There must be a lot of hungry dogs in the world tonight. I have to get that door closed before this place turns into a kennel.*

The little dog cleared the broken glass and wood splinters on the floor and came straight over to Rand at a quick trot. It looked like a three-pound hairball that had been puked up by a washing machine. It was the ugliest dog he'd ever seen. It's stringy fur appeared dingy in splotches of tan and white. Curiously expressive, bulgy eyes gazed up at him as it tilted it's head. The tip of its tongue stuck out of a pushed in nose through exposed bottom teeth that showed even though its mouth was closed. Amazingly, it didn't stink.

Sniffing the air, it moved closer. Rand reached out slowly as he risked petting the small dog, but it was more interested in the bread on the floor. As he got closer the collie raised its upper lip. The effect on the little dog was immediate. He launched himself at the collie with such a ferocious noise that even Rand flinched backwards. The collie yelped and bolted out of the room. The little dog stood for a moment then snorted and came back, trotting past the bread and directly to Rand.

"You're a tough little guy aren't you? Hungry too by the looks of it." The little dog just looked at him, then turned to look at the pile of food. Back and forth the little dog's gaze shifted. Rand, food, Rand, food…

Suddenly it dawned on Rand. "Oh! You're waiting for my permission." Rand was impressed. Scooping him up, he picked up a small piece of chicken and held it out. It took the offering gently and, without so much as a single chew, swallowed it whole. "Go for buddy." He set the dog down and checked its collar while it ate. There were two tags, one for shots and an owner's tag.

"Spang. Who names their dog Spang?"

The dog looked up at him for a second then went back to his feast. Rand sat and watched him for a minute, sipped his beer and let his tired mind wander.

He would give anything to see Moira walk through that door. Rand fought off the daydream, finished his beer and got up to take stock of his supplies. While he was going through the gear, another dog came in the door but only made it half way in before Spang chased it off. Finished with his meal, the little dog got comfortable and lay down facing the fire. Rand laughed quietly. *You sure know what you like don't you?* Shaking his head he came back to the table.

"A dog with a plan, I like it. Good boy Spang."

Spang just looked up at him then rested his head back down on his paws. To keep out any more intruders Rand put a table on its side and pushed the two doors closed then rolled a keg against it all. He checked around the other entrances to the bar. There was a door at the end of the bathroom hallway that lead to the dance club, with a grunt he slid the jukebox in front of it then nodded with satisfaction. Returning to the bar, he poured another beer and thought about the possibility that there were still other people out there. He had to assume that there were. Whoever and wherever they were it was his mission now to find them and try to figure out what to do next. He continued the trend of talking to himself, but now it was partly to Spang.

"I'm going to need a lot of light." He continued with the list. "Tomorrow I'll pack a lunch and go to the PSNI headquarters for weapons and a heavy armoured van. That will keep me safe and give me a mobile place to hang my hat. Then it's off to Belfast to go shopping. Then we will see what we will see."

He felt better now that he knew what he had some kind of plan. He rummaged around the bar to see what he could find in the way of bedding and finally located a foldout couch-bed with pillows and blankets in the office upstairs. He folded the mattress in half, pushed it down the stairs and dragged it in front of the fireplace. After stoking the fire to a nice blaze he climbed into bed with his clothes on. He had never felt so tired.

"Man, what a day." He said to Spang, trying to act as lighthearted as he could. He knew that if he let his mind drift that the feelings loneliness and loss could overwhelm him completely, so he tried to think of positive things. *Let's see*, he thought, *what's good about this situation?*

Spang climbed onto the bed and began tromping a little circle next to Rand. "C'mon Spang, good boy." He pulled blankets around the dog and scratched his ears. It was good to have somebody to talk to, even if he couldn't understand a word.

"Okay Spang, here's what's good about all of this. Let's see, no more unsolicited phone calls, thank God." He needed to think of more, pushing away the pain that lurked just below the surface. "No more standing in lines, and… holy crap! John Lennon would love this one - no more money! Sorry Mr. Lennon but I'm gonna need some possessions and I'm very attached to my religion." He chuckled at his cleverness and yawned deeply. As he closed his eyes, he said a small prayer - for everyone who used to be.

Chapter 2

Through the hole

*'God brings men down into deep waters
not to drown them but to cleanse them.'*
~John H, Aughy

A loud wind whistling through the cracks in the door roused him from the depths of a troubled sleep. A bitter cold blew across the floor. *Oh great.* A thirty mile-per-hour wind blew wet snow sideways through the leaden sky. He refreshed the fire and dove back into the blankets. Spang curled up next to him as they waited for the heat to build. The little dog proved to be an ample heat source of his own.

"Hell of a day. We're gonna have to find some winter clothes."

It suddenly occurred to him that he was including the dog in his plans. The thought of leaving the little guy to the harsh elements stung him deeply. When he had warmed up a bit he went to the kitchen with Spang at his heels.

"Don't worry buddy, the gas still works." He lit all the burners on the stove, put on coffee and set about getting something to eat. Twenty minutes later he emerged from the kitchen with a large breakfast. He was surprised to see sunbeams shining through the gaps in the curtains and the broken door. Thankfully the snow and the wind were gone and the pavement was only wet. He was eager to get away from familiar environments. Without something for his memory to compare with, he thought, it would be easier to cope. He quickly finished the meal, making sure that Spang had plenty to see him through the day. Then he packed up his daypack and went outside. The little dog followed him.

"Dammit buddy, I hate to leave you in the lurch but this is goodbye. You're still the ugliest frigger I've ever seen but you're the coolest too so it kinda evens out."

Spang just looked up at him and turned his head slightly. He wiped down the seat of the motorcycled started it up. When he looked down to retract the kickstand, Spang was still there looking up at him. Rand grimaced and shook his head. Spang barked.

He knows. He fricking knows.

In a split second Rand made up his mind.

"Okay, if you're game I'm willing to give it a try. Let's see if we can get you set up." He shut the bike off and went back inside. It only took him a couple of minutes to find what he was looking for. The blanket went into the milk crate, then he dug the duct tape out of his pack and waved it at Spang.

"Never go anywhere without it."

The God String

A quarter of a roll of duct tape later Spang was placed in his box. The well padded crate was taped very firmly to the luggage rack on the back of the bike. SPang was secured to the crate with an improvised harness made from curtain tie-backs and duct tape.

"Now, we'll find you a proper harness and everything in a little while but for now, DON'T JUMP OUT." He said, waving a finger at Spang. "If you bail, I'll never forgive myself. I'm trusting you now, you said you could ride." With a grimace, he got on and fired up the bike. "Lord, please keep him safe back there."

He started off slowly through the ruined streets of Omagh. Spang stayed low in the crate but poked his head up just enough to see. Rand was amazed at how calm the little dog was as he turned, accelerated, braked, and turned again through the obstacle course of vehicles. Smoke plumes rose like towers just above the roof lines then smeared away across a heavy sky to the east to merge with the ruddy clouds. Many fires still raged out of control and whole sections of the town had been reduced to cinders. *Apocalypse.* He thought. The term definitely applied.

Their first stop was a gas station. He pulled in knowing that he would have to figure out a way to get the gas out of the tank in the ground. It proved simpler than he thought. With keys and a hand pump from the shop, he unlocked the tank and attached a length of garden hose to reach the gas. When he had fuelled the bike he wrapped the hand pump and hose in a plastic bag and lashed it to the front forks with a bungee cord. "That may come in handy later."

The next stop was the police station. Rand found that the vehicles thinned out the farther he got away from the town center. Ten minutes into the journey they passed a farm field on the left and started to smell the piercing, tanginess of fuel. Car-sized tufts of black smoke drifted by them, increasing in frequency until they blended, making it difficult to breathe. After another quarter mile he had to slow down to avoid sharp shards of metal debris that were strewn on the road. The pieces grew in size as they slowly worked their way forward, some were as large as a bus. As the smoke became thicker Rand struggled to see through it and he slowed the bike to a crawl. Finally they broke through the smoke and Rand stopped. In front of them was twenty-five foot high tail section of a passenger jetliner. He reckoned it to be the source of the big explosion he heard the previous night. The massive fuselage was broken into three sections and scattered in the field among piles of smaller debris. The tail had a giant green shamrock on it.

"Aer Lingus," he said to Spang, "I've flown on them. It's not a big one. Probably came from England." Spang squinted his eyes and gave a small whine. "Yeah let's get out of here, this smoke is nasty."

They carefully rode past the wreckage, picking their way around the bigger pieces. Rand had never witnessed devastation on that scale before.

"I have a feeling it's gonna get weirder before it gets better." Twenty minutes later they came to the PSNI station. He unloaded Spang and looked around. The place was a fortress. A maximum-security building made of meter thick concrete walls, concertina wire fences, bulletproof glass and reinforced solid steel doors. If he had to break in, it wasn't going to be easy.

A row of armoured riot trucks and vans were parked outside. Besides the trucks, there were a few regular patrol cars as well. One of the cars still had the keys switched on in the ignition.

"Out of gas. This one must have run all night. That means that there was somebody in it." *They just vanished and it kept running.* The thought creeped him out.

He spied a key card clipped to the wire of the radio mic.

"This might be our ticket in."

He crossed his fingers and held the card up to the reader at the front door. The lock opened with a small click and Rand let out sigh. The interior was clean but dark.

"Power is on for the locks but not the lights. Must be some kind of battery power for the security system."

He fished his head lamp and flashlight out of his pack. A reception desk was situated behind double panes of bulletproof glass and the interior doors proved to be just as solid as the exterior ones. Rand started going room by room, rummaging for keys and managed to find a large police flashlight.

"Hey, we got an upgrade." He said to Spang. The brilliant beam made the search much easier. Before long the constant opening of doors and scanning of rooms became monotonous. Just when he was considering turning back, he came across the locker rooms.

The lockers contained the standard supplies. The pictures of the officers with their families gave Rand a lump in his throat. A towel lay on the floor in a circular pattern with dried footprints in the center. *Stepped out of the shower and disappeared. Where the hell did they go?* Half packed gym bags gave further evidence of the unexplainable suddenness of humankind's departure. Rand retreated to the hallway and closed the door with his back to it, but across the hall his light came to rest on a sign: Evidence Room.

The door opened easily to reveal a small hallway with a cage door at the far end. He tried the key card but the it didn't work. *Not authorised I guess.* He decided to leave the evidence room alone and went in search of the armoury.

Spang found it before Rand did. He stood sniffing at a drain in the floor at the bottom of a set of stairs in front of a heavy metal door.

"Good job boy." There was no key card slot, just a number pad. "Oh great, well here's an example of why a cutting torch is on my list." He made his way back to the Commander's office. *If anyone is going to have the combination to that door it will be the guy in charge.* An hour later he had gone through every scrap of paper in drawers, filing cabinets, shelves and desks. When the batteries in his flashlight began to run low he took a break and went back to where he had found it. Sure enough there were recharging racks stacked with fresh batteries. He grabbed extras plus a charger. When he returned to the Commander's office, he noticed something he hadn't seen before; a small metal box on the wall next to one of the shelves. He pried it open eagerly only to find rows of keys on hooks. "I don't need keys, I need combinations!" Slamming the door of the small cabinet in frustration he turned back to continue the search.

Half an hour later, he sat in a pile of papers in a room next to the Commander's office, exasperated.

"Damn! Where the hell is it? There's got to be something that has that code on it, or at least some manufacturer information about the door lock." He looked at the dog and rubbed his forehead. It was no use, they would have to try and find what they needed somewhere else. He pointed out the door and said sarcastically, "Spang! Go fetch the code boy, go get it!"

Spang ran back into the Commander's office and ran a circle around the desk, barking. Rolling his eyes, Rand got up and trudged over to him.

"We've already been through this place buddy, there's nothing here... wait a minute," he paused, "what's this?"

On the floor below the little key cabinet lay a white plastic key fob. The fob had no key on it, just the ring. Picking it up he saw that one side was blank, white plastic, but on the other side was a row of handwritten numbers and letters. *There's no way that dog knew about this.* Moments later they stood at the door and Rand prepared to enter the numbers.

"If this works, I'm keeping you, we're partners."

Holding his breath he carefully typed in the code; 1-5-8… 2-B-7-X-R-8… 1.

A solid *ssha-clak* accompanied a motorised whine as huge bolts freed the door.

"No way." He stared at the little dog. "Well, a deal's a deal, partner."

He pushed on the door and over a ton of steel silently swung aside to reveal a room that was surprisingly large. Along the left wall was a rack of firearms. Lockers full of ammunition stood at the end wall. In the middle were large wooden tables. More lockers, shelves and closets made up the wall to the right. Rand went straight to the weapons rack to find a sidearm. *I want to keep it light. I'm going to be wearing this thing a lot.* He went over it several times before his flashlight beam glanced across a shiny nickel-plated Colt .45 1911 with pearl grips hanging in it's holster.

"Classic." He lifted the pistol out. "This has definitely been tuned up." He said, looking over all of the custom work. "I know I was thinking lightweight but this is just too nice to leave behind." He swapped the police belt for a tactical belt with a holster that secured the pistol to his upper leg. *How long will I wear this before it starts bothering me?* He thought, raising his knee to get a feel for the weight. *But then, just when you let your guard down, you'll find yourself facing a hungry lion or a pack of dogs. Better to keep it on until it becomes a part of you.* With that resolve he filled three clips with ammunition, put one in the pistol and stored the other two on the belt. He found large, black duffels bags and began to fill them with equipment.

He picked out an M4A1 assault rifle with a grenade launcher and a Remington 700 sniper rifle that had a massive scope on it. Then he found several sizes of binoculars, a spotting scope, a bullet proof vest and a bullet proof riot shield. As the bags began to fill he reasoned to Spang, "We might as well go gung-ho buddy, never know what we'll be up against."

He picked up anything he thought he might use, and a lot of things he didn't even know how to use, including a large box of plastic explosives and a spool of detcord. Eventually he resigned that he couldn't take it all and began to carry the heavy bags up the stairs.

After he had moved all of the equipment into a pile at the front door, he went back to the Commander's office and located the keys for the armoured Range Rovers.

"Our new ride awaits." He said dangling the keys at the dog. "With one of these babies we can plow through wreckage, plus, we'll be safe from anything falling on us in the city."

He chose the truck in the best condition and loaded all the supplies into the back. Standing in the parking lot he looked at the motorcycle sadly, realising that he had to leave it behind. He sighed, "Ah well, easy come, easy go." He changed into some black combat pants and a fresh, blue police t-shirt. As an afterthought he bundled up a heavy leather biker jacket he had found on a coat hook and tossed it onto the front floor with his backpack. Then, with Spang in the passenger seat, they rolled off towards Belfast.

"Now we're loaded for bear."

The armoured car handled like a four-ton marshmallow, which made weaving through the maze of cars particularly slow. After he got off the smaller streets and onto the motorway things got a bit easier. Rand surmised by the wreckage that the majority of the cars had driven off the road at highway speeds which left the middle of the road mostly clear. Trucks posed the biggest problem. A few had overturned and scattered their contents across the highway. He slowed when they encountered a capsized truck that had spilled a full load of frozen chicken. It had defrosted on the pavement and was starting to smell. He carefully pushed the Range Rover's reinforced bumper up against the frame of the over-turned trailer and was able to move it a few feet to the side of the road. Slowly, he picked his way through the rotting mess and got back up to speed again.

"Man, that's just nasty. I don't think we'll be having chicken tonight."

What will we be having tonight? Rand began to think about his next move. It was becoming clear that the prospect of finding any people was remote. The loneliness of the thought threatened to overwhelm him, so he forced himself to look at it in a matter-of-fact kind of way.

The God String

"It's just us buddy, that's all there is to it. It doesn't mean we have get all droopy about it." More than ever he was glad to have someone to talk to, even if it was just a dog. As they reached the outskirts of Belfast he took the exit and stopped to check his list.

"Right, PSNI – done. Get to Belfast – done. Next stop the BBC. Maybe they have a backup generator and we'll be able to broadcast something."

It took him the better part of an hour to locate the BBC studios. When he did finally reach the building, he was pleased to find the doors open.

"Ready to be a TV star Spang?" He said as dog followed him up the stairs. When they got to the doors, Rand discovered the power was down.

"No joy. Well, while we're here we might as well have a look around and see if there's anything worthwhile. Exploring down several large hallways he found the news studio. He tapped the mouse pad of a laptop on a cart but it was dead.

"There's nothing in here that doesn't require power. Besides, how is a video camera going to help us in any way?" He'd had enough for the day. "How about some food and a nice clean bed?" Suddenly the whole building shuddered with a low rumble as Spang barked and ran back to the door. *What the?* Rand steadied himself against the wall. *An earthquake?* Regaining his footing, he ran after Spang. As they burst outside, the shuddering stopped and was replaced by a groaning and screeching noise like massive amounts of metal being twisted and torn. The sound was coming from the direction of the harbour.

Rand ran around the corner and peered down the street. He strained his eyes but couldn't see anything so he went back to the armoured car, flung open the back and rummaged for the spotting scope. It took him a second to find it and he cursed himself for being so disorganised. The noise had stopped by the time he rounded the corner of the building and raised the scope.

About a mile away, smoke rose in a mushroom plume above the buildings. Down by the main pier, close to the Titanic Museum, Rand could read the prow of a massive ship.

"British Topaz. It's some kind of tanker."

She had impacted the pier and run aground, now she was listing to the right at a steep angle. A huge, bent pipe was attached to the side of the ship and a geyser of white spray shot into the air from it. A flash went up as the geyser turned bright yellow and orange, the fireball billowed skywards.

"It just explo—"

As the words left his mouth the smack of the explosion hit them. Seconds later he saw another fireball erupt. This time it was in the center of the street just a hundred feet from the pier. The manhole flew high into the air. A fraction of a second later, a deep *thud* shook the ground, making him step back. Spang was barking loudly. Rand looked again through the scope. Another *thud*, this time louder and only several blocks away. An intersection in the street had a hole in it with a spout of flame gushing straight up like a geyser.

"Holy…" Another *thud* slammed into Rand, this time almost knocking him of his feet. He realised that there was no delay this time.

"Shit! That ship must have lit the gas lines! C'mon Spang!"

They raced to the armoured car and Spang jumped inside just ahead of Rand as he slammed the door closed. Grabbing his leather jacket, Rand wrapped Spang in it when another explosion went off, rocking the heavy truck. He put Spang in his leather bundle down on the floor, fired up the heavy truck and got it moving. Thuds and popping sounded more frequently; it was spreading down other streets. They quickly picked up speed and he headed for a side street. *The gas lines seem to run under the main streets, maybe side streets will be safer.* He wasn't a city guy and had no idea how these things worked. Through the smoke and falling debris Rand could make out the front of a hotel. He decided to head for it when he felt something punch him hard in the chest.

His breath left him and everything went silent except for a very high, piercing note. He was weightless, in a sickening slow motion turn as the truck was tossed through the air, landing upside down. The seat belt bit into his shoulder as the roof slammed into the pavement with a teeth clattering crash. The heavy vehicle ground to a stop, precariously resting on a crushed corner of it's armoured roof. Spang crawled out of the leather wrappings and licked Rand's face as he hung upside down from the seatbelt.

"You okay buddy? I'm alright I think." Rand felt around himself, nothing broken. The windshield was still intact. The armoured truck had saved their lives. As Rand got his bearings he became aware of a loud hissing that surrounded the vehicle. He loosened the seat belt and turned upright in the cramped cab; a position that forced him to kneel on the door with the steering wheel up by his chest. He tried the door above him. Jammed. The frame of the truck had twisted and sealed the front doors tight. He fumbled under the seat and found his crowbar. Positioning himself between the seats, he tried to lever it into the handle of the small door that separated the cab from the back, but he just couldn't get it to bite. Outside the window flames shot up around the front of the vehicle.

"Oh hell, we're on fire!"

His mind raced through the options. *No way through that bulletproof windshield, the doors were jammed... the door to the back... the back...* panic seized him as he remembered the box of plastic explosives and spool of detcord he had loaded into the back. If the temperature got high enough, there were enough explosives back there to vaporise the truck and everything in it. He kicked at the small armoured door with everything he had but it didn't budge. They were trapped. He kicked mightily, again and again but the door was so solid it barely even vibrated. The cab was beginning to get warm.

How did this happen? I was stupid, I didn't think ahead, I wasn't organised.

"I'm so sorry buddy."

Spang licked his hand.

Rand looked at the little dog, he had just killed the little guy, he knew it. Then he realised, Spang was licking the hand that was resting on his shiny new forty-five. Rand pulled out the gun, drew back the slide and pointed it at Spang with a knot in his gut. Spang barked, turned and jumped up toward the window above him. Rand's eyes went wide with understanding.

"Oh, right. Good boy! I'm sorry, I'm sorry! Now come here! Get back."

Rand rolled up Spang in the leather jacket again and stuffed the dog behind him. Then, with the barrel of the gun only an inch away, shot one round into the passenger side glass. He flinched, fearing a lethal ricochet but the bullet stuck. He fired again at the exact same spot and blew out a hole as cracks splintered out through the layers of armoured glass. He quickly made four holes at the corners of a square pattern, just big enough for him to fit through. He used up the rest of his rounds, spacing the holes evenly around the square and one in the middle. It had taken less than a minute and the cab was already getting uncomfortably hot.

He took up the crowbar and hacked viciously at the glass, chipping away at the spaces between the holes. *This thing was built to withstand firebombs. It's the only thing saving your ass right now.* But he knew the heavy truck was built to drive out of fiery situations, not stay in one place and cook. Time was not on their side.

He kept hammering at the glass around the holes, chiseling away, creating distressed points where each hole was and in the sections in between. The laminated, bulletproof glass was starting to weaken.

"Go! You son-of-a-bitch!" He yelled at the glass.

He worked furiously, striking in powerful, quick blows. The skin on his palms tore away with each hit, but he was possessed by fear and anger. *I am not going to be the last one. I am not going to die here in this strange world not knowing what happened to the people I love. And I am not going to kill this poor, innocent, ugly, absurdly cool dog!*

He swung onto his back, held on to the edges of the seat, drew his legs back and with all the strength he could summon, kicked a hard blow to the window. The square of glass finally yielded and burst out onto the pavement with a crash. A gout of natural gas fumes rushed into the opening in a fiery blue ball but then receded as the air pressure equalised. Spang ran up his legs and bounded out the window with a bark. It was a rough landing but he was out. Rand was now alone in the cab looking at the small hole. How was he going to fit through that? He took off his gun belt and threw it outside to keep it from being snagged. He decided to go feet first through the hole to protect his face. As he pushed through the hole backwards, his pant legs rode up. He immediately felt the flames on his skin and the chewed edges of the thick glass shredding him.

Pushing hard off the seat edge with his arms, he got his torso through. It was a tight fit around his ribs and the glass cut him deeply but he couldn't tell the difference between the heat of the blood and the heat of the flames. Keeping his arms over his head, he hung halfway out of the glass, each breath jammed his ribs against the sharp glass. He screamed, and pushed again. Finally, he slid out, down the side of the truck and onto the melting pavement. His body seared with pain as he sprang to his feet, wrapping his arms around him as he ran out of the flames. Trailing a stream of blood, he picked up speed into a loping stride. He scooped up his gun belt and threw it over his shoulder, then put on the speed as he ducked around the corner of the closest building with Spang on his heels. They rounded into the alleyway. He scooped up Spang, swung open the lid of a large steel dumpster and jumped in. With a painful cry he landed in the bottom and crouched down with the dog underneath him. He could feel blood oozing down his back. Molten asphalt stuck to his right shoulder blade, burning him but he curled up around Spang and braced for the inevitable.

Without an explosive source to set it off, the fifty pounds of plastic explosive would have just burned passively as it was set alight by the red hot steel. Unfortunately, the thousand-foot spool of 50 g/m detcord was the perfect initiator. Moments after Rand and Spang entered the dumpster the detcord and C4 finally yielded to the laws of physics, splitting the air with a mighty thud. Huge chunks of architecture ricocheted off adjacent buildings and crashed to the street. Most of the windows in the high rise structures on the surrounding blocks blew out.

The dumpster provided shelter for the rain of glass that cascaded down, it's steel hull vibrated with a low, lazy, bell tone as large shards of tough, plate glass dented and dimpled the steel lid. In the dumpster, Spang shivered as Rand crouched around him like a shield, eyes closed, praying that the lid would protect them from the falling debris. It was minutes before the last of the pieces came down. Rand inched up the lid and peered out. Fallen glass covered most of the alley. Opening the lid all the way, he instinctively looked up. Several large, sharp pieces were dangling above them, held only by their rubber seals several stories up.

"Time to go." He clenched his teeth against the agonising pain as he hauled himself over the edge of the bin gently, holding Spangto keep him clear of the glass. Quickly and carefully, he threaded his way through the debris and got out of the alley. Once out of the shadow of the dangerous building, he surveyed the scene.

The armoured truck was gone. A section of the transaxle lay attached to a charred bit of one of the rear tires that still smoked as it cooled into the black ooze that used to be the pavement. Under the street, the gas main has been severely damaged and now roared out a column of flame over a hundred feet high. Up and down streets for as far he could see, similar pillars of flame shot skyward.

Angry and dejected, Rand hobbled with Spang down the street towards the Fitzwilliam Hotel. His blood soaked clothes were shredded and long cuts and burns covered his body. Adrenaline had done a good job of keeping most of the pain at bay and he picked up the pace as he limped towards the hotel. Impossibly, his mood improved as he spied a light on in one of the fourth story windows.

"Thank God, they got power. Here we go Spang." He said with a grimace. "It's our new home."

Spang's ears were still ringing when they arrived. The little dog was badly shaken by the blast. The only thing he wanted was to curl up and hide somewhere. Rand went behind the front desk, trailing blood behind him. He took a towel from a cleaning cart to clean his hands then he sat down behind the computer and tried to figure out how to make a key card. The pain from his wounds became more intense as he tried to focus on deciphering the hotel's computer key system. Finally he figured it out and created an all-access key card. Then he grabbed a large first-aid kit from underneath the desk and took the elevator up to the penthouse.

The burns and cuts were so painful that Rand took no interest in the room. He peeled off his clothes in the tiled bathroom and stared at the gruesome reflection in the mirror. It looked like a bucket of blood had been poured over him. One eye was shot with red. There were over a dozen long, bleeding cuts down the front and sides of his torso. More cuts ran under his arms, all the way to his wrists. His back, calves and shins were black with soot and asphalt that had hardened onto his skin. He knew that the next part was going to be the hardest as he reached into the shower and turned on the cold water.

He went in and briefly let the cool water touch his back and run down his legs. The pain was too much. He sprang out quickly, dancing about cursing loudly and shaking his arms as blood and water splattered over the walls and floor. He felt like he was on fire, but cussing helped somehow. After the pain subsided a bit, he knew he would have to get this done and over with. Through clenched teeth, he talked to Spang for support.

"If I don't do this buddy I'll be in bad shape, maybe even die from infection." He psyched himself up by getting angry at the pain. The pain lived in the shower and in the possibility of infection and slow death. There were no doctors to help him. He had to stay in the water. More than that, he had to pour liquid soap all over himself and scrub. Those were his weapons, this was his war, and he knew it would be hell. He spat at his pain through clenched teeth.

"You're not gonna take me!"

He jumped into the shower and cranked it up full blast. The sharp needles from the shower head tore into the cuts. He screamed in agony then squeezed out half a bottle of shower gel onto his red body. *You're not part of me! You have to go!* He bent his will toward the asphalt that had seared into his flesh. He ground the brush against the hard black rock and chipped it all away, tearing out chunks of burnt flesh. He had to use the wooden handle as a pry bar. Out on the couch, Spang howled in response to Rand's screaming.

By the time Rand had completely rinsed out the soap and hydrogen peroxide, he had begun to get used to the pain, but that did not make it any easier. His body was wracked. He stepped out of the shower and used every towel as he patted down and tried to stop the bleeding. He was completely drained but still awake though he was not conscious of the stream of silent tears that poured from his eyes. Spreading a long, luxurious white robe on the floor, he emptied tubes of antiseptic ointment onto it, rubbing the salve into the robe so it covered the interior. Then he put it on and closed it tight around him. He stumbled over to the bed, lay down gingerly and slowly fell into a disturbed sleep.

When he woke it was well into the next morning, Spang was lying on his back, feet in the air, snoring away next to him. As he got up, he noticed that the pain had eased and he opened the squishy robe to look at his wounds. It was a gruesome mix of blood and ointment but there was no infection. Carefully he made his way to the bathroom. The place looked like the scene of a gruesome murder.

"We're gonna have to get the maid in here buddy." He tried to chuckle, Spang continued to snore.

The first-aid kit was open on the bathroom counter. *Time for round two.* He stripped off the robe and started applying bandages. The deepest cuts were on the undersides of his arms. He slowly went from wound to wound, bad ones first, dabbing on fresh ointment then applying pads to the burns and butterfly bandages to the cuts. Next, he busied himself with the lesser cuts, leaving what he could to heal in the air. When he was done, he surveyed himself in the mirror. His body was a patchwork quilt of tape and bandages.

He decided he needed some clothes since everything he had was either shredded or soaked in blood. Grabbing the master key, he headed downstairs. Luggage in the rooms below yielded a department store selection of items. He decided on a pair of loose-fitting sweat pants, t-shirt and a robe then he took the elevator down to the kitchen and loaded up a cart full of food. Hobbling along in a pair of commandeered Crocs, he rolled the cart through the lobby and picked up a laptop that was plugged in at a coffee table. A cold cup of coffee sat beside a pair of reading glasses and a cell phone in the middle of the seat. He stood quietly, grimacing against the pain of his wounds, wondering again what had happened.

They had disappeared, that much was clear. The footprints in the towel, the spilled coffees, crashed jets and cars, all of it pointed to that one conclusion. The 'why' was impossible to know, but he knew the 'when'. The 'what' was all around him, the evidence at least; they had vanished instantly in the middle of whatever they were doing. Everyone but him – that was the reality of the 'what'. The 'how' was the thing he thought about most, but it was impossible to know and would most likely remain so. He shook his head and shuffled off to the elevator.

As he came in the door, Spang was scratching to go out. Rand berated himself and took the frantic little dog outside. While Spang scrutinised a patch of lawn, Rand stood in his robe and slippers surveying the streets. Little had changed in the city overnight. The fires from the gas mains continued to burn, as did the oil tanker at the quay. There seemed to be a lot of birds around. Rand supposed it was because everything was so quiet. He took a mental note of the state of things outside the hotel then called Spang back inside.

Returning to the room, Rand put together breakfast for the both of them and tenderly reclined on the couch. He took some fruit from the cart and started to think aloud.

"Cities are not the best place to be. We need a better plan." He washed down four ibuprofen then peeled a banana and thought. Even inside the security of the luxurious suite the silence of the city weighed on him. He relented to the idea that had been pressing on him for the last two days.

"I have to get back to the states."

He stared blankly at the wall as he accepted the reality of that choice.

"I don't know if I have the courage to find out the fate of my family, but the truth is I'm homesick. I need to be where things are familiar. I gotta get home Spang."

The little dog just looked up at him.

"How the hell am I going to do that?" He stood and looked out the window at the ship burning in the distance. "I don't have the skills to navigate the seas. I'd be fine out in open water but more than likely I'd run aground somewhere and then I'd really be in the soup."

Literally.

"Fly?"

Why not, I've done it before.

When he was in his twenties a family friend flew in on his little Cessna to visit. Rand was so fascinated with the plane the man showed him the basics of flying. Every day that week they went up. Rand nodded slowly as he remembered.

"Yeah…it might just be possible." He muttered.

He lowered himself to the couch and continued to work the problem. "The runways are probably as bad as the roads so planes are not the ultimate goal here." *Come on Rand, think long term. You're the only one left, you need access to the planet.*

"Right. I can clear the runway at a local airport while I'm learning, but eventually I'll need to land somewhere else."

Somewhere across the Atlantic.

"Holy cow, what am I thinking?"

Distance is just time.

"Take off, fly for a certain amount of time, then land." He turned to Spang, a grin forming on his face. "It doesn't matter how far it is, it's only time buddy. We can do this."

His smile faded as quick as it had come. "A little Cessna doesn't have that kind of range. We're talking about flying a jetliner."

He stared at the wall and let his thoughts settle. Then he remembered what his mom used to say, 'You eat an elephant one bite at a time.'

Start small. You have all the time in the world.

"Yeah. Baby steps. Okay, so I learn to fly a little Cessna then we move up from there."

A picture formed in his mind. He saw himself ten years older, flying supplies in to his ranch on a big military helicopter, Spang in the co-pilot's chair.

Helicopters are really tricky. "But they don't need a runway. Ideally we need something with the range of a plane that can land like a helicopter."

I need more information.

Suddenly the lights flickered then went out.

"That's the generator." He sighed. "It's gonna to be a busy day."

His first priority was pain management. Every little movement brought sharp stabs from his collection of cuts and scrapes. He redressed his wounds, loaded a daypack with essentials and commandeered a little scooter he had spotted while Spang was doing his business that morning. After he made sure Spang was safe in a milk crate he had lashed to the back seat, Rand consulted the map he had taken from the lobby.

"Belfast Central Library…here it is, it's not far."

It was a ten minute ride to the large square, red sandstone library. The doors were unlocked and the power was off, but the windows let in some natural light so Rand began to browse. It wasn't long before he found a section on aviation. Over an hour later he had a clearer idea of his next move.

"This is the ultimate goal buddy. This is the plane we need to fly." He showed Spang a book on the V-22 Osprey. "A sturdy cargo hauler that takes off and lands like a helicopter, but flies like a plane. Problem is, all the Osprey bases are in the states. The closest would be…New River Marine Corps Air Station in North Carolina."

The whole idea seemed ridiculous. Still, somehow he couldn't let it go. He looked at the picture on the cover. The pilot was clearly visible through the windshield as the Osprey banked into a steep turn.

The pilot in that picture, he's just a guy. If he can do it, so can I.

The God String

Spang sniffed the cover and licked Rand's hand. Rand loaded all the books he could find on flight instruction into a library cart. Then left the cart by the entrance.

"We'll come back for these. Let's find some fuel for that generator, we're gonna camp at the hotel for awhile."

It was a slow and tedious process as they circled block after block to no avail. Changing strategies, he headed for the M1 and soon found what he was looking for. A fuel truck had ground itself to a stop against the rough cement wall of an underpass. Rand looked the rig over carefully. Overall, it was in good shape and had a full load of diesel in the trailer. He climbed into the cab and tried to start it, but the battery was dead. He knew that most of the vehicles on the road would be the same; after all, they had been running until they stopped but the keys were still on. He had to take the scooter to the exit and break into a parked truck to get a battery, but after he installed it, the big rig came to life with a gratifying rumble.

"Yes! Now we're cooking with fire." Rand ruffled Spang's fur then jumped out to wrangle the scooter onto the back of the truck. Once he was back in the cab it took several minutes of grinding the gears to finally get the truck rolling. The gearing was complicated and every time he tried to shift he ended up almost coming to a stop, so he just took his time. Finally he managed to nurse the truck into the alley behind the hotel. Once the rig was parked, he and Spang explored the basement of the hotel and found the generator. It took a an hour of connecting hoses and reading the instructions on the truck, but in the end he got the fuel to flow into the tank. The generator fired up after several tries and the power came back on.

They grabbed more food from the kitchen then went back outside and boosted a Toyota 4x4 pick up. With Spang in the truck he went back to the library to retrieve the books. On the way, he spotted a police car and pulled over to see what he could scavenge. He had to use his pistol to smash a window to get to the keys and open the trunk, but he was rewarded with a small arsenal. There were plenty of rounds for his .45, a shotgun, tear gas, and an MP5 machine gun. In a large black duffel he found a full set of riot gear. *These Belfast cops were ready for anything.* He piled all of it into the truck and made his way back to the hotel feeling satisfied with his accomplishments.

Back in the room he did a little cleaning then settled into his stack of books. As evening fell he sat on the couch and formulated a plan -- the problem was, that plan had him flying a big plane on a transatlantic flight. When he considered it, it wasn't the actual take off and flying that was dangerous, it was the landing. That was the risky part and would take a lot of training. He remembered the plane crash he and Spang had come across on the road out of Omagh.

"We don't want to end up like that. Maybe we should try to scrounge up some parachutes just in case...wait a minute, that's it!" He turned to Spang, eyes wide with revelation. "We can bail out! Just let the plane crash instead of trying to land."

He considered it. *Yes.* He was certain that was the answer - just jump out. The risk of parachuting was far less than trying to survive a potential crash landing. It would mean putting Spang in a parachute. *Do they even make parachutes for dogs?* It was a question he didn't have an answer to, but the plan cut a huge load off of the training he would have to put himself through. All he had to do was learn to start the engines, taxi, take-off and set the right course. He didn't even need to be accurate, just end up somewhere over North America. Once he was on the ground he could work his way to North Carolina.

He grabbed a phone book. *Flight schools, flight schools… The Amphibious Flying Club, nope. Jet Assist pleasure flights, nope. Does anyone learn to fly in Northern Ireland?*

"Here's a little one in Carrickmore… too small." He tossed the phone book aside in frustration and went over to his stack of books. "There's got to be some mention of flight schools in these instruction books." He went through the bibliographies in the instruction books, taking notes. After a half an hour he put the last one down.

"Okay, we've got our list buddy." He said to Spang. "Looks like the closest training facility for jetliners is in Cranfield, England. A place called Cabair. Good facilities. They've got simulators and training to take you from knowing nothing to flying the big jets. Looks like the jetliner sims are at Heathrow…oh crap. They're in England."

Spang looked up at him.

"Yeah I know, it's a small stretch of water, but it might as well be on the other side of the world."

He sat back down on the couch and stared at the ceiling.

"England, how the hell do we get to England?" He rubbed his face. "The Irish Sea is no place to try and become a sailor. Boats are lost out there all the time. Hell I know nothing about sailing and even I know that those are seriously treacherous waters."

Leaning forward with his head in his hands, he worked on the problem. "Well, let's go with the obvious - fly. I have to fly to learn how to fly. If I could learn how to fly even a small aircraft, it would get us there. And then…" A smile emerged on his face, "same thing buddy, we could bail out. It would be like test run."

As long as he didn't have to land, he knew that it wouldn't take long for him to get the hang of the small plane. A knot twisted in his stomach at the thought of the risk involved, but he knew it was the only way.

"Okay, like everything else, we take it one step at a time. Let's just learn how to fly a small plane first, then we'll think about the next part. We've got all the time in the world."

He went down to the kitchen and made dinner, the whole time trying to recall his flying experiences. The more he thought about it, the more his confidence grew. After dinner, he went for another round of cleansing in the shower. It was still painful, but much less than the day before. It took an hour to redress his wounds before he finally climbed into bed, weary and sore. Spang climbed in next to him as he said some prayers and they quickly fell asleep.

The next morning the sun made a rare appearance and Rand's spirits were high, even excited as they made their way through the city in the pickup truck with their shopping list. He had to go to several different stores, but he rounded up all the equipment he was looking for. Back at the hotel, he got it all set up and when he was done he stood back and looked it over.

"Now that's what I'm talking about Spangster, a state of the art flight simulator complete with control yoke, rudder pedals, throttle control and three screen surround."

Spang seemed unimpressed.

Montgomery Thompson

Chapter 3

Stepping out

*'I'm learning to fly but I ain't got wings.
Coming down is the hardest thing.'*
~Tom Petty

"I always wanted to do a long stay at a hotel." Rand said as he looked over his wounds. They were starting to itch, it was a good sign. "But I was thinking more about the 'room service' kind of hotel holiday."

Spang barked. Rand thought it was in response to something he had said but a moment later a sharp smell stung his nose.

"Oh nasty, what is that? It's like…burning rubber or something."

He covered his face and looked around the room. *God I hope the building isn't on fire.* He went to the window and saw billows of black smoke cruising by in the brisk wind.

"It's the smoke from the burning oil tanker at the pier."

He scooped up Spang and the medical kit and retreated to the laundry room in the basement. The location proved to be serendipitous as he needed sheets and towels to dress his cuts anyway. After a few hours the wind changed direction and they returned to their room.

"Funny, I was just about to say how I wish we had someplace more permanent to live, but coming back after being in the basement this room seems almost homey."

Spang happily curled up in his blanket on the couch.

The next day he made a short trip to the hospital for medical supplies and antibiotics. The only painkillers he would allow himself were of the over-the-counter variety, and these he tried to take sparingly. Back at the hotel he continued to devote most of his time to the simulator. After several more days he felt like his eyes were going to fall out of his head for all the time spent in front of the video screens.

"Let's get out of here for awhile buddy."

He changed out of the track suit he had been convalescing in and into some more rugged clothes. When he was done he looked himself over in the full length mirror. He had lost weight and his eyes looked sharper somehow. *Recovery time is over. Time to start moving forward.* He checked his watch - October 21st, a week since they moved into the hotel. He left the lights on in the room and headed out with Spang at his heels.

It took an hour to get to Belfast City Airport due to the wreckage on the roads. He had to break through a fence and drive through muddy fields to get around a tractor with a huge trailer full of dead sheep, but the pick-up truck proved up to the task. As they approached the airport he started to see bits of wreckage. The closer he got, the larger the pieces became; the nose of a United jet, the wing of a small twin turbine Cessna, a chunk of fuselage from an Air France Airbus with rows of seats still in it. It was total aviation carnage. He gained access to the tarmac by driving through a giant hole in the fence that had been made by a Virgin Airlines jet. It had rolled through the fence and into a nearby field where it sat bogged in the mud as if parked there intentionally, a chunk of fence wrapped around it's front landing gear.

Scenes of destruction were becoming routine to Rand. He concentrated on steering around wreckage as he worked his way toward the private hangars. He parked the truck, chambered round in his .45, reseated the hammer, put the safety on and slid it back into it's holster.

"Keep an eye out for other dogs." He told Spang as he grabbed the Benelli M4 shotgun. "And stay close."

Of the thirty or so small planes that were parked outside, most of them had been hit by some kind of debris from crashes. Only six were undamaged. He decided that the hangers would be his best option. He had to shoot the locks out of several of the doors, but it wasn't long before he found what he was looking for: a brand new Cessna 206 StationAir. It had cargo doors in the back that would be easy to jump out of and the latest glass cockpit avionics. *It's just like the cockpit in the sim.* He marvelled at his luck

He closed up the hanger and with a giggle and marked the door with a can of bright orange spray paint: *MY PLANE, DON'T TOUCH,* making the letters as big as he could.

"There, that's as close to an official purchase as I can make." He chuckled and climbed into the truck.

The jump school was close by and he quickly found parachutes, packed and ready to go. Rand rifled through the company's files and found manuals and books on the subject of parachuting. With a collection of helmets, goggles, suits and wrist altimeters loaded into the truck he headed back to the hotel, pleased at the haul.

During the return drive he tested the GPS. It showed he was about 32 miles to the northwest of where he actually was. *Now I know for sure that the global position system is screwed.* He wondered when he would start seeing satellite wreckage coming down and hoped they were far away when it did. *Just something else to look forward to.*

***

The hotel generators stayed running as long as Rand topped off the tank everyday. He kept at the training, spending butt-numbing hours practicing takeoffs and exploring the tolerances of the small aircraft. The simulator program had up-to-date maps of the UK and Europe and Rand had grabbed all of the additional expansion packs that included the US, Canada and Mexico. It meant he could actually simulate flying the route in real time down to the last detail. He did it over and over, though the sim allowed him to speed up time on the long, boring stretches. He would slow it back down to normal when he reached different visual navigation points and when he arrived at Heathrow. Occasionally, the he got bored, he would load up the US map and fly around the New River marine base in North Carolina.

"I can't hurt to begin to familiarise myself with the area." He reasoned.

Once he had successfully completed ten simulated trips to England he decided to work on his landings. After awhile he started nailing them on a regular basis. He adjusted the parameters of the flight simulator to include nasty crosswinds and limited visibility as he tried to master the rudder pedal. There were numerous failures but eventually he started to stick even the more complicated landings. However, the thought of actually trying a real landing terrified him. *After all it's not the kind of thing you get a second chance at. It's do or die.* The reality of the situation made him slightly more comfortable with the simple physics of a parachute.

He combed through books and manuals about parachutes and their use. Rand felt sorry for what he was planning to put Spang through. He started to make a list of everything he would take and how he might parachute the dog and their equipment. He wasn't satisfied until he had sketched out the whole plan in detail. As he looked it over he nodded to himself. The whole idea was becoming more feasible.

The next day he and Spang headed off through the streets of Belfast. He quickly learned that the large glass panes of city storefronts were very, very tough. It proved to be a job for the shotgun. In the end, he got most everything he was looking for. Back in the hotel he immersed himself in a project he christened 'The drop cage'. It was a plastic pet travel cage lined with foam and suspended inside a larger pet cage by strong bungee cords. He examined all of the parachutes and selected one that was rated for a two man team.

"It's gotta hold you, the drop cage, the backpack and the duffel bag." Spang looked at him sheepishly. He seemed to know that Rand's project somehow involved him.

"Don't worry buddy, I've weighed everything out, this is the right chute for you."

It took most of the evening to build. Before he turned in Rand dressed his wounds again. They were healing nicely and the cleaning routine was less intensive as the days went by. Finally, he and Spang curled up for another night's sleep. He knew that the day after next might be his last if everything didn't go exactly right.

October 23rd, thirteen days since the 'happening'. This day was all about final preparations. He packed the backpack, strapped and duct taped it to the bottom of the drop cage. The last thing he did was to zip tie and duct tape an air horn to the handle of the crate. Hopefully they would land close enough together for Rand to track down Spang and the gear by the sound, otherwise Spang could be stuck in the crate and starve to death. He felt sick about it, but he just didn't have the knowledge to set up some kind of elaborate, automated escape mechanism. After using two full rolls of duct tape, he weighed the whole thing on a luggage scale. It fell perfectly in the parameters for the chute.

"Now all it needs is you."

Spang was not impressed. He seemed to know that the strange bundle of stuff had something to do with him and it didn't smell good.

Rand selected a chute and tried it on. It was too difficult to put on in the plane so he would have to wear it for the whole trip. He used one of the chutes as a trainer which he took down to the hotel's large meeting room. He pulled the ripcord to get a feel for it and deployed the backup chute to get more familiar with the whole setup. He pulled the parachute to it's fully deployed length and inspected how the lines and harness worked. After lunch it was back on the simulator to do the whole flight to England again. His basic method of navigation wasn't too far off; point towards Heathrow, travel for three hours until he saw the landing strips and use landmarks on the way to compensate for the winds that would blow him off course. Coming from Belfast, Heathrow should appear on his right as a huge rectangle of runways. If the simulator was correct, there would a big patch of field at the eastern end that would serve as their landing spot for the jump. As long as the software maps were relatively up-to-date, everything should go smoothly.

He told Spang that night, "This must be how the astronauts felt the day before they went to the moon."

He fell asleep with his resolve firmly set -- he knew he was going to need every ounce of it the next day.

In the morning, Rand tended his bandages and then made a breakfast fit for a king.

"It's the last day we're going to be on the Emerald Isle," he said as he gave Spang his breakfast, "the country of your birth, at least I think it is. The country of Moira's birth… he was suddenly overcome with heaviness and the tears started to flow. He crouched over and angrily fought back.

"No, no, no I need to keep it together, today of all days dammit!"

He struggled for several minutes and finally won the battle by steering his thoughts toward the equipment check list.

"Right, chem-lights, drop cage, harness on Spang…" He went through everything methodically, keeping his mind entirely on business. There was no room for sentiment, not for a country, not for a loved one, not for anything. He had to be focused and alert. Soon they said goodbye to the Fitzwilliam Hotel and drove the pick-up to the airport. The bright orange lettering greeted them at the hangar. Rand opened the doors and pushed the plane out on the tarmac.

The God String

It struck Rand as funny that he was standing there, getting ready for his first solo flight amid the overwhelming carnage of what was the greatest aviation disaster of all-time.

"J.J. Abrams would loved to have a shot this scene." He stifled a chuckle. *Stop laughing,* he scolded himself. *A plane crash is not funny. No matter how it turns out today, you're gonna make one.*

He grabbed the keys to the plane and did his walk around flight check, then he prepared the drop crate.

He's gonna be fine. He reassured himself confidently. There was no room for skepticism, if there was; he knew he shouldn't be going.

Rand got into his parachute and secured it tightly. Then he practiced getting out of the pilot's seat, going back and putting Spang in the cage (without Spang of course, he wanted to surprise him when the time came), opening the doors and shoving the cage out. He learned a lot from the drill. There were several times he got hung up on straps and hit the rudder pedals with his feet as he tried to get loose. He also became aware that when the doors were opened in flight they might cause drag and steer the aircraft to the right. He would have to be very quick.

Next, he drove the length of the taxiway to the runway. The main runways were dotted with craters and wreckage but, using the truck to push, he managed to clear the taxiway. He stood at the end of the taxiway and looked down it's length to the plane in the distance. *This is what I'll have to use as a runway.* He drove back, measuring the distance with the odometer. *Two thousand ninety-two feet.* It was just a little more than the eighteen hundred and sixty feet that he needed. It would have to do. He drove to the main terminal and took his pick of fuel trucks. It was just a matter of jump starting one and driving it back. After testing and topping off the fuel, he got comfortable in the cockpit and familiarised himself with the controls. He found everything as it should be and was amazed at how similar it was to the simulator. *You're stalling.* He practiced with the rudder pedals a bit more, then bit his lip and went to get Spang.

The sky was overcast but the grey ceiling seemed high enough. He loaded Spang into the passenger seat, clipped his harness to the seatbelt and then climbed in.

"Okay, here we go." He breathed.

He went down the long checklist with no problems. The engine sputtered to life with a shake, then idled comfortably. He throttled up slightly and they began rolling slowly down the piece of taxiway he had chosen as a runway. At the other end, he turned the plane around to face into the wind as he lined up on the ribbon of tarmac. He squared himself, set the brake and the flaps, clenched his teeth and opened the throttle. The small plane lurched forward as the propeller bit into the air. The ground flashed by as he gained speed. He knew there was no turning back now. For an instant the end of the short runway seemed too close, but suddenly he felt the seat sway slightly underneath him and he was airborne. Remembering to breathe he pulled back gently on the controls and let the nose rise up. Suddenly reality hit him fully.

"We're up, we're flying!"

He looked out the window at the landscape falling away, his heart beating furiously. *Check your notes, stay focused.* At four hundred feet he put the flaps up, adjusted the throttle and looked around. He was astounded at what he saw; smoke plumes and fires as far as the eye could see. In the far distance was a great black cloud hanging in the air.

"That's the ship in Belfast Harbour."

Around the airport were scores of large gashes in the earth where planes had ploughed into the ground, scattering debris everywhere.

He gently tried his hand at turning as he continued to climb. He was amazed at what the flight simulator had taught him though the gentle bumping of the plane in motion was something that couldn't be simulated. He was familiar enough with flying in small planes to be comfortable with the experience. When the altimeter read three thousand feet, he pointed toward London, levelled off and set the trim.

"This is incredible!" He said to Spang who was nervously glancing about. "Why didn't I ever do this? Oh yeah, flying was expensive."

The plane stayed steady with only minor corrections, so he unlatched Spang from the front seat. The little dog immediately jumped into the back and looked for a place to curl up. When he looked back at Spang he was lying in the drop cage.

"You like it in there? Awesome. It makes my job much easier."

It had helped that Rand had thrown in the blanket that Spang spent most of his time on in the hotel, and some bacon though at that moment the dog had no interest in it.

As they left Ireland behind and started out over the sea, Rand felt a strange wash of sadness diluted with anxiety. In one sense it was goodbye, but if something happened and they had to bail out into the ocean, there would be no chance of survival. It was October and the Irish Sea was no place to go swimming.

He cracked open the twist lid on a travel mug full of coffee and scanned for landmarks. A smile leapt across his face as he recognised a landmass in the distance to his left.

"The Isle of Man, no doubt about it." It looked a little different that it had in the sim, but going by the time he had travelled along his current heading, The Isle of Man was the only thing it could be.

The Irish Sea crept slowly by, mile after mile of cold, dark water. Then slowly, as if from a dream, the coast came into view. Soon he was floating along over the green landscape once again.

"It's England Spang! I can't believe we made it."

Spang stayed put in the wonky cage. After about an hour the weather started to get misty and little drops streaked off of the windshield. Then the drops became more frequent until a fine rain fell on the airplane. To Rand the problem wasn't the rain, it was that the clouds seemed to be getting lower and lower. He had read that parachuting got much riskier if he jumped below twenty six hundred feet. Even at three thousand feet, he had to open the chute right away. Now he was watching the cloud level dropping down on him. He guessed the clouds were somewhere between thirty three hundred and four thousand feet and descending. According to his rough navigation he had thirty minutes to go before the jump.

He kept his eyes peeled to the right of the plane for any sign of Heathrow. Thirty minutes passed by and there was still no sign. He scanned back and forth to try and get his bearings. Out of the grey and off to his left the signature pattern of Heathrow's runways finally appeared. It was hard to make out at first because of the amount of wreckage that covered the airfield. Rand's heart leapt in a gush of relief.

"There it is! We almost missed it boy!"

He flew over the airport and surveyed the scene on the ground in amazement. The carnage was on a much larger scale than Belfast. Heathrow, the busiest airport in the world, was now a smoking mass of wreckage. Over fifty crash sites cut into the landscape like giant divots from a violent golf game, marching in a line to the horizon. Whole sections of the terminal had been wiped out.

Of course. Every nav computer flew every plane to it's destination. He shook his head in disbelief. *It's a jet plane pile-up*. With a knot in his stomach he banked his little plane and searched for the farm field that was his jump target. *Almost time.* He was starting to envy Spang. *I wish someone would put me in a box and just push me out. It would be a whole lot easier than doing it voluntarily.*

Rand checked his altitude; twelve hundred feet and descending. He was too low. The clouds had been pushing him down. Still, he had just enough room to get the plane up to twenty five hundred feet. Once he was at the right altitude he trimmed the plane and took off his headset. The noise was startling. *Man this thing is loud. Poor Spang.* He put on the odd little helmet and goggles, checked his straps and turned out of his seat to the back of the plane. Instantly the plane turned slightly and started to nose up. Rand quickly turned back around and grabbed the controls. He adjusted the trim then quickly went back and clipped Spang's harness to the top of the cage and closed the door. By the time he had finished all of this they had flown past Heathrow. He scrambled back to the front, leaning over the chair to get the plane level again and check the altitude. He looked back at Spang, the little dog seemed to be secure so he climbed back into the seat and turned back to the airport. Threading his way through the columns of smoke the field came into view as the top of the plane brushed the bottom of the clouds.

Okay buddy, time to earn your wings. Again he made the scramble to the back of the plane. Spang peered at him from behind two sets of bars as Rand zip tied them closed.

"If something goes wrong, I'm really sorry." He yelled over the engine noise. "You've been a good friend."

The little dog looked scared but there was nothing for it.

"Good boy!"

He depressed the button on the horn and quickly opened the doors. The door to the rear flew back against the side of the airplane, the other flapped loosely in a closed position. The cold air bit through his clothing. *You idiot.* He hadn't counted on the extreme temperature, but there was nothing he could do about it now. Rand grabbed the line that held Spang's ripcord and looked out. The field flew by beneath them. Holding his breath, he shoved the cage out and down then hauled back on the ripcord line. The drop cage fell quickly and, to Rand's relief, the chute deployed. Spang was on his way. Now it was his turn.

With over a hundred pounds gone from cabin, the plane began climbing into the clouds. Standing in the flapping door, he had lost sight of the ground. The grey mist swirled around the open door like a seventies rock show. Something in him went very calm and he just crouched and dove into the grey. He hauled on his ripcord right away and expected to be snapped up like in the movies, but nothing happened. When he cleared the clouds he glanced at his wrist altimeter. The ground looked awfully close at twenty three hundred feet, especially when his chute hadn't opened. The Earth seem to leap at him, wanting him back. The roar of the airplane faded away as the rushing wind filled his ears. Then a gentle tug pulled him upright. His feet swung down and he suddenly felt his weight against the straps. He looked up at a white and orange canopy above his head and realised he had been yelling. Fear had turned seconds into minutes.

Suddenly it all caught up to him, he was nearly down. Adrenaline pumped through his veins and he checked his altimeter again; one thousand feet. He felt like he was much lower. He looked around; to the west was the drop cage, it's yellow chute splayed out on the ground. He looked down and to prepare for impact. *Roll when you hit, like the old WWII movies.* Then he remembered the handles hanging down from the straps. *Focus dammit!* He grabbed them and steered the parachute into the wind. The fast approaching ground slowed as he pulled on the handles. Then, with a final haul down, he took a couple of steps and he was standing on the ground. In the still air the chute slowly collapsed behind him into a heap of nylon.

He stood for a second, shaking. The adrenaline raging through his body. In the distance, there was a loud, splintering crash. At the far end of the runway a plume of smoke heralded the end of his plane. *I've done it.* He thought in utter disbelief. *Spang!* He tore off the parachute harness and ran. He had seen the drop crate from the air, but then he had turned. He stopped and listened. Sure enough, the horn sounded in the short distance to his right. The field was muddy and he fell several times, but finally he arrived at the drop cage. It had come to rest against a rugged line of scrub bushes, just past a large tractor.

"Hang on buddy!" He couldn't hear anything over the shrieking horn. As he peeled the duct tape back the horn stopped and Spang's barking came flooding into his ears.

"Spang! You crazy little fuzzball you made it! I knew you would!"

He opened the two cages and Spang jumped out in a wiggling flurry of fur and licking. Finally, Rand let him down to the ground where he turned towards the cage and barked at it. Rand sat on his knees in the mud, in tears, laughing. The joy of being alive, the joy at having seen his friend safe and the pride of his brave accomplishment washed over him like the rain on the field.

After a minute, he looked up, sobering. The rain was coming down harder. He cut the backpack from the drop cage then made for the cab of the tractor. The keys were in the ignition. Rand studied the controls. It was just a bit different than a car. It wouldn't turn over at first but then Rand remembered that most heavy equipment only started in neutral.

"We're on a roll buddy." He left the tractor to idle and went back out to retrieve the drop cage. He hung it on a set of bars on the back that were normally used for hooking up implements, then he climbed back in the dry cab.

"I know you don't want to hear this but we're probably going to need that thing again." Spang just looked sheepishly at him. They bounced their way onto the far end of the runway and cautiously picked their way through the smouldering wreckage of Heathrow.

Chapter 4

Digging in

'Never weather-beaten sail more willing bent to shore.'
~Tomas Campion

The mosaic of debris covered every inch of ground. Seat foam, food trays, rice, and shards of aluminium and plastic paved the path through corridors of giant broken cylinders of fuselage and towering tail sections. Wings jutted skyward, embedded in the ground like a melancholy sculpture in monument to the motion of man. The smell of smouldering synthetics and fuel hung in the lolling breeze as the day descended around them, soggy and droll. Rand knew he would feel very differently if there had been any victims, but he found the whole scene fascinating.

"We need to ditch the tractor and get a real ride." He told Spang who was clearly not enjoying the rattling contraption. He headed in the direction of the terminal. There he found a selection of vehicles in an odd variety of shapes and sizes. The problem was that they were air industry specific and moved slowly. He was starting to think the tractor might be the way to go when he came across a line of white trucks and SUVs with red and blue *ServiceAir* logos on the side. He passed the neat line of trucks and went into the office for the keys to a large white Ford truck. Once outside the airport they stopped at a gas station to get a map and he checked his notes for the route to the flight school. It was going to be tricky finding the place, but then they had all the time in the world. Between the congestion of cars and getting lost, it was over three hours before they found it.

The building was cream coloured, topped by a sign that read *Cabair Flight School* with a picture of a big yellow palm tree. Rand went in and looked around. He was pleased to find that it was a clean, professional, state-of-the-art facility.

"These people knew what they were doing buddy, but I'll be their hardest case. Teaching someone based on the notes you've left behind? Now that's tricky."

Spang launched into the daunting task of sniffing every inch of the place.

The first night they slept in a tent set up in the main area. From that point on, life was a continual project for Rand. He set up the power on generators, knocked down walls and painted, brought in furniture and appliances, kitchen cabinets and sectioned off an area for a bedroom. He discovered a workshop attached to the facility that taught airplane mechanics. It had a huge shop floor, three hangar doors, and enough space for three small planes and the tools to tackle just about any job.

He hit the books and started spending a lot of time in the school's flight sim. Eventually he knew he would have to go back to Heathrow to get into the sophisticated Airbus A350 simulator, but for the time being, he focused on learning the training plane. He drank bottled water and ate from huge stores of preserved foods from the various shops around the area but he began to crave fresh vegetables and fruits. A collection of various fuel trucks and construction machines began to fill the parking lot which he had cleared with a bulldozer. Searchlight trailers were moved in to light up the landscape and the sky as a signal to anyone who might see them. The nearby town of Cranfield had a university which Rand made full use of to research everything from growing gardens to raising farm animals. He focused on goats for milk and chickens for meat and eggs. Growing up in Montana he knew more than a few people who kept animals, so it wasn't entirely new to him. Over a two week break from training he established his farm.

With everything he needed from a local farm supply store, he fenced the fields and put up shelters for the goats and chickens. Finally, when all was ready, he went in search of animals. He left Spang behind and drove to every farm in the area. More than once he ran into hostile dogs and was unable to get out of the car. He finally had double luck at a farm over half an hour away from the school. The cattle and goats seemed to be doing fine grazing in a massive field along with over twenty chickens. The hen house was industrial sized and had, at one time held hundreds of chickens, Rand assumed that foxes were whittling down the flock. It was a full days work herding the animals into the trailer and pens, but when he was done, he had three goats for milk, six chickens for eggs and one cantankerous rooster.

In subsequent weeks he made every effort to stay busy. The more he worked, the less he thought about being alone. He would catch himself stopping to take a breather and staring out at the landscape. In those times his mind always tried to reflect and inevitably, thoughts of his family would come rushing to the surface. He thought too of Moira. Though he missed her he became aware that he didn't miss her as much as he felt he should.

Keeping melancholy at bay was a constant battle. Being stuck in the middle of a project was the thing that helped the most. He added more fuel trucks to the growing equipment inventory in the parking lot. When he finished parking the last truck in place, he knew he would have enough diesel and gas for at least a year. Straw was stored in a large workshop next to the flight school. Once he had the animals sorted out he began work on the garden.

He knocked down a wall that joined two large conference rooms in the northeastern corner of the building. Taking out the wall gave him one room that was about two-thousand square feet where he replaced all the regular ceiling lights with grow lights. Windows on the east and north walls, though not as ideal as south facing windows, provided some extra light. It took him the better part of a weekend, but he managed to move practically half of a local garden center into the room, raised beds and all. He planted what he would eat for two weeks, every two weeks.

Using railroad ties and a forklift, he built a large square bin. The doorframe took a beating, but the ends justified the means. After filling the bin with soil, he had an indoor, waist-high place to grow his root vegetables. Planting day was every other Sunday. This allowed him to rotate the beds, keep the soil fresh, and adjust what he wanted to plant. He was fed up with eating out of a can. It would take a while until the first harvest, but from then on, he planned to eat fresh every day. When he was done with the root beds he surveyed his work proudly. Then he said a prayer over the garden that it would grow like crazy.

Rand set up a regular schedule for himself and stuck to it religiously. Morning began with a workout, then breakfast and care of the animals and gardening. Lunch was time to play with Spang and the afternoons were for flight training. In the evenings, after dinner and checking on the flock, he would practice with the weapons, clean house, do laundry, make butter or try his hand at cheese. It was exhausting, but he had to constantly make sure that he kept his mind busy. It was getting much colder now and the first snow had fallen though it didn't stick to the ground. He knew it was just a matter of time until the snow came to stay.

"The place is starting to feel almost cozy." He said to Spang one evening. "Could use a fireplace though. Hey, maybe we should pick up one of those fake ones." *You need to get out for a day*, he thought *or you'll get cabin fever*.

He started a list of things that he wanted, but couldn't get locally. It was all just to give him a reason to go to London. *London means Heathrow and the 737 simulator.* The thought gave him a shiver. It was only a step away from actually making the trip across the ocean. His mixed emotions finally came to a head one night as he sat on the couch with the list.

'"We could just live the rest of our lives here you know."

Spang looked up at him from the other side of the couch. Rand pulled him into his lap.

"Just you and me, living out our days at this school in the middle of a field in England. You would get old and die. I would bury you out by the fence. Then I would get old, eventually get sick, and end up collapsing on the floor, dying of thirst. It's more likely we'd die of boredom long before that." He plopped Spang back down on the couch. "Okay, enough of that. I'm gonna learn to fly that big crate and we're gonna get outta here." That night he stayed up late, working the simulator in 737 mode.

In preparation for the trip to London, he welded a huge push bumper to a moving truck. The job took him a whole day. Spang watched from a sofa Rand had moved into the shop. When he finished the modifications he stood back and admired his work.

"I sure hope this works."

The God String

The next morning he grabbed Spang and a cooler full of food and water and headed for London. Everything started well enough, but the road got worse as he got closer to the city. The big bumper held up as he pushed his way through the mess of vehicles, but the truck was a bit light for the job. He knew he would have to come this way on a regular basis to use the big flight simulator so he took the extra time to make a clear path. He plowed his way into the city first and he and Spang spent the day shopping for everything from music gear to ATVs. He picked up everything from ridiculously overpriced watches to a bunch of stuffed toys for Spang to tear into. It was November 19th, the sun was shining and he and Spang ran rampant all over the city. Several times they caught sight of packs of dogs and once even spotted a zebra down a long street, but the animals avoided them. Still, Rand kept an eye out for any zoo predators that could be lurking about.

On the way out of London, the sun was going down and he knew he wasn't going to make it to Heathrow but he thought there might be just enough time to make a detour to the Lakenheath RAF Base for the last of his winter supplies. Three hours later, under a cold canopy of stars, they rolled up to the entrance.

"Looks like we're spending the night here." Rand said grumpily.

He drove through the open gates and headed for the armoury. Lakenheath was home to a fighter base but had all types of aircraft. Rand wondered how well he'd do in an

F-15 or one of the massive C-17 Globemaster III cargo planes. He thought he'd probably end up killing himself more than likely. The armoury was unlocked. The evidence revealed that there had probably been a full staff on duty when they vanished. Rand chalked it up to good luck. The first thing he picked was a shotgun that functioned like a machine gun called an AA-12. It was perfectly balanced and came with large drum clips of different types of ammo; exploding, armour piercing, flechette, slug and buck shot. He also found an M110A1 CSASS sniper rifle with a huge day/night scope and suppressor. He added to that a collection of other optics including spotting scopes, binoculars and night vision goggles. He was tempted to take some of the other weapons that were around but thought twice, remembering the explosion in Belfast.

"We have no use for grenades." He said to Spang who was busy filling his nose with some new scent in the far corner of the room.

Exploring the lockers and clothing yielded another haul: tough military grade clothing in a variety of camo patterns.

"I'm gonna look like a Ninja SWAT goat farmer once I get into all this but hey, it's sturdy."

He took everything in his size, especially the boots, of which he took six pairs. It all went into the truck along with an entire pallet of various types of ammunition, strapped all together with a roll of stretchy film.

While he was loading, he noticed the silhouette of a massive vehicle across the parking lot. After he was done he went over to investigate. The wheels on the thing were huge. It was twenty-four feet long and over ten feet high with a turret on top and heavily armoured. The windows were several inches thick and covered with steel louvers. It made the old Range Rover look like a toy. The door was unlocked so he climbed inside. The manufacturers stamp on the inside of the door read: *International MaxxPro MRAP Cat II Dash (Mine Resistant Ambush Protection vehicle).*

"Wow. No wonder this thing is built like a tank. It's IED proof."

The cab wasn't separated from the back like the Belfast Police Range Rover had been. Inside there were four chairs facing each other across a center aisle. The turret mechanism was enclosed by a steel box that Rand had to duck to get around. The rear door opened into a staircase because the vehicle was so far off the ground.

"I'm loving it buddy, what do you think?" Rand said as he came down the back stairs. "I bet I could weld a small dozer blade on the front. And look, it can even tow a trailer. This baby will move some cars."

He climbed in the driver's chair and discovered another bonus; he could control the turret from the driver's seat.

"Let's go find the keys."

They spent the evening nosing into everything they could find. Rand paid particular attention to finding classified and secret information. A safe in the commander's office was unlocked. The commander was clearly in the middle of working on something out of the safe when they had vanished.

"Holy crap buddy look at this. The RAF was training pilots to withstand terrorist torture techniques." Rand picked another file. "Here's an Army colonel that's under investigation for using heavy metal music to confuse the enemy during raids. Says here that the affect on the enemy wasn't the problem, it was that some of the soldiers felt that that kind of music compromised their religious beliefs."

A search through the ready room found flight gear that the F-15 pilots used including flight suits, gloves, helmets, and most importantly, parachutes. Rand held the military grade chutes at a higher standard than the civilian ones so he took two each for he and Spang then went through the medical facilities.

There was a robust medical presence on the base so he took everything he thought he could use on himself.

"Why didn't I think to check out military bases first? They are little cities all to themselves with everything we need to survive, and all of it is built for long-term storage and use. Even the food has a long shelf-life."

I took him awhile to find the manuals for the equipment he had gathered but it wasn't until he found the motor pool that his eyes lit up.

"The keys and the maintenance manual. Score."

He was so excited he went out to the big vehicle and started it up. The big engine roared to life.

"Oh yeah, that's the stuff buddy! Where have you been all my life you wonderful machine!"

He played with the turret and took the big rig for a spin around the lot. He was hooked. He shut it off and went back to the armoury where he found ammo for the minigun. It took over a half hour to figure out how to load it and he was nervous that he did it correctly. He started the engine and turned on the optics in the turret. From the driver's seat, he used a joystick to aim the gun. The motors whined as the heavy, steel turret swivelled at his command. A well-lit cursor appeared on a flat screen display in the center of the dash. The night vision mode worked perfectly. He aimed at a tree across the lot and pressed the trigger. The noise was only moderately loud, but much more subdued than Rand would have thought. It sounded like someone was using a chainsaw outside. He only held the trigger down for a two count but the tree, which was about six inches in diameter, was now sawn completely in half and toppled over into the parking lot. Spang barked at the noise and Rand just looked at him wide-eyed.

"Definitely not a toy."

They pitched the tent in the lobby of an office building and slept only marginally well. Rand missed his big new bed, as did Spang. The next morning he hooked the new vehicle up to a large trailer and transferred everything from the moving truck. With the road mostly cleared he thought the Maxx, as he called it (not knowing that its official name was an M-RAP), would have no problem dealing with whatever they encountered. It took until noon to gather everything he wanted from the base and hook up the trailer. He knew he was looking at a full day of driving, but in the end he would be completely stocked for winter and he would have an excellent vehicle.

On the way home he discovered that the Maxx's top speed was somewhat lacking. It took a full two and a half hours to get back to the school, but he still wanted to go back for the cargo truck. *After all,* he thought, *it runs, has a full tank of fuel and a push bumper. It would be stupid to waste it. Besides,* he reasoned, *that way I get to pick up another load of MREs, ammo and tools.*

He jumped a small Peugeot 208 that had been left in the school's parking lot, threw in the new auto shotgun and headed back to the base. Spang, as always, took the passenger seat. With the road clear the trip was much faster. As he approached the base and a heavy snow started to fall.

"We better get a move on before this snow starts to cause us problems."

When snow came in Montana it came hard and fast. He didn't know how it was in England but he didn't want to take any chances. He went straight for the forklift and loaded the pallets he wanted and then the forklift itself. As an afterthought he took a set of cold weather combat clothes. He tossed the gear into the passenger seat and put the white and grey camo coat on.

"Just in case we get stranded in the storm." He told Spang.

He climbed into the moving truck and headed back out again. The roads began to get slippery but the truck was heavy enough to push through. The snow increased in size and volume and by the time they arrived back at the flight school it had accumulated over an inch. Once everything was inside he closed the doors and they hunkered down for the storm which didn't let up for four days. By the time it was done, half the country was covered in over two feet of deep white. Rand ventured outside only to take care of the flock, turn on the searchlights at night and check the fuel levels in the generator. The back up was ready to go just in case. He used the time to his advantage and pulled the Maxx into the shop for a refit.

He wanted to be able to light up a 360-degree circle around the vehicle for as far as possible. He installed airplane landing lights on each corner and face of the vehicle and two on the turret. On the front, he welded I-beams to the frame and then attached the blade from a small bulldozer. It was an eight-hour job from start to finish and he had to use a small backhoe to hold the large pieces in place while he welded them. Next, he stripped out everything from the back, including the chairs, to make as much cargo area as possible. Spang just sat on the workbench and watched.

Several days after the snow storm it began to melt and Rand hooked a flatbed trailer to the Maxx and loaded it for a trip back to London. As always he threw in his pre-packed survival backpack which contained everything he would need to keep them alive and find their way back to the school.

With everything packed they took the newly converted Maxx out on its maiden voyage. The vehicle performed better than expected, easily towing the trailer and pushing cars out of the way with it's heavy-duty bumper. It took three hours to get into London. He chose the Westfield Center where there was a large selection of shops. From there he could take the M4 to Heathrow.

Rand pushed the Maxx into the entrance of the parking lot. It was heavily congested but opened up once he worked his way further in.

If people had vanished in the morning, then that would explain why there aren't a lot of cars. He thought. *No one made it out to the mall.*

Once the Maxx and its trailer were parked, Rand surveyed the massive lot with the turret optics. He wasn't stepping out until he knew it was safe. Sure enough, he spotted a large pack of dogs watching him from the corner of the farthest building. He wound up the turret and fired and long burst across the lot. Raking the stream of fire across the side of the building, chunks of cement went flying as the pack frantically scrambled over each other to escape. Flocks of birds burst from nearby trees as the roaring noise from the gun shattered the silence of the city.

Rand chuckled quietly. "That should keep any beasties at bay."

The God String

With the auto-shotgun in hand and .45 ever at his side, he felt safe to climb out. He lowered the loading ramp and drove the ATV and its small trailer down onto the lot. Spang rode in a chest pack and the shotgun was placed in its mount on the handle bars.

"Okay buddy, let's go shopping."

He checked his list against the map of the mall and made good time. After the trailer was loaded they plowed their way to the A4, which turned into the M4 to Heathrow.

The Heathrow Airside Tunnel was a death trap for the Maxx as far as Rand was concerned. Even a bulldozer would have had trouble moving all of the vehicles that clogged the way so he decided to go off-road and barge through the fence. It was early afternoon as the Maxx trundled over chunks of wreckage on the tarmac of Heathrow. Rand was looking for the wreck of the plane he had flown. Finally he spotted it -- crumpled nose first just at the verge of a stand of trees, the tail protruding from the ground.

"There, but for the grace of God go we." He still couldn't believe he had pulled it off. "One more to go buddy, then we're on our way to real living."

He turned away and went looking for a dry spot to park. What he found was an empty hangar for a jumbo jet.

"It'll do." He laughed.

He packed Spang in his harness and took the ATV to the terminal. Spang leaned into the breeze from his chest-pack perch.

"It's going to be a bit of a hunt buddy."

They barrelled through the melting snow toward the terminal to start looking for the 737 simulator. As the busiest aviation center in the world Heathrow was vast. He tried to keep some kind of a map the massive complex, but even that was proving difficult. Finally after an hour and a half of driving around and blowing locked doors open, he found what he was after. Upstairs above the main security checkpoint he found a map of the whole airport in the security director's office.

"We're in the wrong area entirely." He said to Spang who dangled over the map from his chest carrier. "The Airbus training facility is over here, about a mile away in a separate building."

The trip took fifteen minutes but they finally pulled up outside the facility. A well placed shotgun round to the door gained access.

The layout was fairly straight forward. There was a small reception area, a briefing room, locker room, main frame and networking room, control room and the sim. The simulator was impressive. It was in a two story high space, painted entirely white with what looked like a small metal shipping container mounted on heavy steel, hydraulic scaffolding. Rand anticipated that it would require a bit of training just to get the whole thing working. He dug around for any information he could find. In the end an entire shelf full of manuals, four laptops and a pile of notes and checklists from the engineers all went into plastic tubs in the ATV's trailer.

As they sped across the middle of the field on the way back to the Maxx, Rand heard a strange noise behind him. It sounded like his rear tire was rubbing on the fender, but as he turned he saw a pack of over twenty dogs running hard after him. He gunned the throttle, but he had to swerve to avoid all the wreckage while the dogs just bounded over it. He looked back again, they were gaining. He knew that the closer they were, the less time he had to react, so he slammed the brakes in a skidding turn. As the ATV slid sideways to a stop, Rand grabbed the shotgun from its mount. In one fluid motion he brought the big gun to his shoulder.

Slide back, safety off, aim low, squeeze. The fully automatic shotgun began tearing through the ranks of dogs as the pack came at him. He fired in controlled busts. It only took seconds to kill or injure all but two of the dogs, who fled in panic. Adrenaline washed into him.

"Holy crap. That was close." He sat on the ATV with a hand to his forehead. It was the first time he had ever shot at anything in self-defense. Blood and fur were spattered across the snow. The painful whimpering of the wild dogs sounded in grisly chorus. With a heavy sadness he drew his pistol and walked to them. Several dogs were trying to limp or crawl away with severe injuries. He carefully took aim and finished them off. The event hurt him grievously. He loved all animals, especially dogs. These poor creatures were just trying to survive. In the chest pack Spang whined.

"You're right, let's get out of here."

They loaded everything into the Maxx and headed back home. As soon as he arrived, he went to take care of his flock. He had named the two hens Henrietta and Beatrice. The Colonel, a plucky rooster, serviced them. Daisy and Adeline were the two nannies and the buck goat was simply Bucky. Bucky was kept far away from the females as he was only needed to mate occasionally. All the information Rand found about raising goats for milk said that if the male goat was kept too close to the females the milk would taste funny. After taking care of them he got to work unloading. Using the forklift, the large shed came off the trailer and became a new home for the flock. He kept himself busy and tried to put the incident at Heathrow behind him.

He continued to practice what he had learned on the simulator at the flight school and put himself through tests in navigation, take off and landing procedures. With each new success he began to enjoy the process more. It was tempting to stay up late into the evenings working on the simulator, but he knew that he had to stick to his schedule to give everything the attention that it needed. Balance, he learned, was another key to survival.

He was pleased that his flight training was starting to stick. When he took the tests the school had prepared, he scored well and his confidence began to rise sharply. Soon it was time to move on to the A350. Over the course of the next week, he focused his studies on operating the simulator at Heathrow. There was no 'quick step' guide so Rand diligently plowed through the data trying to figure out how to simply start the thing. It was going to take a lot of homework.

As December came on he cut down a small tree and decorated it with some lights and ornaments, but it was a strong sentimental trigger. After only a day of having it up, he took it down, though he kept one small bough.

On Christmas morning Rand went to a small chapel in the village. Kneeling at the altar he said the *Our Father* and then struggled as he tried to find the right words to pray.

It's the why. That's really why I'm here. Yeah, happy birthday and all but what the fuck?

His stuttering thoughts piled up behind the pressure of his battered emotions.

"You have to see me here!" He shouted at the ceiling. "I'm just…" He trailed off. *Just what? Waiting? Waiting for what, to die?*

His anger boiled over and he swept the altar clear, the cups and candle holders clattered across the marble floor.

"I brought this for you," he spoke through gritted teeth, "for your birthday." He placed the bough sprig on the altar.

"It's a reminder, I'm still here. HEY, I'M STILL HERE!" He roared at the heavens then slumped against the altar and let the flood consume him.

He talked to the angels and to God until he could no longer speak. Spang sat patiently. It was well after noon when he finished. Exhausted and spent, he crossed himself with an 'amen'. Suddenly the sun blazed through the chapel windows, bathing the room in a golden light.

He breathed deep and stood.

"You heard me. Sorry about that."

He bowed to the altar, but as he turned to go he saw, through the golden beams of light, the faint image of a congregation. The little chapel was full of people, but they were separated into layers of colours like a video that was out of sync. The people were just getting up after the service and many of them seemed to be looking at Rand and pointing with astonished looks on their faces. Rand quickly looked back at the altar where the apparition of a priest was looking at the pine bough and then at him. There was no sound as this went on. Then as suddenly as they came, they disappeared. A wave of dizziness washed over Rand. He sat down hard on the steps and everything went black.

***

Shining in brilliant gold, the strand stretched from him, into the blackness. He was following as it twisted, immensely taut but coiling. So much speed! The cord ran into him, through him, *was* him. It curved upwards ahead, or had he been going down? Maybe it was going to level out, he couldn't be sure. There, far ahead, another cord split from the one he connected to. He was far off, but coming to it soon. Gold became silver, silver grew white, white grew larger and then, he was opening his eyes, lying on his side on the steps of the altar.

***

Spang was licking his face. He sat up expecting to feel dizzy, but he felt completely normal.

"I'm okay buddy, I'm okay. What the hell was that? Did you see that? Holy… I mean, wow!"

Looking around he could see no trace of the congregation or the priest. He stood, perplexed. Walking out of the chapel he was convinced that he had just had the most incredible vision. As he went out the doors he squinted his eyes in preparation for the bright sun but it was behind a solid ceiling of grey clouds.

The sun wasn't out.

He turned and looked back inside, the chapel was dark. He shook his head and felt around to see if he was hurt anywhere, but he was fine. He drove back to the school in a daze. Later that evening, as he sat on the couch trying to read but the vision kept playing in his mind.

Maybe there's a gas leak in the place or something.

Spang looked at him and snorted.

The daily routine continued. The garden was coming up nicely, but it would be another month until the first harvest. The animals were producing milk and eggs and they had more milk than they could drink, so Rand learned how to make butter and started looking into making cheese. In the mornings he would look at himself in the mirror. It was the only pair of human eyes he could look into. He was lean and healthy. His handsome features showed the stress that he was living under but also the satisfaction of having achieved so much. He wore a goatee and his hair had grown longer. He made sure he stayed clean and civilised looking, but the loss and loneliness still crept below the surface, creating lines that hardened his features. He knew that it was crucial to his survival to stay mentally and emotionally balanced, and that meant staying very busy. His library grew into six tall bookshelves arranged by topic alphabetically; it started with *animals* then went by type – *chickens* then *dogs* then *goats* and so on. He'd never been so organised in his life.

On a cold, clear evening he was distracted from playing guitar by a sound that reminded him of fireworks. He bolted outside with a large pair of binoculars, hoping beyond hope that someone was signalling their presence. Far to the west, a fiery streak lit up the sky. Spang barked at the light. Rand's heart sank and he felt like an idiot for having been fooled.

"Yep, looks like the satellites are starting to drop." The disappointment put him in a melancholy funk. "It's coming down in one piece, there's no other chunks that I can see." Rand watched it fade from view. "Get used to that, and just hope one doesn't land on us."

The God String

***

Far out in the surging dark of the Atlantic, three parachutes sunk into the waves, pulling an empty capsule down with them.

Montgomery Thompson

Chapter 5

Earth angel

*'In the world you will have tribulation.
But take heart; I have overcome the world.'*
-John 16:33

It was sunrise on a sodden, winter's day when Rand returned to Heathrow. He had done his homework and knew how to get the big simulator running. His first task was to connect the building to a large generator he had towed from an equipment rental business close to the school. The Maxx easily pulled the weight of the large generator, freshly loaded with fuel. Without possessing the skills of an electrician the task proved difficult. Nevertheless, he had come prepared and after running numerous extension cords to the simulator systems he finally had it up and running.

The initial thrill of flying in the realistic environment faded with the tedium of having to climb out of the cockpit and run down the stairs to reset the system every time he crashed, which was often. Spang sat outside the door, he didn't like it when the whole room moved. Rand worked on take-off and navigation at first then worked his way into approach and landing. Hours ticked by as he tried repeatedly to master landing the huge jet. Finally, as the sun was getting low outside, he nailed it.

All the way back home he rode a wave of elation. Even the low hanging clouds couldn't dampen his mood. The school came into view just as night had settled in cold and dark. Rand sensed that something was wrong and turned on the array of lights he had installed. Spang became frantic as the lights swept over a churning sea of fur and teeth. A huge pack of dogs were swarming the compound, trying to get at the flock. They scattered as the lights hit them, but soon came slinking back. Rand knew that fear and adrenaline amongst his flock would spoil whatever they made. Other than a few vegetables, he had no other sources for fresh food. He had to eliminate this threat, and quickly.

He fired a burst into the air with the chain gun. Again, the dogs scattered then returned moments later. He couldn't use the chain gun on the pack or he would risk hitting the flock and chewing through the fence. He spun the Maxx around and backed up to the front door, then went through the back of the vehicle to open up the hatch. With his forty five at the ready, he lowered the ramp. As the electric motor whined, Rand peeked through the slowly expanding crack. Five sets of flashing teeth on the left. He fired and two went down with a yelp. Again, they ran off, but quickly came back. Seizing the opportunity, Rand tensed to lunge for the front door. Before he jumped he checked to his right just as an enormous Alsatian charged the opening. He quickly fired and missed, but the dog turned at the sound and sprinted a short distance away. Rand darted through the front door, but as he turned to close it the German Shepherd's head rammed through the gap, the powerful jaws snapping at Rand's arm. He quickly put his shoulder to the door and squeezed the dog's head. The Shepherd yelped and backed out. Rand let the door go loose for a second so the dog could pull his head out then slammed the door shut and set the bolt.

"Son of a bitch, those dogs are mental!"

Heart racing, he ran to the shop and grabbed the fully automatic shotgun off the ATV. Then, he stopped himself short.

"Okay, slow down. Everyone is safe. They're not going to get through the fence, it's just a pest problem now."

Calmly, he put the shotgun back on the ATV and picked up the case with the sniper rifle. He practiced with this one as well and had sighted in a variety of different ranges. The roof had an access hatch from the shop. He had considered building a greenhouse up there but the roof was thick with pitch. Now, he used a ladder to get up to the roof and stepped through the pitch. That was the end of a pair of good boots. *From now on, they'll be the roof boots.*

From up high he could see everything very clearly. The Maxx was idling, its bright lights lit up the front of the building and the parking lot. With dogs circling the large fenced field, the flock stayed in the center but seemed calm. Spang was pouting in the cab of the Maxx, unhappy to be left out of the action but completely safe. As Rand surveyed the scene, a quiet anger rose in him. He was the guardian of the last bastion of human existence and this was his family they were threatening. It was easy once he got his range dialled in. The rifle had a stern kick to it but it was a piece of precision military hardware and it delivered on its promise – one shot, one kill. It took a total of five minutes. Rand finished off the last ones even as they were trying to run. He knew if he didn't, they would eventually come back. He came down and let Spang inside. The little dog was indignant and marched off straight to bed. He put away the Maxx and retired to the shop to put away supplies and clean the weapons. The next day he would clean up the carcasses.

A month later, he brought in the first harvest. It was so good to have fresh garden vegetables. He had radishes, spinach, snap peas and beans, some small broccoli and even a few beets. He quickly learned that he had grown way too much of some things and not enough of the others, so he changed his planting accordingly. Every other day he made the trip to Heathrow where he flew over twenty hours a week in the sim. He was beginning learn how to address in-flight emergencies and how to handle landings in difficult crosswinds. In the course of his training he learned that flying a 737 was actually easier than flying the Cessna. He could put the course into the flight computer and the plane would takeoff, fly the route, perform the approach and land practically all on it's own. He had assumed that the navigation system was based on GPS but that was only partially true. The traditional guidance systems played a major role as well and the plane could navigate either way.

At the end of his last week he made a crucial decision. He would land the plane, not jump out. Being a pilot was key to his survival and he needed to know as much as possible. Knowing that the plane could land itself was not enough. He needed to know how to do it in case something, as it always did, went wrong. The decision took a weight off of him. The thought of jumping again was daunting. It was one thing to jump out of a Cessna at seventy miles per hour. It was another thing entirely to jump out of a huge jetliner going two hundred. First he would attempt a real takeoff and landing at Heathrow. The date he set was May 1. It was February 27, he had two months. He called it 'live day' in hopes that he would be alive at the end of it.

The trip to London was a breeze now that the road was clear. The snow and ice didn't hamper the Maxx at all, although the thing only got about eight miles to the gallon. Several times he almost gave in and took one of the nice Range Rover SUVs at the side of the road. Then he thought of the possibility of getting wholloped by some piece of space junk and concluded that it was best to travel in the Maxx.

The next two months passed without incident and after every sim session he spent extra time clearing one of the less damaged runways. The massive sections of crashed planes had to be towed off the tarmac. In the end it was a combination of bulldozer and crane that proved the most useful. Then he took a large street sweeper and scrubbed the tarmac clean. He knew he had to be vigilant for little pieces of anything that could get sucked into the engines. The best bet was to make sure the runway and taxiway were well cleaned. Without knowing the weather he might have abandon his trip return to Heathrow. It was essential that there was a place to land.

The snow melted quickly and as an added blessing the spring began early. A month out he decided it was time to go plane shopping.

"This time we're going big." He told Spang as he drove. "None of that mamby-pamby small plane stuff – been there, wrecked that." He giggled.

At Heathrow he simply chose the largest of the intact hangars and hoped for the best. He found several planes that would do the job but he settled on a shiny new Airbus A350-900 that had been a part of the DHL fleet. He hadn't been training on this particular variant but it was new, in a hanger, designed for cargo and as a bonus -- it was outrageously yellow. He rounded up the tug, cargo lift and fuel truck and made sure they were all fuelled and ready. Once a week he opened up the hanger and did a complete check over including starting the engines. Then he would shut it down and put it back in. He used every available means to gather information about how to check the aircraft for flight readiness. All seemed well with the plane though there was no way to be entirely sure. Before he knew it, live day was upon him.

Five to eight mile per hour winds out of the east and clear skies, couldn't ask for better.

After scrubbing the taxiway and runway one last time, he pulled the plane out and prepared to make a practice run. If he was successful then he would go, if not, he could just bail out and head back to the school. In the hangar, Spang sat in the front seat of the Maxx. The little dog watched grumpily through the thick glass.

"I'll be back for ya buddy don't worry." Rand assured him. He parked the tug then climbed into the plane with an extension ladder. *Okay…bat belt, survival pack, parachute – all check.* He mentally went through his equipment in case he had to bail out.

After he stowed the ladder he climbed into the pilot's seat and ran through the initial taxi check list. The butterflies in his stomach began to flutter, but he focused on the task at hand. He had stopped at every gas station on the way trying to find fuzzy dice to hang in the window but to no avail. *What is the world coming to when you can't get fuzzy dice at a convenience store? Ah well, maybe once we're back in the states.*

The plane's two giant Rolls Royce Trent XWB engines wound up to speed. With a sigh he released the brakes and began taxiing to the cleared runway. The feeling of the big plane moving underneath him made the butterflies flutter harder but he chased them away with bravado.

"Yeah baby, this is how I ride!" He concentrated on regulating his ground speed and cruised at a comfortable pace to the end of the taxi way and onto the cleared runway, facing east into the wind. There, he throttled back, entered the data into the nav computer and went through his preflight checklist. Anxiety rose like a high tide but he stuck to his notes and checked everything off. Taking a deep breath, he gave himself a pep talk.

"You've done this hundreds of times over the last three months. The training is accurate and the plane is in great condition. Just stick to the plan."

So far the controls felt almost exactly like the sim. Same feel, same look, everything was where it was supposed to be. There was nothing else to delay him. He looked down the runway. Wreckage was piled on both sides as far as he could see. It was like driving down some dark cathedral of airplane death. Squaring himself, he clenched his teeth. His eyes narrowed as he throttled up the big liner.

"Lord, please see me safely back down." He prayed as the plane shuddered into motion.

The acceleration was much faster that the little Cessna and Rand had to fight the instinct to hold onto the controls. Instead, he let himself be pushed back in the seat

The God String

and slowly the wheel came back when he reached take off velocity. A veteran pilot would have a long list of things for Rand to improve on, but he was in the air. Breathing out a sigh he repeated the scenario he had trained for. Get up to level flight, turn around, pass the airport, turn around again and land into the wind. He stuck to the checklist. The computer performed the manoeuvres flawlessly but Rand tried to stay ahead of every move as if he were flying it himself. He had severely underestimated how much he was going to need his notes. The confidence he had on the ground in the days leading up to the flight evaporated completely now that he was aloft. He had to work hard to calm himself down.

One thing the sim didn't do was communicate the sensation of forward movement, the feeling of the immense size and weight of the airplane and the detail of the world outside the cockpit. All of those factors, in that moment, made those notes the most important thing in his world. He followed his finger down the list to the next manoeuvre and started talking himself through it.

"Okay," he stammered, "seven minutes, and then the turn."

He swallowed hard. "No biggie, turn on heading zero nine two at fifteen degrees for three minutes."

The airplane responded as if on cue. It was still flying itself, but Rand anticipated it's every move.

"Okay, now come level at two thousand feet, heading two seven two and pass the airport to the right."

He kept a close eye on the clock. It was working. The huge craft was actually flying itself.

"Now begin the turn."

The plane was a masterpiece of aviation engineering and smoothly followed the flight plan. The next series of manoeuvres brought Rand to his approach.

"All right, here we go. Flaps, gear down. Keep light on the stick and remember to breathe."

He checked and rechecked that everything was in order. Rate of descent, speed, flaps, altitude. He took note of the adjustments being made as he came in. No crosswind and a gentle headwind made it all the easier. He anticipated the timing of the flare a little early which used up more runway before the wheels touched down. The reverse thrusters came on hard and then brakes as the plane's speed dropped. He was coasting to a smooth stop in the middle of the runway. All of a sudden it dawned on him – he was back on the ground.

"I did it!" He yelled and punched the arms of the chair.

Then the voice in his head said, *Do it again, right now, but this time no nav computer.*

"Huh? Yeah, that's right. Stick with it until you can do it without freaking out. C'mon before fear stops you, go, go!"

He taxied the plane around and headed back down the runway, his pulse racing. Once again, he positioned himself with the wind coming at him and fired up for the takeoff. He started to relax.

"Stay cool, no victory dance until you've done this at least three times."

Part of him couldn't believe what he was saying.

He lurched a bit on take-off and seemed to use more runway than the nav computer, but he was up. He came smoothly up to altitude and levelled off as he started to time the turn. In training he had the habit of starting the turn too soon. This would result in him missing the line up for the landing. He would be to the right or left and then would have to compensate by manhandling the rudder. Then he would forget to check his speed and consequently have to abort the landing. It had been weeks since he made that mistake, but he was very conscious not to do it this time.

He eyed the controls intently as he began the turn.

"Keep it like clockwork Rand." He talked himself through the ordeal.

The huge plane came about and he was rewarded with a view of the runway perfectly aligned in his windshield. The descent was equally as successful and he remembered how to make small adjustments on the way down. Then it was just the flare and touchdown.

As he eased the engines out of reverse a sudden wash of complete elation came over him. He was practically in tears from relief.

The voice spoke, *again.*

He kept at it the rest of the day, determined to get the fear out of his gut. He did several touch and go landings, as well as three more complete landings. Each one was a solid performance. He went from being scared to death to really enjoying it. As the sun was starting to get low he taxied the big plane up to the hangar and shut her down.

Opening the cabin door, he stood at the top of the ladder he raised his hands in the air, "Thank you Heathrow!" and let out a whoop.

He was exhausted but felt like a rock star. He let Spang out and sat down to think about the next move. "The time has come to leave here buddy. He sat with Spang on the tug sharing a sandwich and scribbling notes. There was always the chance that they would have to bail out. Rand had no way of knowing the condition of the runways and even though he had coordinates for alternatives, they might be forced to jump due to lack of fuel. It was a chance they had to take. Either way, he had no doubt that they could reach America and get safely to the ground.

"Marine Corps Air Station New River, North Carolina Spang. That's where we're going. That's going to be our new home."

With grin glued to his face, he closed up the hangar and headed back to the school.

It only took him two days and three trips to Heathrow to get everything prepped and loaded. On May 5th he stood in the door of the school and said a prayer of thanks. Then he left a note stuck on the inside of the door.

The God String

If you are reading this, know that I am alive. My name is Rand and I somehow survived. What actually happened is still a mystery to me, I just woke up and everyone was gone. I used this place to train to fly a 737 to America. I had very little flight experience before this but have since done very well both on the simulator and the actual aircraft at Heathrow (you will see that I cleared a path for you). I'm hoping to find a home in New River North Carolina at the Marine Air Station. Don't give up hope. Grow a garden, raise livestock and train yourself to fly. I'm very confident I will make the journey and would dearly love to meet you. Stay peaceful, sane and know that you are not alone.

All the best.
Rand and Spang.

He signed it and drew a picture of a paw to indicate that Spang was a dog. Then, with Spang leaning out the window, he drove the Maxx to the airport. It was a several hours of work but, in the end, he got everything loaded and balanced. The DHL terminal had special aluminium containers that were used for packing the plane. He used some of the containers as feed bins, leaving them open for the animals to graze and drink and some of them to partition the cargo so the weight was balanced. After securing the ladder he climbed into the cockpit and put Spang in his special chair; milk crates topped with his favourite couch cushion that gave him an elevated position in the co-pilot's seat. Rand made sure the little dog could see out the windows but a harness attached him via a short lead to the seatbelt so he didn't accidentally hit any controls. The Maxx was parked in the hangar with the battery disconnected and a spare battery on a cart next to it. Both batteries were connected to a solar powered trickle charger that Rand has staked into the ground. He left a note stuck to the wall.

You can thrive, not just survive at Cabair Flight School in Cranfield. We flew to New River Marine base in North Carolina, on May 5th. You will be able to catch us there for at least a year.

Good luck.

Rand and Spang

P.S. The keys are in the Maxx, take good care of her.

P.S.S. It's possible we may come back here, so don't shoot!

Up in the cockpit, he peeled his eyes away from the big vehicle.

"Okay, here we go buddy. We've earned our jump wings, now it's time to take it to the next level. You ready?"

Spang looked at him, panting out of anxiety. It was 9:06 a.m. when the bright yellow A350 lifted effortlessly into the sky. Rand had topped it off and done a full check, it was as ready as he could make it. The weight on the plane was noticeable, but for a cargo plane he knew it was still underloaded. With no weather information he just set the course and hoped for the best.

The God String

As the navigation system flew the plane like a seasoned pro, Rand went back and let the animals into an open area between two containers. Then he watched some Marvel movies, played with Spang and tried to pass the time occupying himself as best he could. Underneath them the cold blue of the Atlantic streaked by.

At the eight and a half hour mark he put the animals back in their pens. Then, waiting until the last moment he put an unwilling Spang into the drop cage, put on his chute and strapped back into the pilot's seat.

"Sorry buddy, but if we have to jump it's gonna be on short notice."

Right on queue they approached the North Carolina coast. He took over manual control and dropped to an altitude of five thousand feet. An airport appeared in front and to the left and Rand looked through his big binoculars.

"It's too big to be a municipal airport, but it's too small to be an international airport. Let's have a look."

Spang was whining in the drop cage. He didn't like it at all, bacon or no. Rand slowed the plane and came down to fifteen hundred feet, it felt like they were going to clip the tops of the trees. He saw rows of V-22 Osprey lined up on the tarmac.

New River.

His navigation had worked.

"Thank you Cabair."

He circled the Marine base in a wide, left turn so he could look down more easily. The place was a disaster. There had been a massive explosion on the primary runway. The crater was so large that it cut the runway in two.

"Looks like a bomb must have went off." He felt his suspicions were confirmed when he identified the wreckage of what was once a massive C-17 Globemaster military transport scattered across the field. Several of the Osprey had been capsized by what must have been a tremendous blast. The debris from the explosion was scattered all over both landing surfaces and Rand could see the blast marks radiating from the center.

Rand sighed. "Change of plans buddy. Good thing we accounted for this."

He pulled the plane out of its turn, throttled back up and headed south. When he regained altitude, he quickly turned to his plan-B flight notes and set in the course. He still had plenty of fuel so he relaxed in the knowledge that it was short flight to Cape Canaveral.

"Sorry buddy, let's get you out of there." He set Spang free.

It was another two hours to the Cape. At 3:27 p.m. Rand dropped his speed and altitude and began his pass to survey NASA's Space Shuttle Runway.

"God that thing is huge. I could land at full speed and still have room to stop."

It was one of the largest runways in the world, stretching into the distance like an eight lane highway surrounded by sandy flats and water canals. It was every pilot's dream of the perfect landing strip and to make it even better, the Florida weather was sunny and calm.

He headed out over the ocean then, turned about for the approach. The long runway took some of the worry away and he brought the A350 in for a perfect landing, braking lightly and letting the plane gradually roll toward the building complex at the north end where he taxied into the landing facility and braked to a halt.

His feeling of accomplishment was somewhat diminished by the mundane nature of the landing. "Can you believe we just flew across the Atlantic?" The full reality of his accomplishment hit when he opened the door as a sunny, Florida spring day slapped him in the face.

"Wow, smell that!" A fresh ocean breeze was drifting in from the cape. He carried Spang down the ladder with the shotgun slung over his shoulder.

"No more rainy old England for us."

He stood with his face to the sun as Spang sprinted through the tall, green grass in wide circles. Rand came back down to earth and thought about the other animals. It was time to get moving. On the other side of the fence a marshy field of reeds waved in the breeze. He suddenly remembered, *Oh hell, they have alligators here.*

He put Spang back on the plane then he used the construction grade forklift to unload onto the runway. He felt light, awake and elated at just being there. It made the work easy. The goats were rounded up and put inside a circle of containers on the grass, except for Bucky who was once again relegated to a pen of his own. They began grazing immediately. The chickens went into an impromptu fence made from a roll of chicken wire, staked rebar and zip ties – all of which he'd brought along for the purpose. Then he placed the little hen house inside and bird netting over the top. It formed a loose octagon about fifteen feet in diameter. He gave the animals food and water, then explored the grounds with the ATV. Driving around the facility, he checked out the buildings. The first was a small, hi-tech hospital where astronauts would be examined on their return.

Rand had always loved the space program. He watched as many shuttle missions as he could. Now, standing and looking at all the mission patches on the hospital wall brought a lump to his throat. He left and continued to drive around the facility. Most of the buildings had back up generators but none of them were working. He stopped in front of Mission Control to plan his next move and couldn't resist having a peek inside. The front door was open and a large, white lobby filled with pictures of NASA memorabilia greeted him. He decided he would have to come back and tour the place properly.

Out in the parking lot he found a white NASA pickup parked up against a beamer. He jump started it and headed south on the Kennedy Parkway. Surprisingly the road was mostly clear of wreckage and he made good time to the Cape Canaveral Air Force Station. The destination was no accident. He had learned that military bases were great

The God String

survival locations. Driving through the base he searched for unusually large vehicles, ones painted either desert tan or forest green camo. It wasn't long before he located the military security motor pool. He found what he was looking for in a long, six-bay garage.

Though the armoured vehicles weren't as large as the Maxx, he found one large enough to do the job. The four wheels came up to his mid section and a turret on top housed a fifty-caliber machine gun and auto grenade launcher. Like the Maxx, the turret was automated and controlled by the driver or front passenger.

Rand climbed in and began rummaging around. Inside were two M4 carbines in a weapons rack, a box of ammo, Kevlar helmets and vests and radios. He continued looking and found the military manual. The manual introduced him to the M1117 Guardian. As he reviewed the capabilities of the weapons systems he just shook his head. *And I thought the Maxx was deadly.*

The garage was attached to the motor pool maintenance shop which made it easy to do what he needed to do. Around the corner from the security pen there were numerous construction vehicles. He located a forklift and a small bulldozer and got to work.

With a cutting torch, he removed the blade from the dozer and used the forklift to hold it up. This time, the whole operation was faster due to the fact that he'd done it before and knew what to expect. The military also kept things very organised and maintained so it was easy to find what he needed. By the time he had the blade installed on the Guardian it was 6:30 pm and he was exhausted. He calculated the time difference and determined that it was about 4:00 am in the UK.

Maybe I tried to do too much today. He was starting to get a little light headed. He hooked a trailer to the Guardian and drove it back to where the plane was parked stopping by to pick up the side-by-side ATV on the way. The animals were doing fine. No alligators had emerged from the marsh. Rand was sure that NASA had some kind of animal control in the works, but he had to be careful. It had been almost a year since anyone had been there and it was feasible that a family of gators could have moved in. He rolled out his mattress in the back of the plane and curled up with Spang.

"Tomorrow we get find better digs buddy."

The morning came hot and bright. Rand crawled out to a beautiful day. He could actually feel the bags under his eyes, but he felt very awake. Jet lag. He knew the feeling well after travelling back and forth in the early days of his relationship with Moira; body trashed, mind on fire, or vice versa. After a fresh breakfast Rand got busy lifting the garden beds out and onto the lawn with the forklift. Because of the intense Florida sun, he placed them so they would get mostly shade. After that, he took the side-by-side to look for fuel trucks. There were plenty on the base and in within the hour he had the backup generator at Mission

The God String

Control up and running. He took another fuel truck to the little hospital and fired up that system as well. Then he tended to the flock and retrieved some of his gear from the cockpit. Suddenly he remembered Mission Control. "Hey Spang, what say we take a tour."

Of all the reasons he had to go there; equipment, set up a broadcast, try to get weather information – the truth was that he wanted to see the place where man had been the best, gone farthest and accomplished so much. In the wake of his new flight experience it somehow seemed more important than ever. The main hallway was lined with pictures of NASA missions.

"This is where it all happened." He looked at the images in awe.

They wandered the hallways for awhile looking on various offices, copier rooms and meeting rooms. It was boring and mundane. Just as Rand was starting to get deflated he poked his head into a room that was set up like a small version of the modern control rooms in the movies. He went in and flipped on the lights. Five gigantic flat screens were mounted on the wall with and array of smaller screens above them. Rows of workstations all faced the large screens. Behind this was an upper section where guests could watch and where administrators could meet. On a side wall found a fuse box. The main fuse had tripped, but when Rand reset it all the computers and screens flickered to life. He stood and watched for a minute as the systems booted. He could imagine all the busy men and women working away on missions and talking to astronauts.

"I wonder if all this stuff is actually tracking satellites or something?"

The computers seemed to automatically boot the programs they ran. Soon they were chattering away, many with big red letters flashing warnings and alerts. The large screens showed a detailed picture of the earth with a series of lines like giant waves. Other screens showed windows full of programming language and graphs. The largest screen seemed to be a camera that was pointing at something that was an off-white texture. Rand walked down between the workstations. *It's probably the lack of the GPS that is causing most of the problems.* He looked at the screens trying to figure out what they did, but he hadn't a clue. He stopped at a workstation labeled 'Communications' on a piece of blue illuminated glass. He picked up the headset mic lying on the desk and put it to his ear. The cord ran to a box with a switch on it. Rand keyed the mic jokingly, "Uh, testing one two three, is this thing on? Apollo this is Cape Canaveral, we have a seriously, major problem."

He giggled and set the mic back down. "That should take--"

"Hello, hello?" A voice crackled over the speakers.

Spang barked

Rand Froze

"Hello? Cape? Cape Canaveral come in this in the International Space Station. IS SOMEBODY THERE?

The God String

The voice sounded frantic.

"Oh my God buddy, shit!" He fumbled with the headphones and keyed the mic again. "Yes! Yes! I'm here! Hello? Is this really the International Space Station?"

"Oh my God!" Screaming and crying came over the mic. Rand realised he was crying as well.

"What," He tried to break in. "what is your name?'

"Elsie, Elsie Clay. Who are you? What the hell is happening down there?"

Rand looked at Spang and breathed deep. "My name is Rand, I just got here--"

"Oh thank God. Rand it is so good to hear a voice. I thought I was going to go crazy… up here… waiting to die…" Her voice trailed off into tears.

"No! You are not going to die! Listen, I woke up one morning and everyone was gone. I haven't seen a single human being for over nine months."

"Oh my God. Yes, That's what happened to me. I woke up and everyone had vanished from the station. No response from mission control at the Cape, Houston or anywhere. So, are you still alone?"

"Yeah, I met a dog called Spang. He's been great company."

"Oh." He could hear her heart sink. "So, you're in Cape Canaveral right? Are you NASA?"

"We just got here from England but I'm not NASA, I'm just a guy."

"Okay, well…listen Rand. I don't have much time left up here. You need to send me my coordinates so I can figure out where my orbit is. Then we need to see about trying to get me down from here."

Rand smiled, "It's good to hear you say that, but I have to tell you, I'm not a scientist or anything. I just got here…"

"That's okay, I know I'm not out of this by a long shot but I might be able to show you what to do if you're willing."

"Hey, I taught myself to fly an Airbus from England to here, I'm up for anything!"

Laughter now came over the speakers, "You what? You taught yourself? So, you're not a pilot?"

"Nope."

"Unbelievable. Well I guess you are now."

"She sounds so cool!" Forgetting that he wore headset mic he whispered to Spang who was turning in circles and barking.

"Thanks Rand. I can't wait to meet you and Spang… did you give him that name?"

"No, it was on his tag, weird huh?"

On the giant screen something moved against the off-white background. It was a shadow, then a bare ankle emerged in sparkling clarity.

"Hey! I can see you! Or your foot, at least I hope that's your foot."

The God String

"Oh yeah, I forgot that camera was even there." The foot disappeared as she rotated.

The next thing Rand saw was a mass of dark hair floating into the frame, then her forehead and finally her whole face. She drifted backwards, away from the camera. She was pretty, but very thin and gaunt with long, dark pony tail that bushed out behind her.

"You are real right? I'm not dreaming this?" She slapped her face.

Rand was beaming pure joy. "No Elsie, I'm real. I'm the one who should be slapping myself!" They both laughed, then Rand's face softened. "I never thought I could need somebody to talk to so badly."

Elsie just nodded, unable to speak for the tears.

"But you… Elsie, I've had blue skies and rain and green fields, you've been stuck in that tin can surrounded by hostile space."

A sob burst out of her as she nodded. "Yeah, you don't know how bad I want to get out of here."

"It's gonna happen. We'll get you down." *She doesn't need any more stress. Subject change.* "So tell me about you. Where are you from?"

"Austin, Texas. I have a husband, Bob and two kids – Marty and Megan."

"I'm sure you're worried sick about them. I had…have a girlfriend, Moira. No kids, just Spang here." He laughed and held up Spang. "Can you see me?"

"Hang on." She came closer to the screen, obviously operating some kind of controls. "There you are!" She said as she backed away. The look on her face was one of surprise. "Wow."

"What is it?" Rand said, concerned.

"No, wow…as in, I haven't seen anybody for so long I almost forgot what other people look like!" She said, hiding embarrassment.

Rand let it pass. "So what's your situation up there?"

"The plants are all gone. We had a botanical pod full of edibles. You know, research for the future Mars missions so that lasted me awhile with rationing. Unfortunately I just don't have the resources for rejuvenating the soil on a scale that keeps up with my dietary needs. They were never intended for primary consumption."

"But you have rations for the whole crew right?"

"Yes but different crew members were here for different lengths of time. Unfortunately the…event, occurred right around the time that most of us were to return. Of course I began rationing immediately as we do in any emergency but the last of the food has been gone for awhile now."

"So…what are you eating?"

"I'm not really. I'm ingesting paper goods and bit of leather for bulk and roughage but even that is running low. Water systems are way past their due date for filter changes as are the air scrubbers. The one thing I have a lot of is fuel and power."

"We gotta get you down from there, now."

"Yes, but not right this minute. I didn't plan for this... for you, so I need to think about how we're going to do this."

"Right, is there anything I can do here?"

"Well, for now I would say sit tight. I'll know more by tomorrow morning."

"I'm not going anywhere."

"Rand…do you have any idea what happened?"

"No, I just woke up and everyone was gone. It took me a while to come around to the idea that I was the only human being on the planet, but that's the only conclusion I can come to."

"Yeah, me too. The first week I expected a rescue, but after a month I was at a loss. As a scientist I used every method I know to try and find an explanation that was at lest plausible but nothing yielded a positive result. There were no nukes, I would have seen them fly--"

"Yeah I can confirm that because London and Belfast are still there as well as all the military bases."

"What does it look like down there?"

"Like everyone vanished all at the same time. The airports are total disaster areas and the roads are littered with cars. All of the have the keys in the ignition but none of the doors opened. I was in a Police station gathering equipment and there was a towel laying on the floor in a circle with the dried foot prints still in the middle."

"Jesus, it's like the rapture."

"Well if it is then that poor cop arrived in heaven completely naked."

"It's not Rand…you…don't believe that stuff do you?" She said hesitantly.

"I am a believer yes, but not a nut case. If this was the rapture then there would be plenty of other people who got left behind."

"Okay, well we're not going to solve this over the comms in one night. Let's focus on one problem at a time."

It was Rand's turn to become emotional. "It's so good to have someone to figure things out things with." He covered his face.

"I know Rand. Just knowing you're down there is like a miracle. I'm so grateful. Now, I'm going to get to work. You probably have things to do as well."

"Yes, I have to secure the animals and find a place to sleep."

"In the viewing room, the one with all the glass there behind you there are cots in a closet. I know more than a few engineers who have spent the night there."

"Great, I'll start there."

"Wait, Rand you don't have a place to stay? How long have you been at the Cape?"

"We just landed yesterday. We were going to New River Marine base in North Carolina but the runway was completely trashed. Cape Canaveral was my back up plan."

"So…you just flew an Airbus jet, for the first time… across the Atlantic and landed at the Cape?"

The God String

Rand just smiled and nodded.

"Jesus. That's un-fucking real. I'm sorry, but you have got to be the smartest or the luckiest man alive."

"I guarantee I'm both." He laughed. "I'm also the coolest, the best looking, the most talented, the richest and the--"

"Ah now the narcissism rears it's head!" She giggled uncontrollably. "Well when I get down there we'll set you straight!"

"Yeah I definitely need a good slap. I can't wait!." He wiped his eyes. "Okay, I'm off to take care of things for the night. I'll be back in about twenty or thirty minutes."

"Great. I'll be..." she levered the camera to point at an open area on the station, "floating right over there. See you in a few."

It was difficult to leave, but they left the video on so she could see him come back. When he returned he set up in the control room and they talked until he started to fall asleep, mid-sentence.

"I'll be here when you wake up Elsie."

"So will I Rand. Good night and sweet dreams." Elsie floated off the screen and Rand climbed into the cot with Spang at his feet.

You heard me Lord. You always do. I knew I wasn't the only one.

He said a few silent prayers then fell into a deep slumber.

***

Elsie floated out of sight of the camera. She had run out of toothpaste months ago so she used a tiny smear of baking soda from one of the experiments. Those missions had stopped being a priority a long time ago, but her frazzled nerves now had a faint flicker of hope to cling to. Rand. Strange. She thought how she was the one floating above him, but he was her saving angel. *My earth angel.* Elsie hoped he really had learned to pilot a jet plane. She had a plan forming in her head, but it would take more piloting from Rand. The kind that only the best of the best could pull off.

"Long shot indeed honey, who are you kidding?" She said looking in the mirror. "Okay castaway, it's time to put on your Commander's cap again."

Her options were quickly running out. She would need her earth angel to pull another miracle out his own hat or she would join a short but illustrious list of brave astronauts who had given their life for the betterment of mankind.

Chapter 6

Reach

'Please dear God, don't let me fuck up.'
-Alan Shepard

Her voice penetrated Rand's dreams, "Good morning Rand, are you up yet sleepyhead?"

She had been up all night doing math. Rand sat straight up. After so long, waking to a human voice was shocking. He quickly recovered and rubbed his face as the joy of having someone to talk to grew a smile on his face.

"Good morning Elsie, did you sleep well?"

She didn't answer the question, but instead jumped straight in.

"Listen Rand, I've been doing some calculations and I think we might actually have a chance to get me down from here."

Rand took a seat as he pulled his boots on. "I'm all ears."

She floated in front of him and held up a laptop to the screen. There was a picture of what looked like a small version of the old Space Shuttle.

"This is the X-38. It's a prototype of the proposed CRV, that stands for Crew Return Vehicle. The X-38 project was cancelled in 2002 but was reinstated when Obama ordered NASA to develop a lifeboat for the ISS. It still hasn't been installed."

Rand's attention was rapt. She was serious, there might actually be a way to get her down.

"So it's like an escape pod?"

"Kind of, but there's more to it."

"Okay." He let her continue.

"The X-38 has been developed up to the test phase. They built one, remote controlled only, for orbital testing and launched it just after I arrived at the station. One of our mission days was going to be spent working with it. It was going to dock, then we were going to practice emergency escape procedures."

Rand just looked her in disbelief.

She shrugged, "I know, ironic isn't it? Anyway, the X-38 should still be orbiting though I don't know where it is. I need you to give me some data."

"Okay." Data, he could handle that. "What do I do?"

She came closer to the camera and he was surprised as the tone in her voice became even more serious.

"If we can find the X-38 in orbit I can do the calculations that might get it close enough to the station for me to grab it with the arm. Then I can EVA… I mean, spacewalk over to it. Then I get in, stay in my suit and strap myself down as best as I can. Then… you pilot it down by remote."

Rand just stared at her with his mouth open.

"Rand? Say something."

"No Elsie! I'm not okay with that! I can't fly that thing! Especially not with you in it, I'd kill you! Are you crazy?"

"Listen to me Rand, I don't have much time left up here. I'm running out of water. I'm not going to tell you all the details, but let's just say if you can imagine it being really bad, then it's worse than that. I need to get back to earth or I'm going to die, and soon. Do you understand? You have to try. We have to take the risk. If I die in the attempt then I'm better off having tried than just sitting here and dying of thirst while I'm watching oceans, lakes and rivers go by."

"Jesus." Rand realised she was right, he was her only option. He squared himself and took a breath. "You're right Elsie, I'm sorry. Tell me what to do."

Elsie wasted no time putting Rand to work. He found the data she was looking for and she told him how to create uplinks to the station. He had to drive to several different buildings, turn on generators and reboot systems. He kept a radio on him at all times that was taped to the headset at the communications desk. It was set to voice activate so whenever Elsie spoke, it broadcast to Rand. He was her eyes, ears and hands through the morning as she sent him from one building to the next hooking up generators, rebooting supercomputers and routing information. After he had finished, Elsie had full access to the Cape's computers, weather data and satellites.

"Listen Rand, the X-38 is a NASA run program in it's entirety. That means that all the developmental information is there at the Cape."

Rand shook his head, "I still don't think I'm even remotely close to being qualified to fly this thing. I have only spent time on sims Elsie. I barely have enough hours to even qualify for my private license."

"That's okay, the X-38 was designed to be flown remotely, even when you're in it."

"What do you mean?"

"There are no windows, the pilot flies by camera. Essentially, it's just like a big simulator. You'll do great. It was also designed to fly itself. Remember that it's a rescue vehicle, so it's meant top be piloted remotely, like a drone."

"So it either by a pilot on board or remotely from here."

"Exactly."

"But it's never been tested."

"No, but all of the technology is based on drones, which have thousands of actual mission hours."

"Okay, I see where this might be feasible."

"It's going to work Rand, it has to."

She told him where to find the control station for the X-38 then Elsie busied herself with the calculations necessary to capture the craft. Rand took Spang to hook up

The God String

a generator to the X-38 control building which was a converted long-range drone trailer. When he was finished he tended to the flock. Feeding goats and chickens didn't exactly make Rand feel like he was being proactive in Elsie's rescue, but it had to be done. He ate while he worked, not wanting to eat in front of Elsie. When he was finished, he headed out in the fuel truck and got the X-38 building up and running.

The simulator itself was like a complete cockpit at a specially built desk. The main flight control was a joystick. Following Elsie's instructions over the radio, he began flipping the switches to enable a communications link. Once again, Elsie's instructions were dead on. On the main screen of the large control monitor, a small window on the left side of the screen showed Elsie looking back at him.

"Okay Elsie, I have you on the monitor."

"See, no problem."

"Yeah, it wasn't hard, I just did what you said."

She laughed. "That's more than a lot of folks can manage."

"Okay, what now?"

"See that set of controls to your left? There's a knob that says 'C.A.C.', that stands for Camera Array Control, switch it to 'Live'."

He did and instantly the screen went black. "What the? Hey the screen just--"

"Went black. Right, it's supposed to do that because you're looking at space."

"Really? Where are all the stars?"

"They don't show up on camera. The light is too dim for the lenses to pick up. That's normal."

"So… I'm not in simulator mode right now?"

"Nope, you're live, seeing through the eyes of the CRV. You're officially the Captain of America's confidential X-38 program. I'll sign the papers when I get back."

"Okay, so why did you want us live from the X-38 right now?"

"You see the glass cockpit? It represents all the normal flight instruments only on a computer screen."

"Right, the A350 was the same."

"Wow Rand. You said it was an Airbus, but never mentioned it was an A350. I'm even more impressed."

"Yep, brand spankin' new. It's sitting outside in DHL bright yellow."

"Okay, you'll notice that in addition to your conventional flight instruments you have a whole range of things you've never seen. Those are for flying in zero-G. They will tell you everything about your orientation and where you are. So just sit there for a second while I upload the telemetry."

"Roger."

"No, I'm Elsie. Ha!"

"You are way too happy about this crazy scheme."

"No, I'm happy I get a chance to stay alive. Yesterday morning I still thought I was a goner. The more we get into it, the more I'm thinking we really stand a chance of getting me outta here."

"I sure hope you're right."

In a matter of minutes Elsie had finished the upload then she had Rand go out of live mode and start the training sequence.

"So the actual controls for the X-38 are also the training sim, clever." Rand made double sure that he wasn't in 'live' mode.

"Right, nothing like practicing on the real thing. Okay, the way the simulator works is to run a whole scenario. The only scenario we have available to us are the SSEER procedures. That's Space Station Emergency Evacuation and Rescue."

"Gotcha."

"That means that for the simulation, we have to start at disembarking from the ISS and go all the way to landing at the whatever facility is available."

"Wait, can't you program it to land at the Cape?"

"Yes, but for the actual run, where we land depends on what window is available. In other words: where were are in orbit when we start the SSEERS operation will determine where on Earth we can land."

"Elsie, all the runways I've seen are covered with wreckage."

"Well…" she thought for a second, "then I'll just run it through the computer to find out when the soonest opportunity is for us to land at the Cape. I'll do it while you're practicing."

"Good. Unless you plan on landing in London, the Cape is only runway I know is good."

She talked him through the whole emergency procedure - from disembarking the station to landing at the Cape. Without all of the inspections that a normal return would go through, the reentry could be complete in about eight hours. The X-38 Crew Return Vehicle had to orbit the earth several times to decrease its altitude and line up for the perfect return angle. Too steep and she would burn up, too shallow and she would ricochet off the atmosphere and shoot into space.

"Rand you're looking really stressed. I know from experience that you'll perform best if you're relaxed. How bout you take a break and tell me what's on your mind."

He paused the sim and sat back. "This is life or death here Elsie, of course I'm stressed."

"Yeah, but it's not just the rescue. You have your own survival to look after as well not to mention Spang and the other animals."

"Well yes, but getting you back down is more important."

"It all important Rand. You also have to factor in the fact that you just flew over the Atlantic a couple of days ago."

"Yeah, I have a little jet lag but--"

"Not only that, but also it wasn't exactly your run of the mill commercial flight. You piloted a passenger liner in solo flight across the Atlantic for crying out loud."

"Well, you have a point. But what are the options?"

"All I'm doing is making you aware of it. Simply acknowledging the source of stress can go long way toward alleviating it."

"Yeah, I actually feel better already."

"Great. Now go play your video game and I'll coach you through it." She teased.

"You'll have to perform four crucial manoeuvres during this rescue. Let's practice the mission as a whole, to give you the big picture then we'll focus on those four manoeuvres."

When they had run through everything several times she left him to practice on his own. Just as his did in England, he practiced a manual landing as a contingency. Each full run took forty-three minutes. He spent all day doing it over and over again, keenly aware of what was at stake.

While Rand was training, Elsie had NASA's Columbia supercomputer look for a window of opportunity that would allow the X-38 to return to Cape Canaveral. While the massive computer crunched the numbers she made plans for the capture of the vehicle. The X-38 was floating freely in orbit. The first phase of the rescue was to get it close enough to the International Space Station for her to use the station's robotic arm to latch onto the craft and dock it to the station so she could board it. Based on the information that Rand had sent, the orbit of both the Space Station and the X-38 had degraded severely. Initially she was going to try to get the station back into a stable orbit, but then it would be impossible for the X-38 to catch up. The prototype ship just didn't have enough fuel. Battling the brain debilitating effects of starvation, she spent the day crunching numbers and running scenarios. Finally she had a plan.

"Rand?"

"Hey Elsie. Man, my eyes are about to fall out of my head. I've run that sim so many times I think I'm going to be dreaming it for years."

"Welcome to astronaut training."

"Geez, you guys really get the grind don't you?"

"You're only getting a small taste, but hey listen, I think I've got a plan for the really difficult part of this whole thing."

"I'm all ears."

"The X-38 is orbiting way over here." She held up a laptop and pointed at a picture of the earth that had two circles going around it. One was more horizontal and the other more vertical. "And I'm over here. Now this all looks like it's bad but…" she turned around so he was looking over her shoulder at the laptop then spun the earth around on the screen "…if I can decrease the space station's orbit so it's low enough, I can catch the X-38 where the orbits intersect." She adjusted the two lines so they came together in an 'X'.

"Aren't you travelling like a hundred-thousand miles-per-hour or something? How are you going to do that at those speeds?"

"Actually, it's a little over seventeen-thousand miles-per-hour, but the trick is that the path of the X-38 actually comes along side the station's for a short while. See that 'X' where they intersect? It's very long and steep. When I degrade the station's orbit it's going to slow down, which should help, but I'll adjust course to make sure we're not crossing paths at right angles to each other."

"I get it, the shallower the angle, the slower you intersect."

"Exactly."

Rand shook his head and whistled. "That's gonna be tricky." He had a hunch that he was making a vast understatement.

"Yeah, but possible. Thing is, that's not actually the tricky part. You have one manoeuvre to orient the X-38 so that the Canadarm can grab it. Now that's pretty tricky, but the really hard part belongs to me. I have to get over to the X-38 and get inside."

"Why don't you just use the Canada arm thingy to drag it over closer to you?"

"I have to be on the station to release the X-38 from the arm. So, I'll just use the arm to stop and stabilise it, then, when I release, they will fly together for a short time. It's in that short window of time that I go over to the X-38 before it starts falling behind."

"Why can't it just dock to the station?"

"There's not enough fuel to set up the approach for docking and the angles are all wrong. Remember the X-38 isn't fully developed. It isn't set up for this kind of mission. We'll have to settle for close."

"Oh man." Rand rubbed his head in frustration. "So you say that the CRV will start falling away. How much time do you have to get to it?"

Elsie gave a sigh. "It's about five minutes. It'll start falling behind right away but it will be five minutes until I can't reach it anymore."

"And what then? You haul yourself back to the ISS and we do another burn and try again?"

"No Rand."

'What…what do you mean 'no'?"

"It's a one shot deal."

"No way! Elsie I just stopped being the only person in the world and I'm not going back to that. I need you here, we have to come up with a better plan."

Straightening her commander's cap she sighed and said. "There are no other possibilities, that's just the way it is. But listen Rand, I'll make it. I've done hundreds of hours of EVA practice in the pool and I hold the record for the most EVA's for a female astronaut. I can do this. I'm comfortable being out there and if I'm gonna go, I mean, what a beautiful way to go... just, floating over the earth." She pulled he cap off and covered her face.

Rand didn't know what to say. He knew she was right.

"Does your husband…"

"Bob."

"… does he ever win any arguments with you?"

She wiped her eyes as she laughed. "No."

Several hours later NASA's Columbia supercomputer came up with the available window for the operation.

Elsie relayed the findings to Rand. "Good news. Our window of opportunity is in thirty hours."

"What?" Rand balked. "I can't be ready that fast, I need at least a week!"

"We have to go when Columbia says we go. Besides, I'll be dead in a week."

He stared at her dumbly. She wasn't being dramatic, just stating a fact.

"You have one more day to practice and six hours to sleep," she grew somber, "then we're a go."

Elsie stuck to the supercomputer's plan. After organising the Columbia's data into a structured mission plan she focused on the first item: lower the space station's orbit immediately.

"Okay Rand, in a few minutes I'll do this burn."

Rand paused the sim. It was clear that Elsie needed some support. "I'm picking up some anxiety from you."

"Yeah, if this burn goes a fraction of a second too long or too short, the X-38 might collide with the Space Station or miss by miles."

"I'm assuming that your controlling the burn by computer then right?"

"Absolutely."

"It's going to go fine. NASA spent a lot of money on their systems. I'm sure that they're pretty fool proof."

"You're right. We rely on Columbia for mission critical data and it never fails to do the job."

"So why the long face?" His tone was mildly sarcastic knowing full well the implications of what they were attempting.

"It makes me sad."

"What do you mean?"

'The space station is our wonder. It's not only an incredible achievement, it's a symbol of unity, of countries working peacefully together. Even old enemies like Russia and America. They still have… had, their political problems but when it came to the ISS we were like best friends."

"And that's a bad thing because…?"

"Because when I do this burn it's going to kill the station."

"Ah, I understand now. But it will save you. Besides, it would eventually come out of orbit anyway right?"

"Yes, but not for a long time. There is still so much to do up here."

"There's more to do down here Elsie."

"It's a tall order."

"Well, we have to try don't we?"

"Yes, absolutely. If not then you should just leave me up here."

'Elsie, not to change the subject but I've been meaning to ask you, wasn't there a some kind of soy sauce vessel or something attached to the station?"

Elsie burst out laughing, "Soyuz!"

"Well, yeah that's what I meant."

"Yes, there used to be. The last one was sent down with the trash about a week after I got here. Another was sent up, but by then there was no one to get our orbits synchronised for docking. It just fell back to earth."

"That sucks."

"Yeah. It was full of food and replacement parts to extend our water making capabilities. I watched it go. The stages separated and the capsule ejected then just fell into the Atlantic."

"Capsule?"

"Yes, this particular Soyuz was to remain attached to the ISS. It had an escape vehicle, a capsule for emergency reentry. There's that irony again. It cruised past me by a few hundred yards, the engines still burning. It was very close. If it would have hit the station I wouldn't have been alive to answer your call. How did you know by the way?"

"Know what?"

"To call on the comms."

"I didn't. I just wanted to see mission control. I didn't know when I'd have the chance again so I wanted to see it. I've always been into space stuff."

"Are you kidding me?"

"No shit. I just picked up the mic to goof around."

Elsie was stunned. "Oh my God. What are the chances?"

"None to impossible I'd say. But then God has a way of pulling off the impossible."

"I'm a scientist Rand. I'm not exactly religious but if there is a God, I have to give this one to him for sure." A beeping sounded in the background and she became very focused, her eyes scanning a monitor above her head. "Okay here we go. Set to burn in five, four, three, two, one, mark."

A sound like an air leak came out of the speakers for twelve seconds then stopped.

"Burn complete. Okay Rand that's that. I'm getting closer to earth as we speak. We have twenty-seven hours to get ready for the first manoeuvre."

Rand went to bed that night going over everything that would happen on the mission. After making several notes to himself he quickly fell asleep.

The next morning, after taking care of the flock and grabbing a quick bite to eat he went over the notes with Elsie.

"I understand what I need to do to get you here, but what do we do once you've landed?"

"Well, I'm going to need some medical attention. I won't be able to walk and will need time to recover my strength. There's a small but well equipped medical facility right at the runway, so you should get that going and check on the status of the meds. I'll need saline and lots of nutritional drinks. The nutritional drinks are used all the time for returning astronauts and they have a very long shelf-life so that shouldn't be a problem. Saline stores for a long time as well but you'll have to insert an IV. I may very well be unconscious by the time I land. I have very little strength left and what I do have will be spent trying to get through the station in my EVA... um, spacesuit."

"Okay, I'm taking notes here. How do I get you out of the X-38?"

"Hatch in the side. Use the flat-lift. It's a big drivable thing that raises a large flat platform up to the door. Have a gurney loaded onto it. Make sure the gurney is all the way down. You should be able to roll me onto it after you get me out of the suit."

"Oh, that's something I hadn't thought of, getting you out of the suit."

"Don't worry, I'll tell you how to do it."

Elsie continued to give instructions detailing his every move for not only immediately after the landing but for the weeks of her rehabilitation. When she was done he sprinted out the door to get everything ready. It took him over an hour to locate the keys for the flat-lift, but in the end he installed a new battery, fuelled it and parked it by the runway. Next, he readied the medical facility and prepared the gurney and everything she would need. As the afternoon wore on he wrapped up the preparations and went to run the mission a few more times in the simulator. Elsie monitored him closely but only spoke to answer his questions in order to save the last of her energy for the coming challenge. It was nine o'clock in the evening when she stopped him.

"Okay Rand, I think you're as ready as you're going to be. The most important thing now is to get sleep so you'll be fresh and sharp in the morning."

"I'm worried I won't remember all the steps."

"Just talk them out, 'ready to initialise manoeuvre one-orientation, execute on my mark, five, four, three, two, one, mark,' and so on."

"You sound cool when you do all that astronaut talk."

"It serves several purposes. First it calms the nerves, second it keeps you focused on what you have to do next, third it prevents you from getting too far ahead of yourself and there are more reasons I won't go into right now. Test pilots developed it and it's been the way things have been done around here ever since. It just works."

"It's like learning procedure with flying. It gives you something to focus on so you don't realize how scared you are."

"Exactly. See you'll do fine."

"Elsie I just--"

"And talking about how scared I am makes me more scared so goodnight!"

"Sorry. Goodnight Elsie, and don't worry. By this time tomorrow you'll be on the ground. Soon we'll be standing together looking up at the stars instead of you looking down at Earth."

"That's right Rand, don't stop believing it."

"I promise."

Rand went out to take care of the animals. When he was done he looked up at the sky. *She seems so close on the monitor, yet there she is for real, all the way up there.* He went back in with Spang on his heels and they climbed into the cot. In his head he kept going over the manoeuvres he would have to perform flawlessly to save her life. Sleep was the last thing on his mind.

Rand surprised Elsie by waking twenty minutes early.

"I have to take care of the flock. They haven't been getting much attention and we really need them. Besides, it helps me settle my mind."

Elsie smiled, "Good, anything to help stay calm. Funny, I'm teaching you what to do now, but that's going to do a complete flip when I get there. I have so much to learn from you."

"I don't think milking a goat is going to be a steep learning curve for an astronaut."

He left to do just that. When he was done he took Spang to the X-38 control building. Elsie was still in the little window in the left corner of the monitor, waiting with a smile.

"Ready Captain?"

"Yes Commander." He feigned confidence.

The first manoeuvre turned the X-38 so it faced the station at the correct angle. Rand's screen showed green lines that he had to match up to his red lines. He calmly moved the joystick as Elsie monitored his progress through the uplink. The tricky manoeuvre only took seconds, but it was vital to the rest of the operation.

"Rand you did it! And fast too. You're a natural." Elsie cheered.

Rand blushed. "Thanks, I just matched up the lines, it was pretty simple really."

"It's going to take an hour as the X-38 and the International Space Station catch up to one another."

Elsie started to get into the first layer of her space suit; a tight fitting jumpsuit with an array of tubes covering the outside. It showed just how emaciated she really was. Rand watched through the eyes of the X-38 as the International Space Station grew from a small dot of light in the distance and began to fill more of the screen. The little window in his monitor showed that Elsie was almost finished wrestling into the first layer of her suit. When she was done she floated over, breathing hard.

"Okay Rand, just keep off the controls for the X-38 and let me do this capture, but if I screw it up you are welcome to try and save it. If the worst happens and whole thing goes south then don't do anything and we'll take a minute to make a quick plan. There's only so much fuel on the X-38 and we need it all."

Rand heard a groaning sound over the speakers. "What was that?"

"The station is in a really low orbit. Gravity and the atmosphere are starting to effect her. She's not designed to fly this close to the earth."

He sensed that she had enough to worry about at the moment. "I won't mention it again."

"Thanks. Okay here we go."

Rand watched Elsie work the controls of the Canadarm on the monitor but he could also see her in the distance from the X-38, the silhouette of her head in the station's window. As the rescue ship drifted close to the station, the view became obstructed. He waited for seconds that seemed like hours. Finally, he heard Elsie say quietly, "Gotcha." Then she came on the screen, her face beaming.

"Rand I did it! The X-38 is connected to the Canadarm. Now I have to go get into the suit." She paused and took a deep breath. "This ain't gonna be easy. It's not meant to be worn inside the station. Once I'm wearing it, it's going to be difficult to get back in here to release the X-38 from the arm, you'll hear a lot of bumping around, but at this point I don't care what I break."

She came close and held onto the monitor.

"The next time you see me, I'll be on Earth." Then she smiled and disappeared off the screen.

His heart was beating faster. He turned to his notes and set the uplink to receive comms from the suit. He went through the menus and options on the computer and was rewarded by the sound of Elsie struggling.

"Elsie, I've got the suit comms turned on, can you hear me?"

Sounds of her straining to get into the suit came over the speakers. She sounded like she was far away then suddenly a hollow clunk and "Rand? I can hear you, I'm in."

"I was starting to get worried."

"Not yet, I'll tell you if it's time to worry."

"Great."

"Okay, forgive the strange noises while I try to fit through the station to the robotic arm controls. I've got to release the X-38 now, the station is falling faster than I expected."

"Then why are you talking to me? Go!"

The sounds of the enormous effort she made to muscle the huge suit through the station were agonising to Rand. He could do nothing. Finally, she emerged on his screen as her bulky white suit bumped into the camera. She was at the controls and breathing hard.

"That was tough going. As soon as I hit the release I have to get to the airlock, get outside and then jump over to the X-38. Hopefully it won't be too far away." She reached for the control station and paused. "Rand, if I don't make it,

I want you to just turn off the comms. Remember me this way, alive and happy, sailing over Mother Earth."

"Stop that. You're going to make it." He rebuked her sternly.

"Release on my mark... three, two, one, mark."

On the X-38 screen he saw a vibration as the robotic arm released the little craft.

"Release good." Rand confirmed, "X-38 stable."

Elsie passed by the camera quickly, then came more sounds of struggling.

A digital counter ticked down the time in the corner of Rand's screen. It sailed past forty five seconds. The X-38 screen showed a close up of the station pulling away.

"Damn! I can't get through this door!"

"Go Elsie, go!"

Her strains turned to screams of exertion.

Of the five minutes she had, two minutes, fifteen seconds had passed. The X-38 now showed the end of the Canadarm. It had made a successful disconnect and was drifting further away.

"Move it ELSIE! MOVE YOUR ASS!" Rand yelled through the comms.

Sounds of struggling came from her suit, then a hiss as the station airlock door opened. Four minutes, forty three seconds had gone by.

"Okay! I'm outside. Shit, that's far! Oh my God, oh my God--"

He heard the grunt of her effort as she pushed off the station.

"Elsie?"

...

...

"Elsie?"

...

...

"Rand? I think it's too far. It's moving away too fast."

"Just wait Elsie, you'll make it!"

...

...

"No. It's no good. Oh..." She sobbed "God, I really wanted to touch the Earth again."

"NO! This is not happening!" Rand took the controls and squared himself, praying. "Not now..." He made a small bump on the joystick. The little shuttle rolled left so the opening faced down. "...not today..." The joystick edged forward about the width of a human hair sending the craft floating toward Elsie.

"Rand...'" she breathed in disbelief.

"...not on my watch." With a minute flick backwards he stopped the craft eight inches directly above Elsie's head.

"Now get in there!"

Elsie reached up, unlocked the hatch and pulled herself in.

"I can't believe it!" She was breathless, her small body completely exhausted. "That was a million to one."

"Okay Elsie, you've got to come up with a way to strap yourself in--"

"Seats!" She interrupted

"What?"

"They put seats in here."

"Well then shut up, sit down, strap in and hold on!"

"Okay Rand, I'm in."

"Hang on."

Rand began the first manoeuvre to pull away from the station and position the X-38 for reentry.

"There's a problem. It's not handling the way it did in the sim."

Elsie's breathing was ragged. "Damn! It's the weight, the extra weight of me and my suit on one side of the craft. You'll have to fly it in manually."

Rand just stared at the screen. "Elsie…"

"Yes you can! I just saw you do something that was practically impossible… just…try." She was starting to fade.

"Elsie? Elsie, I'll get you down, just hold on!" On his screen, the little ship's calculated trajectory was a line in green, the optimum trajectory was shown in red. On the side screen, figures in green showed him his real time speed and attitude, the optimum speed and attitude was shown in red. Rand worked to make the lines and figures match, but no matter how he tried they always seemed to pass each other. He continued as the numbers vacillated from slightly higher to slightly lower. He knew he had to have them exactly on. After what seemed like hours Elsie came back on the comms. Her breathing was laboured and her speech slurred.

"Hey. Try some of that astronaut talk for me."

Rand looked at the mission clock, it had only been two minutes. He took a deep breath and tried to calm his heart rate.

"That's usually your job but, okay. First manoeuvre complete."

"Good. What's next?"

"Start course correction." Rand glanced at the second monitor, the numbers were way off. His altitude was half of what it should be. The X-38 was falling instead of gliding. At this rate it would smash into the atmosphere and burn up.

"Right. And after that?" Elsie had no idea.

"Yeah, I get it. But we have a bit of a change."

"I'm not sure I can do surprises right now."

"We're a lot lower than planned. I have to make a burn to get even one orbit for approach."

"Shit. Okay, I need some data."

Rand relayed what she needed to know.

"Rand I have no laptop, no pen and paper, though I couldn't use them with these gloves on even if I did."

"Well, I'll just have to wing it. We have no option."

"Just wait a second." She thought hard, then resigned herself to the inevitable. "Okay, yes, you'll have to wing it.

But if you can run the simulation on top of the live view. It will show you where you should be and give you something to line up with."

"Already doing that."

"Okay then give me a sec to calculate the burn time you'll need." Her breath was weak as she fought to stay conscious. With the last of her energy reserves, she struggled on, fighting through a mental fog to come up with a solution. In the end she just couldn't do it. But she didn't want this valiant man to have her death on his hands so she gave it her best guess.

"Rand, it's about three and a half minutes. You won't have any fuel for retro brakes when you land and you'll probably have to do some fancy flying to get her to the Cape. There never was a big chance of success. Thank you for trying, you did everything you could, always know that."

"Hey! We're not done by a long shot. I'll put you down in the desert somewhere it doesn't matter. I can fly to you, the 737 is right outside and ready to go. I just have to get you down that's all, and gravity is doing most of the hard work. Elsie?"

There was no reply.

"Hang in there Elsie I'm here, I'll get you home."

On the screen was the 'Burn' command. He clicked it with the mouse and two fields came up: 'Time Til Burn' and 'Burn Length'. He left the first one at zero and typed in 3:30 in the next, then hit 'Execute'. Rand heard the engines fire through Elsie's comms. Instantly his orbital speed increased while his rate of descent slowed considerably. The X-38 was now running more laterally to the Earth. The red line that the simulator wanted him to be on, ran down at a gradual rate to intercept his path. *That's what you're aiming for.* Once he was back on line he would get one chance at entering the atmosphere. The fuel was gone. Rand remembered Elsie's advice and used his astronaut talk.

"Velocity in the green at 17,000. Manoeuvre two complete."

The X-38 rocketed into a nose dive through the atmosphere. Rand adjusted the attitude to match up with the simulator's recommendations as the red and green lines intersected.

"Reentry attitude manoeuvre in five, four, three, two, one, mark."

The nose came up exposing the heat shields to the friction from the denser air. A strange orange and red light filled the edges of the black screens. Rand eyes danced from one set of stats to the next. Red and green lines travelled together, red and green numbers were within a fraction of each other.

"Manoeuvre three complete."

The little shuttle screamed towards the earth.

"Elsie, I know you can hear me, hang in there."

As the X-38 slowed he levelled out the nose. He was high above the Gulf of Mexico. For minute he was disoriented because all he could see was water. Then the

Florida Keys came into view. The tip of Florida followed as he turned in a wide circle and levelled out above the Bahamas. Following the red line he aimed for a spot between West Palm Beach and Freeport, rocketing past at over seven thousand miles-per-hour. The bottom of the little craft was now only red-hot and cooling as it slowed. Rand couldn't see the shuttle runway, but the simulator said it was there so he continued on faith.

"Preparation for final approach and landing in--"

"Rand? You don't have to count down each time."

Rand exhaled in relief, "Hey, there she is. You okay?"

Elsie laughed weakly. "Are we there yet?"

"Almost, just lining up now."

Sure enough, the red and green lines brought the Florida coast into view. The X-38 had slowed to four-hundred miles-per-hour. When the computer prompted him Rand deployed the air brake. As Port Canaveral slid by on the left, the familiar view of the shuttle runway grew larger on the screen. Slowing to a hundred and fifty miles-per-hour the little craft drifted over the inland waters and on towards the long Shuttle Landing Strip on Merritt Island. He kept the craft lined up with the computer guide and lowered the flaps then the landing gear. A small window opened on the screen next to him. He could see the yellow Airbus at the end of the runway. Suddenly he remembered that he was on the ground and not in X-38 at all. The window displayed the view from a special landing camera located underneath the craft. He looked from his instruments to the camera as, first the rear wheels touched, then the front. He let it roll for a bit then triggered the parachute. He had no way to taxi it so he just let it roll to a stop.

"That's it Elsie, your down."

There was no reply.

She must be out again. "Elsie, I'll be about five minutes."

He jumped up from his chair and sprinted to the side-by-side ATV with Spang on his heels. He scooped the little dog up, put him in his box in the passenger seat and sped off to the runway. Careening through the gates, he swung past several buildings before the runway came into view. There, at the far end was the X-38, smoking slightly. He screeched to a halt next to the lift-truck, jumped into it and turned the key. It fired on the first try. He floored it and drove a bee-line down the cement to the waiting craft. As he approached he slowed and lined up the lift. Then he climbed out onto the platform and raised the lift up to the door. He unhooked the gurney from the straps, cranked the door open and peered in through the dark interior.

Oh right, there are no windows on this stupid thing.

Entering from the bright Florida sun, he fumbled forward pushing the gurney.

A muffled voice said, "Who the heck would fly in something like this?"

"Elsie!"

He went to her side and fumbled with her helmet. She had managed to get the visor up. The seats weren't built to accommodate an astronaut in the suit. Elsie had belted herself to the harness with equipment straps. The suit had taken a beating from the chair arms, but it had held up.

"It twists off." She reached up to the helmet but lacked the strength.

He brushed her hands away and released it with a gentle twist then gave her a long hug. They both wept for what seemed like minutes.

"I don't know how to thank you. You saved my life." She said looking into his eyes.

Rand blushed "It's just good to finally meet you. Now. Let's get you out of this suit and on to terra firma."

Rand slashed the equipment straps holding her in place and helped as she slid to the floor. Then he set to working on the suit, doing just as she had instructed him. Piece by piece it came apart until, at last, she was just left sitting in a hard torso section with a huge backpack. He rolled her one her side and the backpack came off after disconnecting all the tubes and wires, then they got the torso section off her through a rear opening.

"No wonder I heard you struggling so much. I can't believe you even got into this thing by yourself."

"Yeah, it's supposed to be a two man operation." She was breathing hard from the effort. "God, gravity is so intense."

Rand gently picked her up. He'd carried loaves of bread that weighed more. Elsie's fragile body had wasted away to nothing. She was so weak she could hardly hold on.

"It's okay, I gotcha." He carefully laid her down. After he had gently strapped her in he wheeled her out to the flat-truck. The bright Florida sun made them both squint.

"Ow." She grimaced. Rand put his sunglasses on her. "Much better. It's so great to be under the sky again!" She cried, but her body was so dehydrated that she couldn't produce tears anymore.

"I'm going to leave you on this for a short ride to the hospital." He said as he lowered the platform. "Just enjoy the fresh air and I'll go nice and easy. Here's a radio if you need to talk to me in the cab."

He climbed down from the lift then drove slowly to the small hospital with a short stop to pick up Spang. Carefully, he wheeled her into the recovery room he had prepared. He gave her a foam ball to squeeze to make the vein on her arm easier to find. Even though she could barely make a dent in it, it was enough and Rand got the IV going on the first try. She slipped in and out of consciousness as he talked to her.

"The saline is coming now, very slowly though like you said. I'm gonna use the scissors to get the last of these clothes off of you. No modesty for astronauts." He repeated the phrase he had learned from her.

He made a single cut from the ankle to the neck line then one more for the other leg. Keeping the sheet over her he gently rolled her from one side, then the next, slipping the suit undergarment out from under her. "Now, let's see how you do with just a taste of water, it should be safe in very small doses."

The God String

She woke at that and reached for the plastic cup with just over an eye dropper full of water and a straw.

"Oh my God this is good! You have no idea!"

She was grinning from ear to ear. Then he picked up Spang and lifted him up to her.

"Oh! You must be Spang! Oh look how sweet he is!"

Spang went completely sheepish, tail wagging and head down, gushing at the attention. He put Spang back down and brought over a warm, damp cloth. He washed her down as he talked softly.

"It's a miracle you survived and a miracle I called. It's a miracle you heard me. It's a miracle you caught the X-38 and another miracle that you got into the suit and yet another that you made it back into the X-38. On top of that add another four miracles for each manoeuvre it took to land. That makes it a ten miracle day."

"What day is it?"

"It's...oh my God you're not gonna believe this. It's May tenth."

They looked at each other in astonishment.

"Not only that," he continued, "It's ten minutes after ten in the morning."

"What?" She looked at his watch, then back to him in shock.

"Unbelievable." He laughed.

From then on, they called the tenth of May - Miracle Day. Since she was keeping the water down without any problems he gave her more. Several hours later he gave her a nutritional drink which she had to restrain herself from guzzling.

"I never liked these things, now it's like a gourmet meal!"

By the time evening rolled around she had consumed three more and downed over a pint of water. He increased the saline trickle until the two-liter bag was empty. She was feeling better, so when she asked to be lifted into a wheelchair so she could take a shower, Rand happily obliged. While she was showering he changed the sheets and ate a quick dinner. He handed her a hospital gown through the door and she wheeled out a few minutes later looking, and smelling, much better.

"I feel like I've just been birthed back into the world." She was beaming.

"You're emerging from the layers of your ordeal. You look better already."

"It's going to be awhile. There was an astronaut, Scott Kelly, who spent a year on the station. It took him over a year to fully recover. Some of the effects never went away."

"You were up there for over nine months."

"Yeah, and I had to conserve energy so I couldn't workout. No nutrition to keep my muscle mass and bone density up either. I'm sure there is some permanent damage, but at least I'm alive."

"Exactly, and I'll take care of you. You'll be back to your old self in no time. Hey, who knows, all the organic food and whole goat's milk may actually help your recovery rate."

The God String

"I'm going to get to work on physical therapy right away. I need to be at full strength to pull my weight around here."

Rand came to her side and lifted her back into the bed. "Elsie, never worry about that. The simple fact that you're here is reason enough for me to be eternally…grateful."

She was asleep again. He smiled and pulled the blankets up around her and added another one that she could pull up if she got cold. He wrote her a note and left it where she could see it, then went and checked the thermostat and the fuel in the generator. Next he made his way around to the flock and took care of them. On the runway the figure of the A350 was a shadow against a dense field of stars. Down the runway sat the X-38, like a toy next to the big jetliner. He realised he had landed it with a tail wind. *No wonder it took so long to slow down. Good thing the runway is as long as it is.* He stood looking at the silhouette of the craft in the starlight, thinking again of the miracle of Elsie. Never in his wildest dreams could he have imagined events turning out the way they had. He climbed the stairs to the A350 and rummaged around for some fresh clothes then went back inside and took a shower.

Rand slept in the hospital bed next to Elsie's with Spang at his feet as usual. He scooted over a table and a chair so the little dog could hop down on his own if he wanted to. She woke him up several times during the night for help getting to the bathroom as her body rehydrated. The next morning Elsie woke to the smell of eggs and coffee and cried again. When Rand came into the room with a tray of steaming food it was like an angel descending with manna from Heaven. The smell assaulted her senses and she practically lunged at him to get to the food.

"Oh my God, real food."

"Easy there tiger remember, go slow. You still could get a bit of nutrition shock from all this farm fresh goodness."

She looked at him with a mouthful of eggs and sighed. "You're right." It required every fibre of discipline not to stuff her face.

Rand just giggled at her. "I have never seen anyone that hungry. It's cruel that you have to restrain yourself."

When they were finished Elsie laid back blissfully "Oh wow that was good. Thank you so much."

"You're welcome. Compliments of the flock." Rand busied with taking the dishes back to the kitchen and cleaning up. Elsie, feeling rejuvenated, made plans of her own.

As soon as Rand got back into the room she had him put her in the wheelchair and asked him to wheel her down the hall.

"Where are we going?"

"You'll see when we get there."

Rand just followed her directions. Elsie looked back at him, "You know you can't be my pilot, chauffeur, chef and doctor forever. I've got to get better. Turn right here."

"Yeah but, it's only been a day."

"Excuses, excuses. I need to get back to normal."

Rand pushed the wheelchair through a set of doors and into the physical rehabilitation room.

"Starting now."

They stayed there for a month. Rand kept busy with the animals, garden, and trying to make some semblance of a home for them. He towed the X-38 off the runway and refuelled the A350, then he began doing weekly checks on the airliner as he did in England, making sure it would be ready to go in case they needed it.

In that time, Elsie concentrated on her recovery. After three weeks, she managed to walk across the room using only a pair of crutches. Rand could visibly see her putting on weight and getting fit. Still, it would be months before she returned to normal. They spent most of their time together just talking. They agreed that it was most likely an effect of months of loneliness. Elsie learned about Rand's plans for learning to fly V-22 Osprey in New River. She thought it was an excellent idea and asked if she could go along. Rand just looked at her like she was crazy.

"Elsie you and I are joined at the hip; the last two humans on earth for all we know. I'm never leaving you, ever!"

She just smiled and said, "That's a first."

When she wasn't doing physical therapy, she was studying. She started on animal medicine for the chickens and goats. Veterinary medicine was new for her, but her training as an emergency medical technician helped a bit.

She stayed busy with recovery, helping with meals and playing with Spang. The little dog would take as much attention from Elsie as he could get, and he got a lot. Soon Spang was following Elsie everywhere. She began making a list of vaccinations for the animals so Rand could go get the medicine from the vets.

Rand kept busy as well, but life was easier now with Elsie. The underlying sadness that always threatened to overtake him was fading. He still missed Moira and his family, but Elsie brought the light back into his life. He was suddenly aware that he was honestly happy, in a way he had never been. He liked it, though it made him a bit nervous.

One day, towards the end of the month, Elsie managed to walk without the crutches. She was so happy that she tried it again and again. After several trips back and forth across the room she was exhausted.

"There. I told myself that if I could do that then I would ask you to take me into town to do some shopping."

Rand had made many trips to the big mall up the road to get clothes and other necessities, but he had been waiting for her to get better before offering to take her along.

"Absolutely! When do you want to go?"

She looked up him from the chair with a smile, still breathing hard from the effort of walking, "How about now?"

Chapter 7

Union

*'There is always some madness in love.
But there is also always some reason in madness.'*
~Friedrich Nietzsche

Elsie changed from sweats into what she called 'shopping attire' which consisted of Khaki hiking pants and a loose-fitting, white cotton shirt.

Not exactly 5th Avenue around here is it? she thought, looking in the mirror. "Well, we'll just have to see what we can do about that." She took up her crutches and headed outside.

Rand had the Guardian fuelled and ready to go. As she walked toward him, she could see had held ear protection and a gun in his hand. There were cans lined up on the fence about fifty feet away.

"A little primer before we head out. It can be kind of dangerous out here with wild dogs and all."

She put on the ear protection took the gun from him, popped out the magazine and checked the rounds. Then she slammed the clip back in, drew back the slide and fired in quick succession. One by one, each of the six cans flew from the railing. Rand stood dumbstruck. Elsie stood, still aiming downrange, smoke rolling from the barrel.

"US Military issue Beretta M9. Nine millimetre, combat loaded at nine rounds, carry loaded at seven. I'm betting there's one more round in this mag what do you think?"

Rand blinked and stammered, "Uh well, I suppose…"

She fired the last round down range, kicking up a can off the ground. She turned, looking up at him with a face he'd never seen on her before.

"I'm an Air Force Major with over ten years of Special Forces combat flight experience. I've graduated the SERE school and been an instructor in mountain and desert survival courses, but all you really need to know is: I'm from Texas. Now mount up cowboy." The smile on her face said it all.

Rand climbed into the cab of the Guardian. "Cheeky git."

On the way, they resumed a conversation they had started many times over the last month, about the cause of their predicament.

"I don't know Rand. It's all completely off the scale. Everybody up and disappears but the animals stay." She was looking at the wreckage along the highway for the first time. "What about corpses?"

"They got left behind."

"Only the living" She shook her head. "Incredible. Somehow, we have to find out what happened and I need to get back to Houston to see if my family is…to see…" Suddenly she wasn't sure if she wanted to go there.

"Elsie, I know. I'm the same way. I came all the way back to the states yet I can't find the courage to go back to Montana. I just don't think that they're there. I'm afraid what it would do to me…seeing the place empty."

Elsie just nodded and stared out the window.

He pushed on with the conversation to help her snap out of it. "From what you have told me, we were both asleep when it happened. But if everyone that was asleep stayed then half the planet would still be here."

She squinted in thought. "Maybe it was certain people that were in a certain stage of sleep, like REM."

"Even if that was the case there would be a lot more people left behind. Besides, what could cause such a thing?"

They pulled into the mall and Rand pushed a few cars out of the way.

"Oh this doesn't feel right." Elsie held onto the handles inside the armoured Guardian as the plowed through a new BMW 5 series.

"Hey, I have to make a parking space."

"It just feels wrong to go ramming into people's cars."

"You're going to have to get used to that. It took me a while, but now I feel like all this is mine. Now of course, it's ours. Anything you want. Want a diamond? How about the largest in the world? It's yours."

Rand pulled out two flashlights and duct taped them to the armrests of her wheelchair. The Beretta and a radio hung in a bag on the right arm rest as well.

"Right now the only use I'd have for a diamond is to cut glass." She said as Rand helped her into her wheelchair.

"Exactly. It's all just stuff. The only thing that gives any of it value is if it's of use to you. Even if it's just for your amusement." He handed her a headlamp.

"Yeah, you're right." She pulled the headlamp onto her head and adjusted her hair. "Okay then, let's go get amused."

Even when she was in the wheelchair Rand had a hard time keeping up with her. While she was in a clothing store he went back out to the Guardian and pulled the ATV off of the trailer. Hitching a small trailer to it, he drove to where she was shopping. She came out smiling, headlamp and flashlights shining, with a pile of clothes in her lap.

"This is great! I can fit into clothes I would have worn in my teens." She looked at the trailer. "Now that's my kind of shopping cart."

"I'm gonna set us up some lunch. I'll meet you in the middle section where all the restaurants are."

"Sounds good." She went back into the store.

Rand left the ATV trailer and took the cooler he had packed to the food court. As he unpacked the cooler, his mind was on Elsie.

She can be so butch. It's the military thing. But then she can be very feminine too. He saw the way she gushed over

Spang. It was wonderful having another person around. She was a fountain of knowledge, but there was something in him that also enjoyed being alone. He felt like he wasn't in charge of his own destiny so much now. *Look at me, I'm here fashion shopping! Of course it wasn't so long ago I was doing the same thing; grabbing watches and electronics in Belfast and London. You've been alone too long Rand and you're being selfish and childish. Appreciate her or you're going to lose her.* The thought scared him.

He found a gas grill in one of the restaurants and fired it up. After a good cleaning he put on some veggie burgers and mashed potatoes with goats cheese and fresh herbs. Canned peaches in creamy goat's milk sprinkled with cinnamon made dessert. Wine was everywhere, perfectly preserved and though he rarely drank, he thought that this was a good occasion. He had brought along a cold Chardonnay just for the occasion.

"Are you at it again?" She stood with her crutches at the counter in a small flowery dress that shouted *spring!* She had put on makeup and done her long dark hair in waves. It took Rand by surprise as his heart lodged in his throat. She was stunning.

"What?" She turned around and looked behind her, which made the dress spin a little.

"Wow." He spluttered.

"Oh c'mon," she played, "this lil' ol' thing?"

"You look… amazing!"

His honesty, blurted out so involuntarily broke her façade.

"Geez Rand thanks." She beamed. "So, what did you find to eat?"

"Just some... uh..." He was still dumbstruck, "burgers."

She flushed and quickly looked for a subject change.

"Oh! Hey I have an idea, let's eat in there." She said, pointing over to a furniture store with a dining room display. After a quick dust off and a good rinse of the dinnerware they settled in at the table, lit a few candles and sat chatting over lunch.

"It's like we're at some café in the mall just after the lunch rush hour."

"This is the most civilised thing I've done in a long time." Rand agreed.

"So when do you want to leave?"

"It all depends how you feel Elsie."

"Listen Rand, I have something I want to tell you."

Rand braced himself. She was leaving him to set out on her own.

"You had plans before I arrived on the scene. You and Spang were going places, doing things. I will always be indebted to you for saving my life, but that doesn't mean that you are obligated to keep me around."

She's trying to get me to send her away he thought, because she doesn't have the courage to do it. For once Rand, don't bail out and don't let her do it either. "Elsie, I already told you that I'm not leaving you."

"Yes, I know, but I'm aware that you've been surviving very well for almost a year now and…"

She is definitely trying to give me a way out. Man, she must have been badly burnt by someone. "Elsie…"

"Wait, let me finish, please. I know that I can be a little overbearing and overly assertive and overly, well everything. You know? So I'd rather stay friends than have a falling out because I did something wrong or made you feel like--"

Then it suddenly struck Rand, "Your husband is having an affair." It just came out. He slammed his mouth shut.

She looked at him like he couldn't be more wrong, then her face changed. "Yes Rand, yes. He doesn't think that I know. How did you know?"

"Because you're trying to give me an open door to leave you. You think you did something to make him have an affair."

She stared at him incredulously and thought about it. "God, you're right."

"Elsie, you didn't. You didn't work too much or not make the right meals or ask too much of him, none of that."

"Then why did he do it?"

"People screw up. They make mistakes. Sometimes it's getting married to someone they don't love. I don't know any of the details, but I do know that we all have a choice to do right or wrong. There has only been one human being in history who has never made a wrong choice and he's the son of God. Yes of course infidelity is a deal breaker, but it doesn't mean you have to blame yourself. It was his bad choice. Just forgive him and move on. Beating yourself up isn't going to reveal the truth. Maybe now you'll never know. We have no choice but to leave that baggage on the side of the road and move on... down another... parallel road... I don't know. Am I making any sense?"

Elsie was looking at him with tears in her eyes, but as he spoke her face changed to one of acceptance then resolution then, at the last, like a light had just come on in her mind.

"Rand. Yes, I know what you're saying. You make more sense than you think. About me and Bob yes, but the last thing you said, the parallel road thing, that may be it."

"Good Elsie. Don't you worry about it any more, I'm so glad. You've gone through enough..."

"No, don't you see?"

"Um, you don't want to come with us to New River?"

"No! I mean Yes! I want to come with you. I'm talking about what happened to all the people. You just said it – parallel universes, parallel existences. Everybody didn't go, just us! We're the ones who got sent into a parallel universe without people!"

Rand was staring at her, again. "Really?"

"Well it makes sense. I don't know why I never thought of it. I took astrophysics, though we only touched on the theoretical quantum side of it, but it's a well-known theory. So much so that it's practically accepted as fact."

"Well how could that have happened?"

"I don't know, it's just an idea but at least it helps me get my brain around it a bit better." She snatched up her burger and chomped it in a very self-satisfied way.

"You really love solving puzzles don't you?"

She laughed, "You have got me figured out so well. It's like you've known me my whole life. By the way, this is one seriously tasty veggie burger."

They finished their lunch and chatted about the move to New River. As they had dessert and touched their glasses she looked at him with a light in her eyes that made him feel like he was standing in a sunbeam. He stood up and came to her chair.

"Well my flowery little genius, now that you've solved all the problems of the world what say we blow this taco stand and get us a few Osprey?"

"Yes, absolutely." She took his hand and stood. For a moment they stood face to face. Rand flushed and swallowed hard. He helped her into the ATV, put Spang into his basket between them and they drove off to finish shopping. On the way back the Cape they were both quiet and thoughtful.

Rand had never been able to be silent and alone with Moira. Never able to just sit quietly, alone with his thoughts while she was there. There was always the need for her to talk, or him to talk. Some unspoken uneasiness that was covered up with chit-chat. His parents used to spend hours just silently sitting together, doing their own thing. To him it was the hallmark of a solid relationship. That ride back was the first time he had ever had that experience with anyone.

That night, as he was watering the garden and feeding the animals Elsie came up behind him.

"Hey, since there are two pilots now, I wondered if I could throw out an idea." Rand noticed how she was offering an idea rather than telling.

"Any idea out of that head of yours is always welcome."

"Well, I was looking at this beautiful lady here," She gestured at the A350. "and I was thinking that though she's a wonderful ship, she's a bit difficult to load. How about an upgrade?"

"Sure, what have you got in mind?"

She looked at him coyly, "Want me to show you?"

"Yeah!"

"Well then, let's take that rig of yours over to the base."

She knew her way around the Patrick Air Force Base at Cape Canaveral like the back of her hand. Under the star bright sky she had him pull up to a gigantic, closed hangar at the far end of the field.

"Here it is." She took him into the pitch black hanger. He followed close, barely able to make out her silhouette in the inky darkness. She wheeled towards the middle of the hanger then suddenly stopped, clicked on a flashlight and pointed it up. She was sitting beneath the nose of a massive military transport. The top of the cockpit stood over twenty-four feet off the ground. She raised her hands up.

"Happy Fourth of July!"

He was stunned, yet again. "You have to stop that."

"What?"

"Surprising me, my heart can't take it."

She laughed "What's the matter, never seen a C-17 Globemaster before?"

"Is that what this is? It's so big when you're this close I can't even tell what it is. I saw one of these at a distance back in England and wondered if I should try to fly it. I figured I would probably kill myself." He shook his head with a smile. "I knew they were big but, I had no idea."

"I flew C-17s out of Lackland in San Antonio when I was waiting for entrance into NASA. I used to have my very own Globemaster, she might even still be there in Lackland. But this one, is yours."

"How about ours Elsie, she can be ours."

"Okay, but I have to teach you how to fly her."

"Oh man, I don't envy you on that one."

She looked at him, smiling. "I bet you'll do better than you think."

They closed up the hangar and went back outside.

"We won't be able to take her to New River until we've repaired the runway. It was a mess when I flew over."

"That's okay, we can come back for her or maybe find another one at New River."

"How about we drive up on an expeditionary mission, scout the place out, do a few repairs then maybe commandeer a small plane to fly back here. Then we'll load up the C-17 with all the animals and the garden and fly it all back to New River?"

"Great idea. Sounds like a plan." Elsie was looking up at the stars. They stood in silence for a few minutes. She was unaware that Rand was staring at her.

To Rand she suddenly seemed about ten years old. Just a little girl dreaming of being an astronaut, staring at the night sky. A smile crept across his face, then Rand said quietly, "Told ya so."

"What's that?"

"When you were up at the station. I told you that you would be here next to me, looking up at the stars."

"You did didn't you? You are one amazing man Rand… I don't even know your last name."

"Carter."

"Well, you really are a most amazing man Rand Carter. I'm lucky that the last man in the world didn't turn out to be a total asshole."

Suddenly, out of the corner of his sight, a shooting star blazed into the sky.

"Did you see that?" Rand pointed, "A shooting star. We got our Fourth of July fireworks after all."

"I don't think that was a meteor." She grabbed his arm, searching the sky. Smaller shooting stars appeared above the horizon. Then a huge streak of bright light lit up the sky like day.

"Oh my God Rand that's the station, it's coming down!" She clung to him.

They stood and watched in awe as line after line of brilliant fireballs slashed the heavens and dwindled with a sputter.

Elsie was crying. "So beautiful, it was so magnificent. My whole life was wrapped up in that station." She was torn between the joy of being saved and the loss of one of mankind's most amazing creations.

"No Elsie, your life is here, inside you. That was your work, and your work won't be forgotten or lose it's importance. I don't know where we go from here, but we'll find a way to make it count, all of it."

They stood watching the most expensive fireworks display ever seen raining down on the Atlantic.

"I know it's sad Elsie, but it was eventual, and I would trade a thousand space stations for just one of you."

She just looked at him as he wiped her tears, feeling like a little girl.

"How about tomorrow you show me around the big plane?"

She nodded, "Okay."

They drove back to the small hospital. Elsie stopped by the runway, "I'm gonna stay up a while."

"Then take this." He handed her his .45. She had left her gun in the Guardian.

"Nice piece."

"Compliments of the Police Service of Northern Ireland."

"That's right, you were in Ireland when this whole thing started, I keep forgetting. Add that to the list of miracles. And you had to learn how to fly a jet plane across the Atlantic. I can see why you made it now; you have an uncanny talent for flying. In all my years I've never seen anything like it."

"All your years? What are you twenty seven, thirty max?"

"Oh Rand, you say all the right things!" She teased him. "I'm thirty eight."

"Wow! I mean, wow you look absolutely... I mean, you do not look thirty-eight. And here I was thinking I was the older one."

"Why how old are you?"

"Thirty three."

"The last people on earth, only five years difference. What are the chances?"

"Yeah." Rand looked at his feet, dodging the implication. "Well, I'll see you inside."

"Nite."

Elsie watched him walk away then looked back at the stars. She sat for a long while just watching the sky. *Too much.* It was all too much to think about. The Space Station, the world, her career, her children Marty and

Megan, her husband Bob. *I can't let them go, not the kids anyway. It's only been nine months.* She thought of Tom Hanks in Castaway. *He didn't give up after nine months. Of course, his wife continued to exist. But I'm not Tom Hanks, and this isn't a movie. Everyone is gone and there is no way of getting them back.* It was cruel and wrong, but that's the way it was. She had struggled so hard to survive in space, worked so hard to recover on earth to what end? Everything she ever cared for was gone. She had the most incredible children that she may never see again. She had the job that everybody in the world wanted, that she wanted, all gone. She realised she was sobbing when she felt a hand on her shoulder.

"I know Elsie, I know." Rand was at her side.

"Oh Rand I'm tired of crying. I cried for nine months up there. But I don't know how to let them go."

"Yeah, I'm trying to figure one that out too."

She put her arms around his neck and let the last of the tears fall away as he held her.

"We can figure it out together okay?" He said softly. "I just thank God we have each other."

They sat that way for a long while, saying nothing. Finally, he said, "Come on, let's go to bed." She didn't want to let go of him. "C'mon now," he encouraged her, "morning will bring clarity and hope, it always does."

"Okay." She relinquished with a sigh.

When they got back into the hospital Rand lead her to a place on the floor where he had made up a large bed with three mattresses put together. She looked at him, "How did you know I was going to ask you to sleep close to me tonight?"

He smiled and shrugged, "I didn't. I was going to ask you."

She hugged him. "Thanks."

Then he gestured with a flourish to a pile of soft clothes on a chair, "Your jammies await."

She picked them up off the chair. "You heated them?"

"That's a lesson from the comfort queen." He looked down as he held his stack of warm night clothes. "That's Moira. She was really good at cozy."

Elsie hadn't heard him talk about her before. "Thanks Moira." Then she went and got changed.

They slept in the big bed together. Both felt a little tension, but it was countered by a security and comfort they hadn't had in a long time. Spang lay on his back, feet in the air, snoring between them. In the morning Elsie lay staring at the ceiling, she knew this hallway. She had walked through it many times on the way to and from pre-flight medical examinations. Never in a million years would she have thought she'd be laying in a bed on the floor with a man she barely knew and a snoring dog. As Rand stirred she quickly closed her eyes and acted like she was sleeping.

Rand yawned and looked over at her. She was beautiful. Her skin was getting tan and her dark hair flowed over the pillow in thick strands. There is no way, he thought, she's thirty eight.

"Good morning." She said softly, "How did you sleep?"

The tone of her voice sent a wave of desire through Rand's body, catching him off guard. He disguised it by rubbing his eyes and stretching, "Um, yeah, I uh… I slept great. How bout you?"

She looked at him curiously, he was hiding something. "I had the best sleep I've had in ages!" She rolled on her back and threw her arms and feet up in the air and laughed. He smiled and got up. "Rand?"

He turned. "Hmm?"

"I don't want you to feel strange because we shared a bed."

"Oh, I don't." He lied.

"Because we're both dealing with some very serious issues of loss, and it would be normal for two people to seek each other for comfort… you know?"

"Yeah, that's… that's probably true."

"But I don't want you to feel guilty. That's not what I'm trying to do, you know? I mean… use you as a way to ease the pain of loss. Do you understand?"

Rand sighed. "Yes Elsie. Listen, there is definitely an attraction. I mean, on my part, I'm attracted to you, but not because you're the last woman in the world. Please don't take that wrong."

She just smiled weakly at him.

"No Elsie, that's not what I mean. I'm still dealing with losing Moira. With her I was never attracted to any other woman. She just did it for me. I had a wandering eye when

I first met her, but then it totally disappeared. It was actually really great, like a burden had been lifted. But now she's gone, and I don't know if I should let her go or wait it out."

"I'm the same with everything in my life, except Bob. I was going to leave him when I got back."

"I woke up thinking about Tom Hanks in that movie Castaway. He didn't give up on his wife after only nine months. He didn't… what? Why are you looking at me like that?"

"Are you kidding me? That's exactly what I was thinking last night when I broke down. Tom Hanks in Castaway, I'm not kidding Rand." Her words spilled out rapidly. "I was thinking about Tom Hanks and Castaway and how he didn't give up but it was just a movie and this is real and I'm not Tom Hanks and I have to let go because you're really hot and why and guilt and kids and Bob and…"

Rand just looked at her with his eyebrows raised.

She stopped ranting and just looked at him the same.

"You think I'm really hot?" He'd never seen anyone go from slightly tan to solid red in under a second.

Her hand flew to her mouth. "Oh." She looked back at him and nodded. "Yeah! I mean, yeah, you're not bad."

He laughed, "Geez, I feel all special."

She picked up a pillow and threw it at him. "Don't let it go to your head!" The pillow missed entirely, falling short on the bed. She burst out laughing. "You brat! Taking advantage of a convalescing war veteran! Have you no shame?"

Rand scooped her up and put her back down on the bed. They both were giggling like a couple of school children. When the laughter subsided he was leaning over her, her eyes inviting him. The air was heavy with anticipation, like the Angels were holding their breath.

"Elsie, I can't. You understand?"

She smiled at him, appreciating his honesty and his wisdom. Then she laughed and pushed him away. "Get offa me ya big galoot! I'm still fragile."

"You? Fragile? Ha!" He pelted her with the pillow and she went down in a heap.

"Just for that you owe me breakfast!"

They worked hard over the next week to get ready for the trip. Rand made plans to keep the flock safe and fed while they were gone and Elsie focused on getting stronger. By the end of the week she was walking full time on crutches and would even occasionally switch to a cane. The Guardian was made ready and the animals were supplied with straw, food and water to last several days without care. He made a new pen for them on a new patch of grass and widened the area considerably. While Rand was busy checking the welds on the plow end of the Guardian, Elsie came cruising around in a golf cart.

"Hey, look what I found."

Rand looked at her in the cart and shook his head. "You want to take that to New River?"

"No, I'm going to take it up the road to look for an RV."

"What? why?"

"You're doing good. Those are two of the big five. Because I'm in no shape to sleep in that thing," she pointed at the Guardian, "for the next two nights."

"But I don't think an RV is going to be able to push vehicles out of the way."

"No, you plow in the Guardian, me and Star Spangled Spangler here will cruise behind you with the kitchen, the soft bed and the bathroom."

"Oh, why didn't I think of that?"

"Because you're a man."

"Okay, okay. Just make sure that golf cart has enough juice and take--"

"A radio and the nine-mil. Way ahead of you." She tossed him a walkie.

"Keep an eye out for dog packs now, I'm serious."

"Okay."

"And take Spang with you."

"I don't have a choice."

She laughed as she drove off with Spang riding shotgun. He watched her go, thinking that maybe he should have gone with her, but there was too much to do so he just kept working.

The golf cart cruised along slowly and weaved between the cars very efficiently. This was actually the first time Elsie had been on her own in the apocalyptic landscape but her mind was on other things. *Am I really falling in love with him?* Since her close encounter with Rand she had decided to be Astronaut Elsie. Astronaut Elsie could work and live in close quarters and still be professional, compassionate and kind without any sexual tension, but it wasn't working so well.

It's like all of the love in the world is channeling itself through me because there are only two of us left.

You are smarter than that.

But it's so strong and unreasonable! I've never felt this before.

You are compensating for the months of isolation. Your subconscious needs to cement the relationship to establish a feeling of permanence.

No, that's why I married Bob. I know that mistake. This is raw... energy... love force and desire. I wasn't even this emotionally charged as a teenager.

Your not thinking straight.

She pulled the cart into the RV dealer and drove up to a mammoth custom machine. It was black and blue with graphics that looked like wings and flames.

"This is the one."

She drove the cart up to the office, walked in and found the keys right away. Then she went back to the big RV. Suddenly she was overcome with a sense of mischief. She decided that, as Rand had said, the world was theirs and she was going to do what she darned well pleased without anyone saying anything about it.

"Say goodbye to mister golf cart." She put Spang in the passenger seat of the tour bus then found a large rock and placed it on the accelerator of the cart. She watched as it sped down the row of RV's and crashed with a bounce through the office window.

"Hey that was kind of fun. We're gonna have to do more of that."

Climbing into the driver's seat of the tour bus she thought, *Not bad Els. So far today you stole an RV and destroyed property. You're becoming quite the criminal.* She chuckled as she turned over the big motor, but the battery was flat. *Aw crap.*

She hobbled down to the golf cart, her crutches making the distance seem even longer. She was sore and breathing hard by the time she got there. The cart lay high centred in the window. It was trick negotiating the terrain with all the glass but she managed to flip open the latches on the back hatch and find the battery.

Okay, now we're cooking with fire…oh shit, I don't have any tools.

It was long way across the lot to the service building but she had no choice. Halfway through the long trip she had to stop and rest. Sweat streamed down her face in the Florida heat, but she gathered her strength and pushed on. Finally she made it into the shade of the big building. It didn't take long to find the rack of new batteries and even less time to figure out that she had no way to carry them. The mechanics had a bike that they used to pedal around the huge lot, but that wasn't an option for her.

Rand warned you. Even little things can escalate into life threatening situations. Dammit Elsie you know better!

There was no way out of this but the hard way.

She gathered the tools she would need and put them in a wooden box. Then she cut a length of rope and tied it around the battery and the tool box, the other end she tied to her pistol belt. With her jaw set, she headed back out into the sun, dragging the heavy train behind her. The one hundred and twenty yards to the RV seemed like miles but she kept pushing. She fell into a trance, like the one she used to get into when she went running. After a couple of miles everything became a rhythm of footfalls and breathing. After what seemed like a marathon, she drug herself into the shadow of the bus and collapsed.

Not yet, you can't rest yet. Keep the momentum.

She levered herself up on her crutches and opened the engine hatch. The battery was larger than a normal road car's and much heavier. Her frail muscles and matchstick bones trembled under the strain but she managed to drag it out of it's cradle and it dropped to the ground. She stared at the new battery like it was a two ton block of steel. *There is no way I can lift that into place.* Her mind at a loss she scanned the area. Suddenly her eyes came to rest on a board laying at the foot of the chain link fence that surrounded the lot.

With renewed energy she crossed the fifty feet to the board and tied it off to her belt, just as she had done with the tool box. She dragged the board back and set it up as a ramp into the engine compartment. Over the course of ten minutes she wrestled the battery up the ramp and finally into place. With the battery bolted down she struggled up the stairs into the cab and was greeted by a perfectly content Spang, who had no idea what she had just been through.

Turning the key she knew it had to start or she would have to call Rand. It was not the impression she wanted to give him on her first solo outing in their new world. The starter turned the engine for a few moments then it finally rumbled to life.

"Thank God!"

She lay on the big steering wheel, panting. After a minute she sat up and looked around. She had always been a quick study with anything vehicular and in no time she was giggling maniacally as she closed the door and headed back to the base with the air conditioning roaring at full tilt. Rand had just finished loading the ATV on the trailer when Elsie pulled up.

"Impressive."

Elsie smiled and leaned out the window, "She may not look like much, but she's got it where it counts kid."

Rand laughed, "Alright Captain Solo, what happened to you?"

"I got in a little over my head, but it all worked out. What do you think? Would she make the Kessel Run in less than twelve parsecs?"

"That cheese brick isn't running anywhere very fast."

"Hey! You be nice when you talk about our home! Isn't that right Spangler?" Spang's head appeared in the back window.

"It's really nice Elsie. Permission to come aboard?"

"Granted." The door swung open automatically.

Rand climbed in. "Wow it's like a house in here. Hey, did you see this?"

A sign was stitched into the leather on the header above the couch in tattoo styled lettering 'The Sambora Sled'.

"Whoever this was built for was named Sambora. They must have been loaded."

Rand looked back at her with a growing grin, "I wonder if his first name was Richie."

She looked at him quizzically. "Who?"

"Bon Jovi's guitar player? You don't know Richie Sambora?" He shook his head. "Space jocks."

Elsie went and got cleaned up while Rand checked the animals and loaded the RV with a few provisions. When she came back out the RV and Guardian stood ready to go.

"Okay, let's blow this taco stand."

They headed North on 95. Rand had to do minimal plowing that day and they made good progress until they hit Jacksonville, Florida. The Guardian had a difficult time with a semi-truck full of milk, but Rand got the big rig started and managed to move it enough to make room for the RV to squeeze through. They pulled off the highway at a wooded rest area just outside of Woodbine, Georgia. As Rand climbed out of the Guardian the dense, humid Georgian air seemed to envelop him in sticky sweat. Elsie slid open the window of the RV.

"We'll camp here for the night." She said, then quickly turned apologetic. "If that's okay with you."

"Sure."

Elsie went to the switches in the kitchen. When all the whirring and whining of the motors finally stopped, the RV had grown to almost double its size.

"Wow. This is not the kind of camping I'm used to." Rand had gone inside and was sitting on the king size bed. "Normally I would say something like, 'I gotta get me one of these', but we already have it. I have to make up some new world sayings. How about, 'We should see what one of these looks like when you blow it up.'"

Elsie laughed, "No kidding, I did a bit of destructive entertainment back at the RV lot." She told him about her recent adventure.

"You little delinquent." He scolded. "You should have called me."

"Yeah, instant karma is a bitch."

"I knew something was up when you came back all dirty and sweaty."

"Oh, thanks."

"No, I mean you just looked like--"

"It's okay, I know what you meant."

"Well you certainly look a lot better! I mean... you've filled out. You were so thin when I took you out of the X-38."

"I smell better too."

"Yeah, wasn't going to say anything about that."

"I appreciate that, but I know it must have been horrid. I was literally sweating out my own urine."

"Okay. Did you have to go there?" Rand grimaced.

"Hey, it's nasty but it's how I survived!"

"I know already. I figured it out when you told me on the comms, you didn't have to say it." He grimaced.

Night settled in but the intense humidity continued to hang in the air. With no city lights to interfere, the stars came out blazing their crystal fire, the colours shifting in the evening heat. Rand gathered wood and made a fire as Elsie brought out the veggie burgers that Rand had prepared for the trip.

"Now for the pièce de résistance." She opened a side hatch on the RV and pushed a button. Again, the whirring of small electric motors unsettled the night as a large barbecue and hood fan folded out from the side of the rig.

"Are you kidding me?" Rand laughed incredulously. "This thing is like the Swiss Army knife of RV's."

The next morning, Elsie woke before him. She lay quietly watching him sleep, a burning desire filled her body.

God I want him!
But you're still married!
It's not like me at all.
Shame on you. What about the kids?
Bob and I are done. Besides, Megan and Marty will absolutely love him.
This is very impulsive and completely out of character.
This is a new world. I'm not going to fall on societal pretences that don't exist any more.
It's presumptuous. How do you know he feels the same?
The way he looks at me, especially in the mornings.
Get a hold of yourself. This is not how an astronaut or a commander behaves.

She bit her lip and quietly got out of bed, not wanting to make life any more difficult for him. While she busied herself with a small breakfast it took every ounce of willpower not to curl up next to him and wake him with kisses. Shaking off the thought, she forced herself to switch hats once again into her astronaut-self. Convinced she had regained her self-control, she woke him.

"Rand, hey! Time to get up, breakfast is waiting and there's cars to plow."

Rand scratched his head and rose, but other parts of him had got up before he had.
Easy there horn dog. She's married with kids.
Not any more.

The God String

That's a shitty thing to say. Good thing no one else can hear your thoughts.

Sorry, but she's so perfect…and so beautiful!

Calm down! She can't know how you feel. You'll freak her out.

He quickly ditched into the bathroom.

"Be right there!" He plashed his face with cold water.

Elsie thought maybe he was taking a shower, but after five minutes there was still no sound of the water running.

"It's getting cold. Henrietta would not be happy that you are wasting her eggs."

"Right, okay, just a minute I'll be right there." He came out a minute later in his robe holding a towel loosely in front of him and pretending to rub his face. She tried to ignore him.

"Oh nice! Thanks for breakfast." He sat, putting the towel in his lap to cover his persistent tent pole. Rand ate quickly then went back to the bathroom for a shower. This time she could hear the water starting up. As his arm shot out the door to drop a towel onto the floor, she caught a glimpse of his lean, naked body.

Elsie stood. Her breathing had gone shallow and her heart rate jumped. Desire burned in her deepest core.

No, no I can't…I can't…

Don't do anything

I can't ignore this. I'll go mad.

It will pass.

No, I don't want it to pass. I want love to win!
You don't know what will happen!
When have I ever known?

...

"That's it."

She marched over to the bathroom and threw open the door.

Rand was standing under the shower, water coursing down his chiseled frame with a look of total surprise on his face. She looked at him, her eyes following his hard, tan angles up to his eyes. She threw her robe off, pressed her body to his and kissed him hard. She kept kissing him, pulling his mouth to hers with one hand while she found the hard horn of his desire with the other, then walked him slowly out of the shower to the bed, still dripping wet. She turned around, pushed him onto the bed and climbed on top of him. He started to open his mouth and she put her fingers on his lips.

"No more talking." She whispered in his ear as she drove him into her. He finally surrendered and took over with a fury as dark clouds gathered over them.

Late morning stretched on as they claimed each other again. A storm thundered overhead bringing with it a strong, warm wind. Naked and unabashed they tumbled outside to get a breath but found they couldn't stay away from each other. Her body against his was the only thing that made sense in a world gone mad. Their repertoire grew as they went from passion to passion, a wild flame raged in them setting the world on fire, burning away the uncertainty, turning loneliness to ash until at last they held each other, drenched, spent, and laughing in the middle of a hot southern rain

Montgomery Thompson

Chapter 8

The Student

'Life is a succession of lessons

The God String

which must be lived to be understood'
~Helen Keller

They stayed that way, holding each other for a long time, taking turns laughing and crying. Crying away the final shreds of hope and despair for their lost lives, laughing because of the outrageous fortune that found them together. There were no words. They felt like they were going mad together. They had taken their choices to action, the choice to move on, a new world choice, the only one they could make: the choice of love. Finally it was clear that that choice demanded action in the form of survival. They went inside and towelled each other off.

"It's a different world from now on." Rand said, his eyes smiling into hers.

"Yes." She said, her eyes still brimming with tears. She felt like there was something else to say to follow it up. *And we'll be okay...* She tried it in her head. *And it's ours... and what now?* She had never been frightened, confused and overjoyed at the same time. *This is the love that all of the songs talk about...* Yes, that one seemed right. She wanted to tel him, but Rand was already busy preparing to go.

They loaded up the RV and continued north. Rain fell heavy on the highway as Rand pushed cars and trucks aside to make room for the RV to get through. Interstate 95 turned into Highway 76 as they drove straight through the heart of Florence, South Carolina. The vehicles on the highway were so dense that they had to take back roads around the town and drive on dirt roads to connect back to the highway again. The storm was growing in intensity and the rain soaked roads almost proved too much for the motor-home but Elsie kept her foot down and, despite a rough ride, pulled back onto the highway in once piece.

By the time the sun went down they estimated that they were only three hours away from Marine Corps Air Station New River and decided to push on through the night to get there. Darkness fell like a curtain as the growing storm put on a dazzling display. Lightning flashed wildly and the rain fell in torrents, dropping visibility so low that Rand had to switch on the gun turret's spotlight. In the RV, Elsie struggled to keep the big rig from being blown off the road. They continued to make slow headway but eventually it got so bad that Rand radioed Elsie.

"It's too crazy out here, I can't see anything."

Elsie's voice crackled through the static of the radio, "You're right, let's call it a night and wait for the storm to pass."

Rand stopped in the middle of the road and ran to the RV as waves of drenching rain pounded them. He had to fight as the wind tried to tear the door from his grip and managed to get inside with only a small bruise to his head. "It's crazy out there!"

She handed him a towel and waited until he finished drying off. Then she slowly pulled him to her and kissed him deeply. He felt his pulse slow and his nerves calm. She pulled back and he breathed a sigh.

"God, you're pure magic."

She gave him a huge smile and steadied herself as the wind shook the RV. "Tea?"

Outside, the first unnamed hurricane in centuries approached the coast. It had glanced off Nassau as a category five and was pushing north up America's eastern seaboard. Now it was aimed straight at a small community outside of Wilmington, North Carolina called Carolina Beach, making landfall as a category three. Only sixteen miles inland on Highway 74 just outside of a tiny housing development called Sandy Creek, Rand and Elsie had no way of knowing that they were directly in its path.

The wind outside shrieked across the black landscape, shaking the big RV like a toy. Rand held on to the back of the driver's seat and peered out the big windshield.

"In Northern Ireland sometimes the winds got up around ninety miles per hour. I think it's pushing at least that out there." He pulled up his hood. "I'm going to look outside and see if I can find out more about our surroundings. I want to know more about where we've parked."

"Be careful Rand, there could be anything blowing around out there."

"I will. Turn on all the lights then get on the camera system on the RV and see if you can see anything. I'm going to make my way back to the Guardian and check it out through the night vision on the turret."

He took a radio and the biggest flashlight he had. Elsie turned on the headlights and every other light the RV had, then Rand stepped out into the maelstrom. Most of the wind was blocked by the wall of the RV, but he could feel its strength on his lower legs as rocks, branches and other debris peppered him. Pausing at the front corner of the motor-home he reached his hand out into the headlight beam. The air was moving so fast that he could barely keep hold his hand up. Elsie could see the top of his head from the driver's seat.

"You okay?" She said through the radio.

"Yeah!" He yelled into the radio. "The wind is really strong!"

"Stay there for a minute, I'm going to pass you a rope."

She tied the rope to the steering wheel and handed it to him out the window. Rand tied it around his waist, and then braced himself as he stepped out into the gale. The wall of air forced him to the left as he stumbled then leaned into it. Step by step he fought his way to the Guardian and grabbed the antenna mount. He pulled himself along side and secured his rope to a handle next to the door then hauled open the top section of the door that opened on the right side of the vehicle. He had to climb over the lower door that usually lowered to create stairs. Reaching around, he shut the top door behind him, instantly quieting the chaos. He climbed into the drivers seat, started the engine and engaged the gun turret's night vision cameras. Sweeping the area for a full view he radioed back to Elsie.

"We're in a low spot and water is coming up over the road. It's about ankle deep now but it's going to get deeper."

"Roger that. How about the trees?"

"It's bad, the whole forest seems to have been recently logged. What's grown back is all tall, spindly and dense. The new growth wasn't managed at all."

Rand's experience as an outdoorsman in Montana had taught him what a properly managed forest should look like, and the horrendous consequences of a mismanaged one. "Basically we're surrounded by a lot of ammunition for the storm, and by the looks of it, it's going to be coming down soon. We gotta get out of here."

"Rand, it has got to be a tropical storm or hurricane. Winds don't usually get this bad here without assistance from storms coming north off the Caribbean."

"If that's the case then we'll be safer in the Guardian. We'll have to abandon the RV. I'm sorry Elsie, I know how much work it was for you."

"That's okay, as long as we're safe."

"I'll back up next to the door. You get into some rain gear get our supplies together. And we'll move everything over to the Guardian."

"On it."

Elsie started piling their supplies next to the door. They didn't have much, so it only took a couple of minutes. By that time Rand had backed the Guardian close to the RV and lined up the doors. As soon as the RV door opened, Elsie started handing supplies to him then grabbed Spang and crawled into the armoured truck. Rand sealed the hatch behind her.

"Whew! I've never seen it so bad." She said pulling back her hood.

"You guys okay?" Rand looked her and Spang over.

"Yep. Let's get out of here."

Just then a loud thump rang against the side of the vehicle. The trees had started coming down.

"The poor RV, I hate to leave it here."

"There will be others. Besides, we can always come back and get it if we want."

A tree crashed over the top of the RV, drooping branches over Rand's windshield. "Or what's left of it."

Rand put his foot down as another tree fell on the Guardian. The heavy vehicle roared off down the road, rolling over and through fallen trees like a Cadillac on a Sunday cruise. Just outside of Leland they cleared the trees and the full force of the wind came to bear, shaking the heavy vehicle with a sound so loud they had to yell just to talk.

"Good Lord, that's gotta be well over a hundred!"

"At least!"

The God String

"WHAT?"

It was no use conversing, they would just go hoarse. Suddenly Spang started howling. They both looked at him, then each other, then burst out laughing which made Spang howl even more. Rand and Elsie were in fits.

"Poor Spangler!" Elsie said with tears in her eyes.

For some reason they just couldn't stop laughing. Maybe it was the crazy weather, or the high from their newly found intimacy or just the ridiculousness of the whole situation. Rand didn't know or care, the laughter shattered the heaviness on his heart. He laughed so hard that had to stop so he didn't drive off the road. Spang kept up his serenade and they both laughed until they got stomach cramps. Eventually they calmed themselves down and gave the little dog some attention.

"Look at him , he's completely disgusted." Elsie cradled Spang's head.

"It's loud to us, I can't imagine what he's hearing."

"I think the metal hull of this armoured beast is vibrating in the wind, obviously at a frequency that we can't hear but poor Spangler can." She wrapped Spang in a blanket and covered his ears.

Rand got back on the road and kept chuckling to himself. The going was slow, but the sturdy machine had no problems going around, over, or through any obstacles. South of the seaside town of Hampstead the road washed out, but even that was no problem. The Guardian waded through three feet of water and stalwartly rumbled on. After a long night of screaming winds and being battered by debris; including bricks and a large pieces of roofing tin that would have sheared a normal car in half, they pulled into MCAS New River. The sun was just coming up, peeking through the thin layer of sky. Heavy clouds filtered the sun light which bathed everything in a golden wash. The Marine base was on the northwestern edge of Morgan Bay which was swollen with storm surge, but the Marines had accounted for this kind of event and the water held at a manageable point.

Rand drove across the runway through rows upon rows of huge CH-53E Super Stallion helicopters, AH-1W Super Cobra attack helicopters, Beechcraft C-12 small personnel transports and the reason why Rand decided to fly to the states; the tilt-rotor V-22 Osprey. Elsie was sleeping, curled up in the back with Spang on a pile of blankets she had taken out of the RV.

"Elsie wake up, we're here." He reached back and shook her. "Come up here and look at this."

Elsie rubbed her eyes and crawled into the cabin. "Wow Rand, this is gonna be great. I was always kind of afraid of helicopters, you know, with the Jesus nut and all."

Rand looked at her, perplexed.

"Never heard of that? Helicopters have one big nut that holds the rotor in place. If that one nut fails…" she pointed her finger in an arch toward the ground.

Rand blanched. "Do you think Ospreys are built the same way?"

"No, they're a standard prop rotor. It's just that the engines tilt up. At least that's my understanding. I'm sure there's a lot more to it."

Tired and sore, they climbed out of the Guardian and went into a building labeled *The Landing Zone - Officers Club*. Inside the smell of mold and stale beer was overpowering.

"No way Rand, this place is rotten." Elsie said holding her nose. "Let's try the BOQ. Oh sorry, the bachelor officer's quarters. You're on a military base now, there are acronyms for everything"

"AFE." Rand smiled

"Exactly."

Elsie's idea proved a much better option. The rooms were clean and though not luxurious, were more akin to something they would find in a motel chain. The water was cold but they took a quick shower anyway then crawled into bed and quickly fell asleep. About six hours later they woke and brought food in from the Guardian which Elsie had begun calling the Thing. The hurricane had passed, but left swirls of storms in its wake. After their meal Rand stood outside and surveyed the base as the sun began to set.

"It's beautiful here. I wonder how many of these aircraft are still in working order?"

Elsie had her ear to the wind. "I dunno..." she said absently.

"What are you listening for?"

"Dogs."

In a flash Rand had drawn his pistol and put his back to Elsie's, covering the areas she couldn't see. "Where?"

"I don't hear anything but I know that Marines use dogs. Camp Lejeune is right around the corner and they use them there too. The dogs are trained so they might have formed into a pack and stayed put on the base."

"Let's wait an hour then we can use the Guardian to check the area with night vision."

"Use the FLIR, it will see their body heat."

They stayed in the room while they geared up for trouble. Then when they were ready Rand let Spang out of the building and they quickly climbed into the Guardian. The turret swung around giving them a full three-sixty view of the area but there were no dogs.

"I've got a squirrel and… I don't know, is that a…"

"Opossum, yep. It's safe to say we're in the clear. Let's do a tour and then come back here. We can get a fresh start tomorrow."

They drove around the base to familiarise themselves.

"If we put in some fencing at the entrances we can completely close this place in. Then the animals can do what they like."

"As long as they stay off the flight line." Elsie reminded him of the hazard.

"I can put up fencing to keep them clear of that too."

After several hours of snooping around, Rand spotted a fenced area full of construction equipment. He stopped and hooked up a large trailer mounted generator.

"Excellent, now I can get the power on at the BOQ."

Elsie liked the sound of that.

When they got back, Rand jump started the generator and passed several extension cords through the window. One for the hot water tank and the others for lights. In no time they had hot water, coffee and a working microwave. They showered, soaking into one another, then fell into bed to sleep in the comfort of each others arms.

In the morning, Rand woke Elsie with a long series of gentle kisses. She responded eagerly, reversing on top of him and, arching her back for maximum tension, drove relentlessly until they both cried out from the powerful, sharp release. Then she pulled off and curled up in his arms.

"I can never get enough of that." She looked up at him through the piles of her dark hair.

"Neither can I." He smiled and brushed her hair back.

"Maybe it's time to get up." She sighed.

Rand laughed, 'Busy day today my love.'

Her face suddenly went flat, "What did you say?"

Rand frowned, "I said busy day today my love."

"Ooh," she climbed on top of him. "Say that last part again."

"My love."

"Oh I like that."

"I love you Elsie."

Suddenly a dam inside her heart burst and she began crying.

"I love you Elsie." He pulled her close and whispered.

She held her hand to her mouth and nodded. "I know, it's amazing!"

"I really do."

"I know, I can feel it! I love you Rand!"

"I've never felt anything like this before. I thought I knew what love was." He laughed with tears coming to his eyes. "I wasn't even close!"

Elsie didn't know if was because they were the only people in the world, but the strength of his love seemed to shine in her like the sun. Rand felt so high he never wanted to come down, but eventually she let him go.

"Tell me that everyday please?"

"Of course I will, because I do and it's too wonderful to keep to myself. Now," He spanked her on the ass, "let's get this place fixed up then you have to show me how to fly my present!"

She looked up, "God I don't know what I did to deserve this man, but whatever it is may I keep doing it for the rest of my life!" Then she looked at Rand, "And I'm not even religious."

The wake of the hurricane had finally cleared to a gorgeous sunny day, but the storm had made a mess of things. After he got a truck started for Elsie, Rand found a proper plow truck and cleared most of the runway. The large pieces he had to push with a bulldozer. The massive crater he had seen from the air was even bigger on the ground and made the second runway completely useless. The debris was obviously from a C-17. As he pushed the wreckage out of the way he found what looked like the remains of an Osprey. Rand figured that the C-17 with no crew aboard, must have dropped out of the sky mid-landing and hit the Osprey. Possibly a bomb went off. It was only a guess. Next, he drove out the sweeper truck and cleaned the good runway completely.

Elsie drove around and found the records, keys and security passes for the base. The Marines were very different from the Air Force but there were a lot of consistencies in protocol. While she was doing that, Rand towed generators to the buildings that Elsie had marked on the map. It took five in all. Thankfully the Marines had built the buildings with emergency power couplings and all Rand had to do was attach a large plug to specially built receptacles. With the generators running, he and Elsie turned their attention to the planes.

Elsie sifted through the roster of aircraft on the base and found what she thought would be the most serviceable units. She radioed Rand and told him which hanger to clear a path to, then she headed to the meteorology department to find out what she could about the weather. There was a spring in her step and she was suddenly aware that she was walking with little difficulty. She thanked God again when she found that New River was an auxiliary control station for the military weather satellite network. Rand had the power up and running so she rebooted the systems and accessed the live satellite video feed.

"Just as I thought, a hurricane." She muttered to herself.

The storm was moving northeast out across the Atlantic, losing force as it crossed into colder waters. She noted several other storms brewing as they swirled off the Sahara at the Horse latitudes and spun out into the ocean. She knew that some of them would make it as far as the Caribbean but the chances of another hurricane hitting North Carolina directly were very slim. She gathered the data she needed and headed to the pilot's ready building. The locker rooms had attached showers and a large hot tub as well as an area for physical therapy, a full gym, boxing ring and hand-to-hand combat floor. It was still early and Rand had just begun working on the aircraft so she got to work cleaning up the place. Three hours later she called Rand on the walkie.

"Hey darlin' you wanna come over here and get naked?"

"You don't have to ask me twice."

Rand floored the sweeper and headed to where the truck was parked on the tarmac. He ran inside the door to find a note hanging at the front desk. *'Good boys to the left, bad boys to the right.'* He looked left, but went right with a grin. Inside he heard the shower running. He quickly undressed and went into the large shower area, sliding in with a "Ta-da!" but it was empty except for one of the showers that was running.

He washed off the dust then continued out the other doorway. Candlelight cast a soft glow in the steamy air. She lay naked on the edge of the far side of a large hot tub, one leg dangling in the water. His eyes followed her arm down between her legs to where her fingers plied the pink flesh of her passion in a small circle. Her eyes smouldered as they rose to meet his.

It was too much for Rand. He waded across the hot tub and descended on her with his mouth, she groaned and pushed against him.

The first time they were together, they made love. Now it was sex, with love in every act. Rand had never experienced anything like it. Elsie was moved to do things she had never dared. The thrill of it was like her first flight. The breathless disbelief of leaving the ground, the utter astonishment at the beauty of the sky, the elation of a freedom never known. It was all of these things with him. She had lost the world to find him. He had found a world in her he knew he would never lose. They took their time, watching and feeling every touch and sensation hungrily. He finished her with his mouth, then again from behind as she braced, thigh deep in the hot water. She climaxed again just before he did, and as he came she spun around and swallowed him deeply. His surprised cries reverberated off the tiled walls in rhythmic echo to his pulsing orgasm. When she had nursed every hot drop out of him they sunk into the warm tub and just floated in silence. Finally Rand pulled Elsie to him and just held her.

"I always believed it could be like this." She whispered.

He pulled her closer, wanting to soak her into him until they became one. Finally, they sank into the hot water up to their necks then he slowly let her go. The heat from the water went to their heads and they swam in slow circles, eyes locked, floating in a dreamscape of steam and candlelight.

After a long soak they climbed out and dried off. When they emerged back outside, the sun was just reaching it's zenith.

"It's only noon?" Rand looked at his watch. "Why did I think it was night time?"

"It's the magic of the pool, it's kind of dark in there." Elsie threw her arms around his neck and kissed him.

"No, *you* are the magic of the pool."

"Well it's there any time we want to use it."

"Again!" His eyes flashed.

She shook her head. "We've got work to do if we're going to make this place a home. I'm not sleeping in temporary quarters for the rest of my life."

"True. Okay, back to work."

"After I got the weather information, it was a hurricane by the way, I came over here, rolled up my sleeves and attacked the place with bleach. I had to mop it all twice but most of the mold came up. The military keeps everything so clean that even after a couple of years it wasn't too bad."

"And all of that before noon. Very impressive."

"The great part is that the generator will keep the hot tub heated. All we have to do is put a bromine tablet in every now and then and we're guaranteed a hot soak everyday."

"Now that's what I call thriving."

"So, you ready to check out your new ride?"

He rubbed his hands together. "This day just keeps getting better!"

She led him to the locker area where they got into flight suits.

"What are these insignia?" Rand pointed to the patches on his flight suit.

Elsie looked, "Let's see… this is 2nd MAW, MAG-26, VMM-263."

"It's a whadda what?"

"Second Marine Aircraft Wing, Marine Aircraft Group twenty six, Tilt Rotor Squadron two six three." Elsie said ripping hers patches off. "Take them off hon. Out of respect for the brave men and women who these belonged to. We haven't earned the right to wear these insignia." Elsie grew very solemn as she looked down at the patches in her hand. "They were the best of the best." She put the patches back in the locker and closed the door. Then she found an unused locker to call her own.

Rand saw the U.S. Marines insignia on the wall. "The few, the proud…"

"That's right." She said suddenly. "Even though I'm Air Force, we were all part of the same team and I'm damn proud of them. On joint ops nobody messed with our Marines without catching hell from the sky." Elsie fought back tears. "They were damn good flyers too."

There are so many sides to her, Rand thought, *and I love them all.*

"Now," she rubbed her eyes and tossed him a flight helmet, "see if this fits."

He put it on. "Like a glove. What's this for?"

"You Mr. Carter, are going to learn to fly today…"

"Yes!"

"…military style."

"Oh. Should I be scared?"

"No, you should be excited. US military pilots are the best in the world."

"Is it okay if I'm a little bit scared?"

He tried to sound like he was joking to mask his slight apprehension, but she saw right through it.

"A little fear is good, it makes you pay attention."

They took the truck across the runway to a large hangar at the northeast side of the base. Following Elsie's instructions hours before, Rand had connected the plane's generator to charge the batteries and parked the tug in the hangar.

"Tell me why we're taking this huge empty thing back to Cape Canaveral instead of one of those smaller planes?" Rand asked. They were standing in the hangar now looking up at the giant transport.

"It's training for you. You will be flying your C-17 back here."

"How much experience have you had in one of these?"

"I flew a Spectre AC-130 gunship with special ops in the Gulf war, Afghanistan and…' She hesitated.

"What is it?"

"It's just hard to disclose something that's been so ingrained as classified. It goes against all my training." She took a breath and began again. "I flew the AC-130 in the Gulf, Afghanistan, Syria, Mali and Uzbekistan. Then I came back to the states and qualified for the C-17 Globemaster. During training I got selected for the astronaut program.'

"Woah, we had black ops mission in Mali and Uzbekistan?"

"We had black ops mission all over the world."

"Wait a minute…so you have never done any *actual* missions in a C-17?"

She looked at him and smiled, forcing a mood change. "Lots of training missions my sweet. I have over three hundred hours in these puppies."

"That's what I want to hear."

"The military knows how to train pilots Rand. And now I'm going to train you."

"Okay, let's do this." He said nervously.

Rand hooked the tug up to the front landing gear then caught up to Elsie as she walked to the rear of the aircraft and lowered the massive ramp.

"God, we could've parked the RV in here."

"She'll hold over a hundred and seventy thousand pounds of cargo. She's got a range of two-thousand, four-hundred miles at five-hundred fifteen miles per hour and a service ceiling of forty-five thousand feet. She can carry one-hundred thirty-five combat loaded troops, or six Guardians, or three Strykers, or one M1 Abrams tank.'

"Wow, I-"

"Her wingspan is one-hundred sixty-nine feet, eight inches and she stands proud with a tail height of one inch over fifty-five feet. She's the fat lady, my big gal, Mistress Moose. Most of the men call theirs Barney, to me she's Aunt B.'

Rand laughed and gave her a short applause. "That's quite a spiel."

She laughed with him, "It's what I used to say in response to the question, 'So what do you drive little lady?' It really put them on their heels."

"I can see why. You're so feminine and then you shift into military mode and it's like… you're someone you don't want to cross."

"I can hold my own most of the time." She chuckled.

Rand saw a strength and confidence in her demeanour. "I want to learn Elsie."

"Well, let's get to it."

"I mean all of it. Teach me everything."

"Sure hon, anything I know is yours for the taking."

"Sweet."

Elsie showed him how to do a walk around inspection then after Rand walked up the ramp and called in Spang, she showed him how to close it up. They walked the interior length of the cargo bay as she introduced him to all of the various systems.

"For what appears to be a big empty space there sure is a lot going on." Rand's head felt like it was on a swivel just trying to keep up with Elsie's briefing.

"Don't sweat all of this. I'm just introducing you to it. As my instructor used to tell me, 'Save your sponge for the cockpit'."

They had to climb up a ladder to get to the cockpit. There were two chairs for observers stationed behind the pilot and copilots chair. Though the cockpit was roomy, it was smaller than Rand suspected it would be. Elsie climbed in the co-pilot's chair.

"Um. Isn't that one for me?" Rand said, confused.

"Nope, you're the pilot on this one. Just get in and I'll introduce you to her."

She took him through the controls using the Airbus A350 as a reference. There were some military specific controls like defensive flares, a smokescreen and the IFF, which she explained.

"It stands for Identification Friend or Foe. Basically it sends out a radio frequency that says 'I'm a friend don't shoot me'. Allied missiles and target acquisition equipment will only look for and lock on to aircraft that aren't broadcasting that they are a friend."

"Is it only on military planes?" Rand asked.

"Good question, the answer is no. Civilian commercial aircraft as well as military and civilian response vehicles and equipment can all carry IFF. Even ground troops carry equipment that uses IFF, like the shoulder launched Stinger missile. Make sense?"

"Yeah totally. Makes perfect sense."

After the orientation Rand used the tug to tow the plane out of the hangar.

Back up in the cockpit Spang was curled up on one of the soft observer's seats. Rand hated to do it but he put him into the drop cage to keep him safe for the flight, then kissed Elsie as he climbed back into the pilot's chair.

"Okay, ready to roll." He said putting on his helmet. "Whoa. Joystick?"

"Yep. No yoke on this baby, she flies like a fighter."

She showed him how to start the engines. "Each one is capable of over forty-thousand pounds of thrust. She may be big, but she's more responsive than you'd think when she's empty."

The four engines began to whine as they spun up. When they had reached the optimal RPMs, Rand eased the throttle forward and began to roll down the taxiway.

"She's a bit bigger than your Airbus so keep that in mind when you line up."

The thought was already foremost in his mind as he tried the unusual joystick controls.

"Woah girl, easy."

He had too much speed and the plane turned very fast. Elsie reacted instantly and the plane slowed into the turn.

"She's more stable than you think." Elsie chuckled.

"Are you sure you want me in this chair. God knows what damage I can do."

"Don't let a thing like that scare you off. When you learn by making a mistake you learn best. Besides, I'm here. I won't let anything go seriously wrong."

"Alright then. What's next?"

"Finish lining up and then begin takeoff procedures just like the A350."

"But I don't have any notes. I…"

"You don't need notes Rand. I watched you fly the X-38 a foot over my head in orbit. This stuff is common sense to you. Just…"

"Use the force?"

She laughed, "Exactly. Feel it."

He laughed now. "I think I understand."

"Just relax. You know where the controls are, now do it."

Rand set the brakes and flaps and throttled the huge engines up to the revs she told him. Then he let off the brakes and let her roll. She shook more than the A350 but she accelerated faster too. Before he knew it, he was airborne.

"Wow she really flies!"

Elsie just laughed. Rand was thrilled. Even though he was flying one of the world's biggest cargo planes, to him it felt much smaller. Elsie had the coordinates for the twenty minute flight to the Cape, but she had other things in mind. She quickly put him on task, making him climb and turn to specific altitudes and headings with only so much time to get there. Her requirements made him take turns steeper than he felt comfortable with. He held his breath and kept asking, "Is this normal?" When he just couldn't complete one of the manoeuvres she took the stick.

"Watch. She's a fighter, and she's no push-over. She's tough and likes to be handled rough sometimes." She gave it full throttle as she pulled the stick back. The giant plane nosed up an incredible angle.

"Holy shit!" Rand blurted out.

"Stay calm Rand I'm not doing anything dangerous."

He took a breath and tried to master his fear. The plane kept climbing steeply, up and up. Rand looked at the altimeter – twenty thousand feet, twenty one, twenty two, twenty three…

"Elsie what the ceiling on this?"

"Forty-five thousand feet, but I'm forcing her into a stall."

The controls started beeping and buzzing. Rand gripped the underside of his chair as the computer started talking; *'warning - stall imminent, warning - stall imminent…'*. Suddenly the plane stopped moving. *'stall, stall, stall…'* the computer repeated. In slow motion, the view outside whirled to the left and Rand felt briefly weightless as the plane fell backward. Elsie's voice broke through his dismay.

"Now don't panic. I want to teach you something important."

Rand realised he had been holding his breath "Wh-what?"

"This is how you recover from a stall."

The plane had turned to face the ground now and was accelerating into a steep dive turning to the right.

"I said keep calm Rand, you have to learn that." Her voice again, cut through the panic. "Do you trust me?"

The huge airplane was gaining speed. The engines started to whine loudly as the spinning ground filled the window.

"I… I…"

"Rand this is Elsie, do you trust me?"

Suddenly it was clear. He made a choice and blocked out everything but her, choosing to ignore even the shaking of his body in the seat.

"Yes." He turned calmly and looked at her. Then he smiled. "Yes Elsie I trust you."

She smiled at him.

"Okay then, take the stick and focus only on stopping the spin. It's going right so you…?"

Rand used the rudder and stick to turn the plane to the left until the spinning stopped. Now they were simply plummeting straight down.

"Now…" She was about to tell him the next step but he was already doing it. The huge plane slowly came up out of the dive. There was no amateur dramatics with struggling and pulling on the yoke, just a gradual levelling.

"Incredible." Rand shook his head.

"It was all you Rand. You did it. Now…"

"Hold it!" Rand looked at her, "I know what you're going to say, do it again."

"That's right. How did you know?"

"It's just like when I landed the Airbus the first time. It was a bit shaky, but this voice came into my head and told me to do it again. I did it until I was nailing it time after time."

"Okay listen to that voice, that's your inner pilot. Let's go through some turns and then end with the stall okay?"

"Okay!" He said with enthusiasm.

She just went on as if it was another day at the office and gave him the coordinates she wanted him to go through. This time he brought the big transport smartly into turns, climbs and dives. His fear was gone now that he knew what the plane could do. At first, he surprised her by reaching the altitude and heading faster than the time she gave him. He had an uncanny knack of managing power in the airplane to get the optimum performance from the engines. She didn't tell him this, instead she told him to hit the time exactly, not before or after. It seemed effortless to him. The steep turns that rattled him before seemed like nothing compared to experience of the stall.

"Now you're flying." She said proudly.

He was grinning ear to ear. "What a difference!"

When she told him to go into the stall he pulled it off perfectly, recovering within five-thousand feet. She was stunned but was careful not to show it. After the stall they headed to Cape Canaveral. As they prepared to land, she talked to him only in little bits, making him recall what he knew about the landing procedure of the A350 and then applying it to the C-17. She was coming to trust in his amazing ability to adapt to the new plane. Sure enough, he made the final approach and landing without her so much as saying a word. The only thing she had to help him with was the application of the reverse thrusters and brakes. With the airplane safely down at the Cape they both stepped off the huge ramp with Spang jogging along beside them. She hadn't spoken since their final approach.

"Now," she said at last, "come with me." They walked to the front of the plane and stood back so they could see the whole thing.

Then she said, "Look at the size of that thing."

He looked at her quizzically. "Yeah, it's big, but not as big as when I first looked at it."

She smiled. "Lesson complete."

He looked at her again. "I did pretty good didn't I?"

She couldn't hold back any longer. "Rand, I don't want to make you overconfident. And that is very important to remember because overconfidence will get you killed. You were concentrating so hard you didn't even realize that you landed the plane yourself. I said nothing. What you did up there in the manoeuvres, the stall recovery, the landing I… I've seen military pilots with over a hundred actual hours and hundreds of sim hours not do that well. If I have the right stuff, you've got the super right stuff. You're a natural. You should have been flying a long time before this."

"Thanks Elsie, that really means a lot coming from you. Learning with a pro makes all the difference. I can't believe how much more there is to know. So how long did it take you to master the stall?"

Elsie looked shifty eyed for a second. Rand frowned. He'd never seen her so unsure of herself. Then a light went on and his eyes went wide.

"You never did a stall recovery in this thing did you?"

"Yes we did, just… not at those heights and angles."

His first reaction was to ask why the hell she put him through that but then he stopped himself. It was because she knew he could where others couldn't, because she believed in him. After a long silence with her looking at him sheepishly he said,

"What a rush!"

She jumped up and wrapped her arms and legs around him.

They had been gone for three days so the first thing Rand did was tend to the animals. With Spang on her heels, Elsie went with him to learn the routine. She tried her hand at milking but found that it was harder than it looked. After trying and trying again, getting kicked once and stepped on twice she finally got the hang of it. Once the animals were all happy they focused on moving everything from the A350 to the C-17. Loading the C-17 was a breeze. The deck had the same recessed wheels in it for pallets to roll on and places to tie things down as the A350, but unlike the Airbus Rand could drive a forklift right inside. It had been designed from the wheels up to be a master mover.

"I wish I would have had one of these when I came from England. I had some really cool stuff there I wanted to take." He was thinking about the Maxx. With the C-17 loaded Elsie closed up the back while Rand climbed up to the cockpit. The flight back was smooth and uneventful. Rand stuck the landing at New River perfectly and they had everything unloaded by nightfall. The animals grazed happily on a patch of tall grass on the side of the runway. After Rand had driven around and closed all of the gates, the base was sealed. The high fence that ran around the whole perimeter would keep any predators away.

The next morning they went in search of a permanent residence. It was an uncomfortable thought, but they knew they would have to move into someone's house. Rand told her that when they found a place, he would go into the house and pack up all the memorabilia and personal belongings and they would make a small memorial somewhere on the grounds.

"We should try to keep close to the base."

"Yeah, maybe something on the water."

"But not within flood range." Elsie added quickly.

"That hurricane was as bad as it's going to get. If a house got through that okay we should be fine."

They spread out a map of the area on the chart table.

"There's base housing all over the place." Rand traced his finger over the map.

"Base housing is… how do I put this… not exactly quality accommodations. We need a big house with lots of room for storage and utilities with easy access. But I also don't want to be staring into vacant houses. It's not good psychologically or logistically."

"Okay, I understand the psychological part."

"By logistically I mean that being around a bunch of houses while their contents are rotting away is going to be smelly and attract all kinds of scavengers from dogs and rodents to bugs. It's best to stay away from populated areas."

"I hadn't thought of that. So, we're looking for a nice house that's remote but close to the base."

"Yep. Like here, to the southwest of the base. Treehaven Lane."

"Sweet, it's close to a Harley dealership, but it's a little far from base. How about here?" Rand traced his finger on a road to the northeast. "White Street."

"Yeah, that runs through the base."

"Then it jumps across interstate seventeen and heads straight where the river empties into Wilson Bay."

"Okay, let's look along that road and see what's there."

White Street ran directly behind the hangars. They took the Guardian north and followed the road as it turned to the east and went through a security gate. After a short series of sharp bends they drove across the interstate on an overpass.

"Looks like some kind of gun range down there." Rand tried to see out of the Guardian's small windows.

"No houses yet, keep going. I'm going topside." Elsie opened the top hatch over the passenger seat and stood up. "That's better."

Another road headed off to the right but they stayed with the well-maintained road they were on. The trees were dense on all sides and appeared to be getting larger and widely dispersed. Suddenly the road ended at a stunning white Victorian house.

"Rand it's gorgeous, It looks practically new." Elsie said, afraid of liking it too much. "I just hate the thought of taking some family's beautiful home."

"Okay, take it easy. I'll check it out and let you know what's going on with it. Be right back." Rand had the automatic shotgun with him as well as his bat-belt. He walked carefully up the stairs of the porch. Slowly he opened the door, a woody, musty smell came from within. It reminded him of a lumber yard.

"It looks totally unoccupied." He radioed Elsie. "Let me check around a bit. Standby."

As he methodically went through every room on the ground floor one thing was abundantly clear; no one had been living in the house. A part of him suspected that no one had ever lived there. In the kitchen came his confirmation. "Elsie, it's fine. Get in here, you have to see this."

As she came in the front door she was surprised at the coziness of such a large house and the detail of the craftsmanship. The woodwork was incredible.

"I'm in the kitchen." She found him leaning over a set of plans. "Look here, it's called *the Practical Magic house*. I have no idea what that means, but the place is definitely magical… what?"

Elsie was looking at him, hand over her mouth, eyes as big as quarters.

"This is the house! The house from one of my favourite movies! Practical Magic. You know?"

Rand shook his head. He was crossing the line into the realm of the chick flick and that made him nervous. Elsie began to explain the movie and Rand just listened and nodded. When she was done he said,

"So this house was designed for a movie? It doesn't look like a set."

She shook her head, "No it's based on the movie. See, here on the plans."

She turned the plans around so she could read them.

"Built for Drew and Amy Ownes, designed by Dietsche & Dietsche Architects, PC, blah, blah. These people loved the movie and had a house designed after it."

"Well, it's a really nice house and most importantly, it's never been lived in. What do you say?" He spread his arms wide and she wrapped around him.

"I love it, it's beyond perfect!"

"Well that settles that. We're home."

The God String

Montgomery Thompson

Chapter 9

Cloak & Dagger

*'There are few problems that can't be solved with
a suitable application of high explosives.'*
~Adam Savage

Returning to the base they hooked up a construction generator to a giant Mk-23 cargo truck and a large enclosed trailer to the Guardian. Rand plowed his way into Jacksonville while Elsie dropped the generator off at the house then headed into town to meet him. She caught up with him just as he stopped in front of a furniture store on the main street. Together they loaded both vehicles and the trailers with everything they needed for the new house.

"It's going to take a lot more trips, but for the next day or two this should do." Elsie wiped her forehead.

"Now that the road is cleared it will be easier. Let's head back and I'll set up the power."

They lit a fire that night and Rand blessed the house before dinner. Elsie pulled out a bottle of aged whiskey she had found and they walked down to the water's edge and sat on the dock as the moon rose.

"You know what this means don't ya?" Rand teased. Elsie looked up at him with a frown, perplexed. "We're gonna have to get a boat and do some fishing."

"Fine with me country boy. You catch em, I'll cook em." They clinked their glasses and drained the last of their drams.

It took weeks to settle into the house. Rand made daily excursions out for tools, fuel, furniture and a myriad of other random things they wanted. Boats, motorcycles, cars, trucks and ATVs began to fill up the huge barn and garage on the property. They took turns trying to out-do each other as they prepared for winter. Rand built a full alternative power system with wind and solar then added water power from the slow moving river that ran into the bay. Elsie saw his bid and raised it with a full workout gym including matching treadmills. Rand countered with a wood fired hot tub and a massive indoor, year-round vegetable garden on raised beds. Elsie fired right back with a wood-fired oven that doubled as a hot water heater with a double insulated storage tank. And so they went on until they had satisfied most every material need they had ever conceived. Rand exchanged vehicles almost weekly just to amuse Elsie.

First it was a Ferrari, then a monster truck. After that, it was a succession of luxury automobiles including Bentley's and Rolls Royce's. These they delighted in taking off-road on the weekends, thrashing them until they were dead. None of the cars lived up to their former price tag. The only car that Rand coveted was a black on satin-black Bugatti Chiron. He had plans to fly that to Groom Lake to see if it really would reach over two hundred and fifty miles per hour. On the weekdays, they went through the full training course for the V-22 Osprey. It took weeks of ground school then Elsie did her flight. Rand stayed on the ground. They decided that in the event that something went wrong it would be better to have Rand there to respond.

Her first flight went off without a hitch and after several more flights she could instruct Rand. In no time he was flying the Osprey solo. The sturdy cargo plane could tilt its propellers straight up so it could land and take off like a helicopter. The onboard systems made it easy to fly and soon they were using it to do runs into neighbouring cities. From the air they could survey hazards and they didn't have to plow through cars. They could do in a day what normally took weeks. And it meant that they could access a much larger area for resources.

The days flew by and soon winter was creeping in. The Marine base had all manner of vehicles including the M1A1 Abrams, the main battle tank for the U.S. military. Rand started driving one around on a regular basis. He called it "Bruiser" and painted it cherry red with racing flames.

Rand had gained a lot of knowledge about alternative energy systems and Elsie had him set up the communications on the base with a full time power system. His began to fly out regularly to gather solar, wind and hydro power systems and set them up on the base. After a month he had the runway lights and field lights running on the base as well and was installing full-time power for the buildings they used regularly. He modified the field and runway lights so they could turn them on from the air. All of the generators were attached to a fuel tanker trailer, which in most cases meant they would run for over a year. Rand continued to hook up generators from all over the area and bring them to the base. Likewise, he parked caches of fuel tankers in the more remote areas outside the base. If 'thrive' was his motto, then 'redundancy' became his creed.

Elsie made good on her promise to teach Rand everything she knew including what she knew of Special Forces hand-to-hand fighting. Though Rand saw no practical application for it but it was fun and a good way to keep in shape. It was December 12th and they were sitting in the locker room cleaning up after sparring in the gym. Rand was telling her about the military base he had broke into in England and the fun of going through all the top secret documents to see what the government was up to.

"Hey, let's do that here." She said, excited for something new and fun to do. "There's all kinds of top secret stuff all over this base."

"Really?"

"Oh yeah, Camp Lejeune Marine Base is the headquarters for the MSOB. It's only a few miles away.

Those guys are black ops all the way. I'm sure there's classified stuff everywhere."

"Wow, I had no idea. Incidentally I only understood about half of what you just said."

"Just look around for safes, they're usually in the high ranking offices. They train people that handle confidential material to conceal stuff in places that look totally ordinary. They call it 'hiding in plain sight' What we really want to find is anything labeled S.C.I. or S.A.P."

Rand looked at her questioningly.

"That's *Secret Compartmented Information* and S.A.P. is *Special Access Programs*. That's the really secret stuff."

Excited for their new adventure they quickly got dressed.

"So, where to first?"

"Right to the top; the base commander's office."

Elsie lead drove them to the building and they soon found themselves rummaging through the desk and files of the base commander.

"So this is where they keep everything?" Rand whispered.

"Um, why are you whispering?"

"I just feel like I'm not supposed to be doing this."

"You're not. Under normal circumstances we'd be arrested as spies. Now, to answer your question this is not where they keep everything. This base commander might have information on where to look at MARSOC... that's M.A.R. for Marines then S.O.C. for Special Operations

Command. It's the Marines contribution to SOCOM which is where all of the armed services band together to form one kick-ass Special Forces solution. When I flew my Spectre missions, it was with SOCOM. Anyway, once we know what to look for we'll go there and search. If we turn up nothing here, then we find out where the MARSOC commander lived, go to his house and search it. Somewhere along the line we might get lucky and find information that might point us to some senate subcommittee chairman or congressman. We might also find connections to the FBI, NSA or some CIA representative that drafts black ops for approval. That's where we find the intel on the ops. It might mean a flight to DC."

Rand was staring at her. "You were a very dangerous person. I'm surprised they didn't have a watch on you day and night."

She kissed him. "I'm pretty sure they did."

The sleuthing was the most fun Rand had in a long time. In the base commander's office they found information on the location of MARSOC headquarters at Camp Lejeune. They flew an Osprey to the Marine base and located the MSOB command center. Inside was an array of intriguing technological combat equipment that Elsie had to pry Rand away from.

"We can check all that out later, it's not going anywhere."

Once in the MARSOC commander's office they found a safe that was empty except for a note that read 'nice try'.

"My guess is that he never used the safe so he knew for sure that anyone accessing it would be doing so for the wrong reasons."

Rand shook his head. "Tough as nails and sly as a fox."

"Yeah, and that's probably an understatement. Let's call it a day and pick up where we left off tomorrow."

That night they sat in the hot tub and mulled over what they had found out.

"It's gotta be at his house, where else could it be?"

"Well it's not possible that there weren't any ops going on, there are always ops going on. If the military isn't conducting ops for themselves, they are assisting the intelligence community. This is the guy that has the intel and it's definitely in digital or hard copy form. The only question is, where did he keep it? He seems like the kind of guy that would keep things close. His house is close and I'm willing to bet that if we looked up his active teams they all live in the same neighbourhood."

The next day they went to the MARSOC commander's home in the Guardian. After a search of the whole house they came up empty.

"So much for hiding in plain sight." Rand said, deflated.

"Okay then, we'll just have to get tough. Start looking behind all the furniture, under carpets, pictures, cabinets. Tear it all apart, turn it over and inside out. I don't like to disrespect the man's house, but he doesn't exist anymore so I guess it doesn't count."

Rand grimaced. He had no problem with driving over cars, but this was different. This guy was a hero. There was nothing for it but to dig in and get to it. The den was first. Rand uncovered a safe hidden beneath the carpet, this time it wasn't open.

"That's okay, just pry it out of the floor and we'll take it to the shop. Keep looking just in case it's another dead end." Elsie told him.

They continued to ransack the place. Underneath a cupboard in the kitchen Elsie found a combination written in pen; 12-44-56-79-01. They tried it on the small safe several times to no avail.

"That means that it's a combination to another safe." Rand said excitedly.

After every inch of the inside of the house had been turned upside down so Elsie went to the shed in the yard while Rand checked out the garage. It only took him a few minutes before he found a large safe behind a tool locker. He decided to try the combination first, and then radio Elsie. His heart leapt as the lock clicked and the handle turned. He stopped short of opening the door and keyed the radio.

"We have a winner!"

"Really?"

"Yep, the combo works!"

"You opened it?"

"I left it closed to wait for you…"

Elsie bounded into the garage. "Well open it, let's see!"

On the bottom shelf was a stack of files, thick with paper. The top shelf was narrow and close to the top of the safe so they had to reach in and look with their hands. Elsie pulled out a stack of yellow, orange and red opaque packets shaped like thin cell phones. They were made out of a hard plastic-gel like material that obviously had to be broken to get open.

"I know what these are Rand." She said excitedly. "These are high security access codes printed on cards. The cards are probably sensitive to the air and will crumble to dust within seconds of being opened. The way it works is you crack open the cases, then memorise the information." She sat back with a wide smile. "You did it, you found the intel. Way to go Agent Carter!" They high-fived as Rand giggled like a kid.

Elsie opened up lawn chairs and they sat down and sifted through the files. There were several personnel files on MSOB soldiers. Sure enough, many of the people lived close by in the same neighbourhood. They didn't dig too deeply in the personnel files out of respect. Other files contained information on new weapons systems, updates to military law and monthly security briefings for the base. When Elsie stumbled on a file containing pending congressional actions she let out a yell. "Here it is!"

Rand practically fell off his chair. "Easy there tiger, here what is?"

"This lists the names of the Senate subcommittee chairman and the CIA rep. Now we move to the next phase of the operation."

"Wait. It's an operation now? Well we gotta have a cool name for it. Operation… what? C'mon, come up with something good."

Elsie stood and looked at him with raised eyebrows.
"Operation um… nosey?"

"Ooh I like it! Commence Operation Nosey. So what do we do now?"

"It's time to go to D.C. and look up this CIA rep. We may need to pay a visit to the Senate Subcommittee Chairman as well."

"Cool, before we go I'd like check out some of that cool gear we found."

"Oh right, back at the MSOB. Okay then. We'll consider it mission prep."

They went back to Camp Lejeune and looked around the Special Operations offices and depot. They found the usual marine issue weapons and gear but behind the MSOB depot was another set of what appeared to be abandoned buildings, including a hangar.

"These are definitely conspicuously inconspicuous."

As Elsie checked out a staging barracks, Rand entered the other building and found the cache of weapons and equipment he had hoped to find.

"The armoury, now this is what I'm talking about."

He started by opening all the lockers, cases, drawers and closets to take stock of everything there. Immediately several pieces grabbed his attention. The first item was a black Kevlar helmet with an opaque full-face visor that looked like a prop from a science fiction movie. From the outside it didn't look as if the wearer would be able to see a thing in it. Various sized clear, red and gold lenses mounted into the top and sides gave it the appearance of a sleek headed insect. The visor was made from the same material as the helmet, a kind of thick, hard plastic. Soft rubbery cloth, like fleece covered wet suit material, completely sealed the chin and neck area. The reason for this became clear as Rand put the helmet on and lowered the visor. As it closed, a thin screen like a big pair of glasses slid down from a slit in the upper rim of the helmet. As soon as the faceplate clicked flush into the helmet, the glasses lit up, giving the wearer a modified night vision. Instead of the green wash of normal NV (Night Vision), a powerful computer approximated the colours of the surrounding environment. The display had none of the 'smear' affect; the blotchy and disorienting light trails from bright lights and abrupt movement that was so characteristic of traditional NV systems. Giggling, Rand put the helmet back into the black plastic box with it's twin and set it by the door.

While Rand was exploring the armoury, Elsie went through the barracks. The place served as a staging area for Special Forces units waiting to depart on missions. As they sometimes had to wait for long periods of time for last minute Presidential orders or Congressional approval, the facility was equipped with beds, lockers, showers, food and entertainment. As with everything in the place, the high, sturdy bunk beds were made of unpainted two-by-four and plywood construction. Opposite the beds, across the wide floor were a set of heavy shelves and hooks. The hooks held the SpecOps team's camo uniforms (called BDUs) and the shelves were packed neatly with each soldier's weapons and gear. The absence of larger small arms like assault rifles and grenade launchers told Elsie that the barracks wasn't in use at the time everyone vanished.

There were a few personal effects like photographs tacked to the shelves. Partly out of respect and partly to keep her head clear Elsie avoided these stations and stuck to the ones that were devoid of anything personal. As she looked over the shelves she noticed something odd about the BDUs. The pants and jackets were lined with thin, gel pads that had been inserted into interior pockets throughout the garment so that almost every inch of the wearer was covered. She searched the rest of the building and found a closet full of BDUs of different sizes that had the same internal pocket system. She picked out several sets of the black BDUs for herself and Rand and made sure they had enough of the gel inserts. She discovered that there were only two sizes of the gel inserts, small and large, and went about stuffing them into their appropriate places. Not fully understanding how the gel pads were meant to be utilised, she hunted for documentation. In the filing cabinet of the main office she found it.

It was a system called LBA (Liquid Body Armour). She failed to see how the squishy gel could stop a high caliber round but after reading through the documentation she began to get the whole picture. The booklet described the chemistry behind the special substance called Shear Thickening Fluid. The gel contained free floating particles that, when disturbed by enough force, bound together to create a material that was over five times stronger than steel. The jacket was meant to be worn over a soft but tough stretchy black shirt called a base layer. The "corners" of the body, like shoulders, knees and elbows, were protected by separate pieces. The knee and elbow pads overlapped with their counterparts and also included thin but tough rubber plates. The shoulder pads attached to the equipment harness and included a vertical collar that protected the neck from side shots. The high tech material boasted a 'full quartering' of traditional body armour meaning that it was one quarter the weight, four times the flexibility, four times the coverage and a quarter the thickness. The result was that ninety-five percent of their bodies were protected as opposed to just the chest and back of traditional body armour. Elsie made sure that they both had two complete suits including the combat harness.

In the armoury, Rand had set his sights on the next item; a small black box that contained a set of ear pieces and a rounded, black plastic control unit. The instruction booklet was in the lid and he giggled excitedly as he read about their amazing capabilities. After a quick inspection and a few battery changes he grabbed two and put the gear in a big black duffel and kept going. Behind a security cage was what he surmised to be a gunsmith workshop. Firearms of every description were stacked in racks, hung on pegboards and piled in cases. In the back room of the caged area was the ammunition. Rand reckoned it was enough for a small world war. He set aside some weapons that had caught his eye then grabbed the big box with the NV helmets and the duffel and headed out to the Guardian. He stashed the case with the helmets in the big armoured vehicle and closed the door just as Elsie came out with her own duffel bags.

"Oh good, you're here. You can take that one at the door, it's yours." Elsie dropped her duffel bag at his feet. "Load that for me could you?"

Rand threw both bags into the Guardian. "What's in there, clothes?"

"Yep, but not what you think. It's a new kind of body armour. Might come in handy."

"Nice, so what was your building?"

"A staging barracks. It's where the spec ops soldiers hung out before a mission. What did you get?"

Rand chuckled. "Armoury."

"Oh you! You get all the fun stuff."

"Yeah well, I thought you would like to pick your own weapons. Maybe you can tell me more about what some of this stuff does."

They went back into the armoury and had a field day playing with different weapons. To make sure they chose the right ones they stepped outside to test fire them into the air. They were both impressed by the Fabrique Nationale de Herstal (FNH) SCAR assault rifle. Each came with a powerful day/night scope and a very quiet suppressor. Besides the fact that it was lightweight, the SCAR was an extremely stable and accurate weapon with very little recoil and loads of options. It was one of the only assault rifles in the world where a soldier could swap out calibers and barrel lengths in the field. The main difference between his and Elsie's SCAR was that his was set up for the heavier 7.62 millimetre round. After the incident with the pack of dogs at the flight school Rand preferred to have something he could snipe with while Elsie opted for the lighter 5.56 millimetre round and an under-mounted forty millimetre grenade launcher.

Rand's favourite weapon was still Military Police System's AA-12 fully automatic shotgun he had brought from England. It was hard to beat a shotgun that fired like a machine gun. The beast of a weapon was so balanced it could unload a twenty-round clip one handed. It was light, waterproof and had a variety of ammunition types including Hatton rounds for door breaches, armour piercing and slugs that exploded on contact in addition to the range of normal shotgun rounds. But he decided that he liked the SCAR too. He could have both, so he figured, why not?

Elsie picked up a finely tuned M9 Berretta pistol then helped Rand pick out some other things that would be handy to have. Rand took thirty feet of climbing rope with a foldable grappling hook and a miniature come-along. Extra batteries were a necessity as well as a handful of compact, super bright combat flashlights that switched from normal to red, to infrared. They also took backpacks and Rand grabbed a video recorder and a small solar battery charger. While Elsie was looking around Rand loaded a box with door charges, a spool of detcord, M84 flash-bang grenades, M67 frag grenades, and 308-1 smoke grenades. He packed the boxes out to the Guardian and stacked them next to the NV helmet box. He came back inside just as Elsie emerged with a large black duffel bag for the weapons. They loaded it all into the Guardian then Rand said, "Okay, here's my first surprise." He took a small plastic case and handed it to Elsie "I was going to wait but I can't stand it anymore!"

She opened the case and looked over the set of wireless ear plugs and smooth beveled black control box.

"They're some kind of headset radios used by the Special Forces." Rand explained. "They fit snug into both ears and work like a normal radio, but the cool thing is that they also function as hearing protection. They totally cut off all sound from the outside but, the really amazing thing is that they also have little microphone so you hear normally. When a gun goes off, they dampen the sound to protect your hearing. You can actually have a conversation in the middle of a gunfight with these things on. AND, check this out."

He had her put the earpieces in and turn them on. He did the same with his then he reached over and turned a knob on the little box, suddenly she heard everything very loudly. He walked about a hundred feet away from her.

"Now you can hear me whispering all the way over here. But..." He drew his pistol and fired into the air.

She flinched, but the sound wasn't loud.

"Your ears are still protected." He walked back over to her. "Pretty killer huh? Their called Enhanced Acoustic Receptors."

"E.A.R.s, why am I not surprised?" She kissed him, "Great find baby! These are going to be much better than carrying a radio around on the harness. I wonder if they can connect through the Osprey's comms? So what did you find in the big building behind the armoury?"

"I haven't gone in there yet." Rand surveyed the large building behind the others. "I thought maybe it was an indoor shooting range."

"Let's check it out." They found the side door to the large building unlocked. Inside, under huge parachutes suspended from the roof they found two flat-black V-22SA Osprey folded for storage. The aircraft were very different from the standard Osprey. The fuselage was sharply angled and the skin had been treated with a rubbery material. Rand also noticed that the tail section was smaller and the nacelles and rotors were shaped differently. Missile mounts retracted into the cargo bay just under the wings and a twin minigun mount dropped down from under the nose; these were open, awaiting loading and inspection.

Elsie whistled. "Oh my, stealth Osprey." She ran her hand along the sleek fuselage. "Hello my sweet stallion."

"Easy Els, I'm starting to get jealous."

She flashed him a smile. "Oh baby their gorgeous!" Her eyes sparkled. "We have to get them running."

"Both of them? Why don't we just travel together?"

"It's the same reason Special Forces does it, redundancy is safety. If something happens to one, then the one left unhurt can save the other. Plus, we can approach an objective from different directions, increasing the enemy's confusion and our lethality."

Rand wasn't sure which enemy she was talking about, but the safety part made sense. It only took thirty minutes for them to locate and swap out the Concorde aviation batteries in each plane. They had already done it several times before on the other Osprey. Then they used a tug to roll them out on the tarmac. Working together on each aircraft, they got both of them unfolded and prepped for operation. Rand drove the fuel truck over and topped them both off. Then they picked one each, or rather, Rand let Elsie choose hers then he took the other.

"I'm naming him Blackie;' she beamed, 'after the book, Blackie -The Horse Who Stood Still. Megan loved that book."

"So it's a 'he' now is it?"

She laughed, "Yeah, it's the first plane I've had that's male. I don't know, he just looks manly. Check him out, he is bad ass!"

Rand had to agree. The aggressive lines and cut down silhouette made the regular Osprey look dumpy by comparison. The military kept a rigorous maintenance schedule and the engines started without a hitch. As the props whirred in idle, Elsie surveyed the cockpit and immediately noticed some changes.

"Rand, radio check, over." Elsie said using the new EARs.

"Loud and clear. Man, I don't even need a headset with these things in."

"You'll see a subset of switches just above your master alarm. There are two for each rotor, turn all four of them on."

Rand did as she said and immediately the sound of both the rotors and the engines was dampened.

"Nice, I could use that technology on the generators."

"I thought you'd like that. Unfortunately it limits our speed and power so turn the dampening back off and let's get back to New River."

"What about the Guardian?"

Elsie thought for a second. "After we drop off your bird, I'll bring you back to Thing, okay? It will just let me play with Blackie more." She giggled.

"Sounds like a plan."

They lifted off and flew the mission. The stealth Osprey handled differently than the standard V-22. Rand thought that there was considerably more power in the stealth version. The cargo bay also seemed to be wider and longer but not as tall. Elsie radioed the command to remotely light the runway and they touched down. Rand shut his Osprey down and then climbed aboard Elsie's. She flew him back to get the Guardian and then took off for New River, leaving him to drive the last leg back. Rand pulled in with the Guardian just as Elsie was rolling Rand's Osprey into it's hangar. They drove back to the house in the Guardian and Elsie made dinner as the sun began to set.

That night they went through the equipment they had found and loaded for the trip to Washington DC. Rand decided to dress the part of a secret agent.

"Where did you get a tuxedo?" Elsie asked, surprised.

"Oh, I was planning to surprise you with a fancy night out on our anniversary this May, so I stopped by the store on one of my equipment runs."

"Uh huh, and what other little tricks do you have up your sleeve mister?"

"Well, you'll just have to wait and see." He teased. "You never know what I'll come up with."

He wanted to put the Aston Martin Vanquish into his Osprey but he knew it wouldn't fit. With the report of no snow in DC, he opted for his Zero DSR electric motorcycle. It was a slightly larger version of the motorcycle he had said goodbye to in Omagh what seemed like years ago.

Between the both of them they had enough tools to break into just about anywhere. Elsie's Osprey carried a car that was specially built to fit in the plane's cargo bay called a Phantom Badger, a spec ops vehicle that was specifically designed to be carried in the Osprey. Speckled in digital night camo, it looked like a mix between and large Mule ATV and scaled down world war two Jeep.

"Where did you get that?" Rand was completely surprised as he walked around inspecting the odd vehicle.

"You're not the only one with a few surprises. I found it on a pallet in the secure area of the C-17 hangar. It was packed up to drop and ready to roll."

Rand was thoroughly impressed. She had clearly trumped him – for now, he thought, but his sly grin didn't escape notice.

"What are you up to?"

"Up to? Me? Now why would I be up to something?"

Elsie just smiled and let him think he was getting away with something. She was trying her best to embrace the role. She had been so conditioned by training to treat these things with an air of reverence for protocol. It felt completely reckless just to go bashing about into secrets that people had probably died to protect, but another part of her was starting to really enjoy the childlike playfulness of Rand. He was pulling her out of that hard shell and showing her how to live again. She decided to play along. Maybe if she acted the part, the part would rub off on her. After all, none of these secrets mattered now. Maybe, she thought, it was best to live in a world without secrets. She took the Badger to the base while Rand rode his motorcycle.

Once they had the vehicles secured in the cargo bays of the two stealth Osprey, Rand disappeared into the back of his plane. Elsie did quick walk around then returned to the rear of the planes.

'Okay, we're ready. She said. 'Now we just wait for… what are you doing?"

Rand was in the cargo bay of his plane pulling a pair of black leather motorcycle pants on over his tux. "This is part of the whole set up!" He put on his movie announcer voice, "We land in a pair black, stealth Osprey. You come out in your night camp buggy and I'm on my jet-black spy motorcycle. Then…"

"Seriously?" Her hand went to her forehead. "Okay, then what?"

"Well, you and I ride up to this Senator's house and park the rigs. I take off my leathers and I'm standing there looking bad-ass in my killer tux and you…" Rand held up his hand for her to wait. "'…just, just a sec. Close your eyes."

She obliged him with a smirk.

"You take off your flight suit and step out in this."

When she opened her eyes he was holding up a deep red, sequinned, floor length dress.

"Oh my." Her hands went up to her cheeks. She took the dress from him and looked at it. "Honey, Jessica Rabbit is going to be looking for her dress. You want me to fly wearing this?"

Rand nodded. "Under your flight suit."

She sighed. "Okay, but I have to do a field modification."

He looked at her in serious anticipation. She stripped down to nothing in the cold night and slipped the dress on. "You do realize that it's December."

Rand shrugged, "It's okay, we won't be outside for long."

She took out her knife and cut a slit down one leg then pulled the fabric back and stuffed it into one leg of the flight suit. Then she pulled her flight suit back on.

"With all this fabric stuffed into my right leg I feel like Quasimodo. And the sequins are poking me."

"Thanks for playing along hon, you're the best!" He kissed her then stood back. "Ready?"

"Not yet silly, it has to be dark to do a secret stealth mission."

"Oh, right. Not much point in going all black without the dark."

Rand sat for a few minutes inside the cargo area before he got bored and started packing extra things into all the extra room in his plane.

"Now what are you doing?" Elsie teased him.

"Your cargo space is taken up by the buggy, but mine is totally empty. I figured I had room for more stuff just in case."

'Just in case of what?'

"We never know what we could get into. From D.C. we could find ourselves flying to Cuba. I want to be fully prepared."

"But Rand we can always come back, take a break and head out a different day. I'm looking forward to sleeping in our bed tonight."

He looked her. "There's one thing I've learned living here for almost a year, that anything can and will happen. I know we're doing this for fun, like a kind of adventure vacation, but I won't take any chances."

"Yeah, you're probably right. Plus we've got a little time to kill before we go green so why not prepare."

"Go green?"

"Oh you have so much to learn. Green, as in green light go. The mission's a go."

"Ah." He felt stupid. "Makes sense."

They went back to the MSOC buildings and threw extra rations, ammo and batteries into cases, loaded the

The God String

Guardian and returned to the aircraft. Elsie hung up a mirror and set up a little boudoir in a corner of the cargo area and made more adjustments to her outfit. She was determined to knock Rand's socks off when she came out of that flight suit. Finally, the darkness settled in. Rand was struggling to take a leak in his tux and motorcycle pants.

"They never show this part in the movies." He grumped.

"Papa bear this is Minx. We're ten from green, repeat ten from green. Go to ready point by five, five minutes to ready point."

Rand fumbled with his zippers. "Darn it." His white shirt was poking out of the fly on the leather pants, but he hurried over to the aircraft anyway. She was in her flight suit, ready to go.

As he approached the plane her voice came over the comms, "Um… Papa bear your cub is out of the cave."

"I know. It's the problem of wearing two pairs of pants." He quickly fixed it and regained his composure. "I don't know how Bond does it."

"Costume department."

"So… Papa bear and Minx huh? Couldn't I be something like, Snake or Ice Man?"

"You could if you wanted a higher cheese rating. Papa bear is about a seven on the cheese scale and I find that I can't communicate above a seven because of involuntary laughter."

"Okay, cheese seven it is then."

She drew close and kissed him. "For luck on your first covert operation."

He grabbed her and kissed her hard. "For luck on your, um…"

"Twenty third."

"Twenty third covert op… twenty third?"

"Yeah. I was a Spectre pilot first. That's a covert ops plane from nose to tail."

"Holy cow. Well then I guess I'm in good hands."

"Oh you certainly are." Her eyes flashed lustily. "See you in the air. Gimme a radio check when you get situated. You got your nav notes?"

"Yep." Rand thought they sounded like a typical suburban couple going off to work in the morning except they were climbing into SpecOps Ospreys and loaded to the teeth with firepower. They both entered their respective aircraft. They had already done their checks so Rand just started the two big turbo-prop engines. The rotors wound up to idling speed and he did his radio check.

"This is Papa bear to Minx, radio check over."

"Papa bear, Minx. Copy loud and clear."

"Minx you know that the Osprey is a bird of prey right?"

"Affirmative."

"When you see a pair of Osprey in flight you're seeing a mated pair."

"Nice."

"And they mate for life."

"I like where you're going with this, but we'll have to save the mating for later. Okay, I'll take off first and wait for you at fifteen hundred feet."

"Roger."

With a huge smile on her face Elsie throttled up the Osprey until it lifted gently off the ground. Blackie handled differently than the other Osprey she had flown. It felt more sporty, almost like a smaller plane. She continued climbing vertically until she reached fifteen hundred feet. Rand duplicated the manoeuvre and came up next to her. They had spent many hours flying both together and solo, now it was like dancing.

Elsie tilted the props forward and Blackie took off, transitioning into level flight. Rand stayed to her left and slightly behind then pulled up level with her left wing.

"You are lookin' good Minx." Rand activated the missile battery and the doors quickly swung open to reveal the menacing weapons system under the wing.

"Papa bear, are you planning on having a disagreement with someone?"

"I just wanted to see how they effect the handling."

"Well?"

"There's just a slight bit of drag, but not too bad. Still, I can see why they went to the trouble of the doors and all."

"That's good to know, just keep in mind that we haven't trained on those so it's best not to use them."

"No, I don't feel like blowing myself out of the air today."

The two Osprey cut through the air at two hundred and seventy five miles per hour. They stayed low to hugged the landscape. Elsie took the time to work with the targeting systems and even sent two missiles into a building on a hillside. The explosion was spectacular and let them know the true strength of the missile system. In fifty minutes they were over Washington DC.

"Papa bear stay tight on my six while I make the LZ."

Elsie swung down low over the water of the Potomac and followed it up to the CIA headquarters. "We'll set down right there on the lawn." She tilted the rotors up and touched down lightly. Rand was right behind her. As soon as he shut down the engines, he climbed out of the chair and went back to the motorcycle. He took the NV helmets out of the black box and strapped Elsie's to the back of the bike with a netted bungee cord. Then he put on his NV helmet and walked back to open the back ramp, he did a radio check for the earpiece radios.

"Papa bear to Minx, rolling radio check over."

"Copy loud and clear Papa bear." Elsie said from the Badger. "Nice landing. Now find me a clear path to Tango one."

They had made a list of the places they were going to hit in what order. The Senator's house was first, designated Tango one. It was just around the corner off Dolley Madison Boulevard. Leaving his lights off, Rand rode his motorcycle down the ramp of the Osprey and over to Elsie waiting in the Badger.

"Woah, where did you get that?"

"Just a little something I found. This one's for you." He handed the other helmet to her.

She looked it over. "Even with that mask over my face I can hear you as plain as day. This is like a layer of Kevlar and that gel armour I found. How can you see through it?"

"Just put it on and lower the visor. I promise it won't bite."

She checked the interior for spiders then slipped it on and clicked the visor in place.

"Woah! What the hell? Rand where did you find these?"

Rand giggled to himself. "I wanted to surprise you."

Elsie laughed, "Wow, this is amazing. I've never seen anything like it. This is some serious experimental tech. God, I bet they cost a fortune."

"Yeah, they were in a heavy case, just the two of them. They looked expensive."

"I'm guessing millions." She looked around quickly. 'No smear either. What the boys in Spectre pool wouldn't give for these."

"Well, let's get to it. I'll scout ahead, you bring the… buggy thing with the gear."

"It's called a Badger and he's my fuzzy little toy."

"Another 'he', Blackie might get jealous."

He took off on the bike and began scouting a path for Elsie through the tangle of cars, but he quickly found that there was no way for even the small Badger to get through to the senator's house.

"Minx, Papa bear. No joy, it's way too congested in our nation's capitol. Stay put and I'll come and get you." Rand swung the bike around and raced back to her. Elsie parked the Badger back in the Osprey.

"Hey hon, I'll ride behind you, but it's gonna be frickin' cold."

"Yeah. You should stay in the flight suit."

"Actually I kind of planned for this possibility. Gimme a sec." She went into the cargo area behind the Badger, opened a duffel bag and rummaged around. "Just stay there."

"Okay." He tried to see what she was up to. After a few minutes she came down the ramp wearing a skin tight, shiny red, one-piece patent leather motorcycle suit with two slim white stripes down the left side. Matching stiletto heeled boots finished off the look as she stepped out and struck a pose.

"Sweet Lord Almighty." Rand's mouth hung open. Once again he was completely dumbstruck. She couldn't help but laugh. It made her even more beautiful.

"I have no words for what you do to me."

"Good. Phase one of the mission complete." She handed Rand his SCAR rifle as she slung hers onto her back and put the NV helmet back on.

"Now, let's get going." She climbed on behind him and pressed her body against him. "I like this better anyway."

He agreed whole-heartedly. The electric bike's incredible speed and virtually silent operation made them feel like

Ninjas as they snaked through the traffic that hung in suspended animation in the D.C. winter.

"There it is, 6121 Ramshorn Drive."

Rand pulled the bike up to a heavy, ornate iron gate. Elsie pointed to the pavement underneath the gate.

"Security spikes." She got off the bike, raised the visor on her helmet and inspected the gate.

Rand admired her. "You look like a superhero. Everything you do turns into a sexy pose."

"Maybe I am a superhero." She blew him a kiss. He just stood there with a goofy grin on his face.

"These spikes are just a sign of what's inside. All the equipment for burning through this gate is in the Badger."

Rand shook his head. "You know what. This is silly. It's too cold out here to be messing around. This lawn is big enough to land the birds on. Let's go."

They went back to the planes and flew to the address. They landed on the lawn, right at the front door of the house. Rand, fed up with all the dilly-dallying, walked to the front of the house with Elsie's SCAR assault rifle and launched a grenade at the front doors. "Honey I'm home!'" The hollow sound of forty millimetre grenade launcher belied it's power. The explosion forced Rand to step back as the doors were reduced to splinters.

Elsie was shocked at first but then laughed.

"That was good, but we're supposed to be more like spec ops and less like the Terminator."

"Right. I just wondered what one of these grenades would do."

"Well now you know. Just make sure you keep your distance, they can frag you pretty bad."

"Okay. So how would the Special Forces take on a place like this?"

"Well, I'm typically in the air while they're doing their thing, but I have had some training. It's called dynamic entry and the idea is to start stacked up at the doors at multiple entrances. If possible they try to enter from the opposite ends like the front and back or the ground and the roof at the same time. Then work through the building rapidly clearing room by room until they meet. They throw flash bang grenades in first, usually through a window away from the entrance so it distracts the occupants. At the same time, they blow the door with a special charge. Then they all pile through the door very quickly in single file, each one picking a separate part of the room to sight and fire on. They have a saying, 'watch your corners.' It means to pay attention to the corners of the room or hallway first because that's typically where people ambush you from."

She clipped his SCAR assault rifle to his harness and showed him how to hold it so that he was always looking through the sight. "Your scope is built for sniping so you'll have to…"

"Wait a sec." As Rand lifted the rifle to aim his thumb touched a pressure pad on the grip and a small window on his visor showed him what the scope was seeing. He could zoom in or out with another control at his thumb. He held the SCAR at waist level and he could still put the crosshairs on target. "Elsie, I've got to show you this."

They figured out that the NV helmets were linked to their scope and digital sights. This enabled them to hold their weapons in any position and shoot accurately.

"This is some serious tech. You see whatever your gun sight sees."

"Okay, let me give it a try." He stood next to the front doorway and quickly moved around the corner. Elsie heard a quick succession of clacks from his silenced SCAR. She peeked around. Rand had blown a bust of Beethoven in half. It sat smoking on its wooden stand.

Elsie nodded at him appreciatively. "That's how it's done. Congratulations, you just saved us from a statue of an old, deaf composer."

They went through the house, practicing clearing rooms as they went. In no time they found the Senator's office. The décor was cliché; dark wood everywhere, deep buttoned leather chairs, walls full of law books.

Rand was unimpressed. "These guys need a new interior decorator."

"It's tradition hon. Stupid tradition to be sure, but tradition all the same."

"So where would this guy traditionally put his Top Secret intel?"

She looked around then opened a cabinet behind the desk. Inside was a small safe, about two feet square.

"Time for the torch?" Rand asked.

"Yeah, but not the Acetylene. I was thinking more along the lines of the plasma cutter."

Rand went and got it from the Osprey while Elsie went through the files and desk. When he came back, she was sitting on the desk going through a thick report.

"This guy wasn't so bad. He supported the Large Hadron Collider and proposed to back NASA funding."

Rand got the plasma cutter powered up from the generator in the Osprey and began working on the door.

"Hang on Rand. Here's the documentation on the safe. It's a class 5-B security safe."

"And?"

"It's gonna take some work to get into."

"Tell me about it. All the plasma cutter is doing is making a trench in the thick steel."

Elsie crouched down to take a look.

"That's no good. When the torch eventually gets through, it's going to set fire to the papers inside."

Rand scratched his head. "I think I might have an idea. Be right back."

He went out to the Osprey and quickly returned with a spool of what looked like bright orange weed-whacker line

He went out to his Osprey and quickly returned with a spool of what looked like bright orange, nylon weed-whacker line. "How about detcord?"

She stood and took the spool from him. "Jesus Rand, where did you get this?"

"Well, it's a Marine base. The armoury has an explosives locker."

"This might work. It says here it rated 250 g/f, that's pretty powerful stuff. If we line it around the seam in the door it may cut through the bolts."

They lifted the safe from the cabinet and placed it on the desk. Then they pressed the cord into the space around the door making a full circuit around the seam. Then Elsie showed Rand how to remove the shunt on the blasting cap and slide it over the end of the detcord. They placed the remote initiator over the slim, cylindrical metal blasting cap then backed off to the other side of the Badger in the Osprey before they set it off.

"Ready?"

"Ready." Rand squeezed abruptly.

The shock blew the front windows out of the house, even peppering the aircraft with a few pieces of glass and wood.

"Holy moly! I wonder if there's a safe left."

They ran back to the house. The office was completely trashed and the biting smell of cordite filled the room.

"So much for stealthy." Most of the desk was gone. Rand started into fits of laughter and pointed a large hole in the wall opposite where the safe used to sit. Elsie bent over and looked through. The safe was embedded in the brick wall in the next room, smouldering with the bottom facing them. The door was lying on the floor by the opposite wall, cut precisely where the explosives had been.

"Well, it worked." Rand pulled the safe from the wall and it landed heavily with the hole facing up. The inside was full of loose cash in hundred dollar bills and documents.

They threw all the cash out of the way and rummaged through the papers.

"Here," said Elsie holding up a thick file. She started to look read through. "I think I've got something here hon."

Rand came over. "Switch off your night vision."

"Oh right." She said, "I forgot I had them on." She flipped the face shield up.

He shined his flashlight on the documents. "The Earthworm Project." They began reading.

"It's a CIA operation, look Rand." She pointed. "Looks like they used the military too, mostly SOCOM guys. That's not that unusual, SOCOM was sometimes used as the heavies for CIA ops."

"Wait, Elsie look at this! Secret underground facility… at an old base in Montauk Point, New York."

"This matches what we saw in New River. They were recruiting soldiers and pilots for this project, but it doesn't say what the Earthworm Project is. The CIA is supposed to brief the volunteers but someone else gives them access to the facility. I wonder if we'll find the rest of the story back at CIA headquarters Langley?"

"Only one way to find out."

Rand cleared away some debris from the explosion to make sure it didn't get sucked into the turbines while Elsie packed the equipment. The flight to CIA headquarters was essentially just a jump over a couple of city blocks. As they touched down, Rand decided it was time to play secret agent. He walked out the back, stripped off his leathers and struck a Bond pose in his tux. Elsie rounded the back of the plane.

"My my, what do we have here?" She walked towards him in long steps on her high heels, like a model on a catwalk.

He cocked one eyebrow and said: "Rand, Rand Carter. Gimme some sugar baby."

She doubled over laughing. He tried to remain straight faced but her reaction started to crack his façade.

"Gimme some sugar baby?" She roared laughing. "Where did you get that?" The tears were rolling down her face and she couldn't stand straight.

"What? It's classic Bruce Campbell."

"You are too much." She said wiping her eyes.

The Central Intelligence Agency building was massive with a long central glass atrium through the middle.

"This place is going to take forever to search." Rand said.

"Maybe not, the Senator's document named Daniel Warwick as the CIA representative in charge of facilitating security on the project. So let's find his office."

The task was straight forward, but there was nothing in Warwick's office that indicated where the access codes would be or who might have them. They kept searching for over an hour but came up empty.

"This is getting us nowhere. With no power we can't get to any of the computer based data."

Rand thought for a moment. "I'll bet this place has a serious power back up system. After a year it probably just ran out of diesel I'm guessing. All we have to do is locate the fuel storage for the generators and get them fired up again. Then we can start up the computers…"

"And what?" She cut him off. "Hack into the CIA's most secure network? I don't know about you but that's way outside of my skill set."

They both sat deflated.

"Well, it was fun." Elsie said with a forced smile. "I liked blowing up the safe. That was really cool."

"I liked watching you walk around in that outfit."

She gave him a smile. "Well, we know there's a secret base under the old Fort Hero base at Montauk."

"Wait a minute!" Rand sat up.

"What is it?"

"God how could I be so stupid, it's obvious. Elsie remember those cards we found? The ones encased in plastic?"

"Yeah, those are like launch codes or something."

"Or they may be the codes we're looking for. Check it out, Warwick is in charge of security for the Earthworm Project. Where is the best place to hide something?"

"In plain sight like I said." Elsie was still doubtful.

"Exactly, I'll bet the Force Recon Commander was in charge of finding the volunteers. Then Warwick and the Senator screened their files."

Now Elsie sat up, picking up on Rand's train of thought. "With the CIA's information gathering capabilities, they could do extensive background checks on the candidates."

"Yep, the candidates just go about their business on the base. Then the Force Recon Commander, what's his name?" Rand never was good at names.

"Donaldson."

"Right, Donaldson calls them in and tells them they've been selected for a special assignment. It's voluntary of course. He can't give them any information, but if they choose to do it he gives them directions to the secret base in Montauk. At the last minute, he gives them the access card."

A smile grew across Elsie's face. "That makes sense. High security military protocol always uses time sensitive data as part of the code. So, where are the cards?"

"Back at home."

"Good. It's getting late. We can go back home and strategise a visit to the base at a later date, whaddaya say?"

"Definitely. I'm bushed and this tux is a bit too stiff."

They jumped up and went back to the planes. When they were all strapped in and set for take-off Rand keyed his mic for a radio check. Elsie just said, "I told you we were gonna sleep in our bed tonight."

Rand shook his head, "Cheeky."

The two black Ospreys peeled off into the night for the flight back to New River. They touched down fifty-two minutes later and went inside to clean up. After a romp in the hot tub, they climbed into the Aston Martin and drove home. That night the winter wind blew in a dusting of snow and they decided to hold off on any more adventuring until the weather warmed up.

They had managed to store ten Ospreys as well as the C-17 into hangars. They took another day to fetch the other C-17 from Cape Canaveral to make sure they at least had a whole plane for parts in the future. Rand began to service the two black Ospreys, but also took pains to preserve the remaining aircraft. He drained the crankcase of oil and then topped them off with an anti-rust oil for long term protection. After he changed out the oil he had to run the engines for an hour. Then he sealed off any place that bugs, birds or mice could get into with tape and plastic sheeting and any exposed metal got a good coat of lubrication. He couldn't complete more than one aircraft a week. It was an ongoing project to make sure that they would always have operational aircraft. Between that and taking care of the garden, the herd and the house, he had a full time job.

Elsie settled into a happy home life. The big movie themed house grew cosier and more homely day by day. After a life of ambition and career challenges she realised that, though she had seen and done amazing things, it was the simple things that brought her deep contentedness. She thought of her children often and would talk to them when she thought Rand wasn't around. Then she started to do something she never thought she'd do, pray. Rand noticed the change in her. He hadn't seen the Air Force Major side of her in several months.

"We'll be ready to fly soon." He said one day in March.

"Yeah." She responded. "I'll do a few practice flights, but I don't know. I just don't have the burn like I used to. Now it's like driving a car. It's good to have the Osprey to go shopping with but other than that I think I'm going to spend most of my time here."

He came and sat down next to her. "It's Megan and Marty isn't it?"

She couldn't hide it from him any longer. "Oh Rand I miss them so much! I don't know if they're safe or anything. They've got to be worried sick with me gone. They relied on me for everything!"

Rand pulled her close to him, "Shh, it's okay. If they are their mother's children they are capable of much more than you think. They will find their way, and yes, of course they miss you, but in the end God always reunites us with him. You'll find them there."

She looked at him. "I know you have a private, spiritual life Rand. I know you hide it from me as well. It's because I've been so cerebral and scientific, but lately I've been feeling like I need that connection. You don't have to hide it from me anymore."

He held her for a long time. "I wasn't hiding anything, I'm just very private about my faith and I don't like to shove it people's faces. It doesn't mean I don't feel it because I'm not jumping around and yelling, 'Jesus saves!' That's just not me. I guess the deeper I feel something the more quiet I am."

"Is that why you always talk so soft, and quiet to me?"

"Yes my love, that's exactly why."

The next week the sun shone through the clouds and within two days everything had thawed out. Flowers were popping up and the trees were showing bright green buds. The spring brought a new life to everything. Rand coaxed Elsie into showing him more about the ordinance and they worked together to learn how to load and fire the Osprey's weapons on the target range. The targets were the vehicles they would trash. It was one of the ways Rand tried to make things fun for her to keep her mind off the children.

"Y'know there were very few people in the world who got to play with these kind of toys!" Rand said over the radio.

"And none of them EVER got to do this without being answerable to someone!" she laughed as she loosed a missile into a disabled Bentley.

On his birthday, Rand woke to a full breakfast in bed, which Elsie served to him in lingerie. She gave him an hour-long massage and spent extra time on anything that really made him smile, then she sent him to the shower. When he came out, she was standing in her red leather body suit holding his tux.

"Ready for some adventure Papa bear?"

He did a quick fist pump and hissed, "Yesss!" He was so glad that to see her out of her sadness.

She had secretly packed their two black Ospreys the day before. Rand emerged outside the house in his tux. She had the Aston Martin Vanquish purring in the driveway. As they drove onto the base she said, "I already took care of the flock."

"You are so amazing Elsie, you thought of everything."

She just blushed and went straight to the waiting planes. They both climbed in without a word and prepared to lift off. She had the coordinates set so he knew to just follow her.

"Papa bear be advised that I am weapons hot."

"Roger that Minx, you're hot."

In the specially fitted stealth Ospreys, the helmet controlled the targeting systems. Rand and Elsie learned that it was an upgrade that was installed only months before the disappearance because pilots complained that the Osprey had insufficient armament. The missiles were small, multi-role and experimental, able to function as air-to-ground, anti-armour or air-to-air depending on what the pilot selected.

Rand now changed out the standard headset for a special helmet that held the visual targeting system visor. When the visor was down, the weapons came out.

"Minx, Papa bear is green for take-off, weapons hot."

They lifted off and laid on full throttle toward the New Jersey coast. The flight was easy with clear, warm weather and a gentle sea breeze. As they approached Montauk, Rand was distracted working on plans in his head for Elsie's birthday when an alarm went off on the Osprey's dash.

"What the…?"

"We're being targeted! Countermeasures! Hit the deck NOW!"

He slammed the controls forward and pitched the rotors back for a fast landing. The beeping continued as he dropped out of the sky.

"Shit!" He set off a stream of flares and chaff to throw off the lock. Then all he could do was wait as the aircraft lost altitude. He wanted to be on the ground. The lighthouse loomed in his view. He was setting down on the lawn at its base.

Elsie came on again, "Engage IFF! Turn it on!"

"Roger." Suddenly the plane made another noise. He recognised it this time, a proximity alert; he was really close to the ground. He put the rotors straight up, pitched the rotors for maximum torque and poured on the power to slow down. The big plane came down hard but still within tolerable limits. Rand gritted his teeth, but the specially designed seat absorbed the shock. The beeping stopped.

"Minx come in! Elsie?" No reply.

He ran out of the plane and stood on the lawn, anxiously searching the sky. Suddenly the unmistakable roar of the Osprey's twin miniguns cut through the distance. A screaming ball of flame flashed over him. It cleared the trees, barely missing the lighthouse, and crashed with a splutter into the sea.

Rand knew it wasn't Elsie's Osprey, it was a much smaller craft, too small for a person to fit into.

"Lord let her be okay, please, please." He was frantic.

Elsie's Osprey burst over the trees only a few hundred feet over head, blowing a hard wind down on everything beneath.

Rand put the visor on his flight helmet down to shield his eyes and scanned the craft for damage. There was a line of small holes in the main fuselage. She landed on the sun lit lawn and gave him a thumbs up from the cockpit. He breathed a sigh of relief and ran around to meet her at the back as the twin rotors wound down.

"What the hell was that?"

"I don't know, it was some kind of UAV. I couldn't get my IFF on in time. Once it had a lock, it stuck to me so I did a vertical touch and go. It flew past me and I popped up at the tree line and hit it with the minigun." She was shaking.

"Nice flying baby! You okay?"

"Yeah, I'm fine, just scared shitless! Jesus!" She said, pacing. "THAT's why we fly two different planes!"

"We should arm up, we don't know who else may be shooting at us."

"Now I'm wishing I would have used a missile. I just didn't have time to configure it. That thing came out of nowhere!"

"Lets hope you got the only one. I don't see any more." Rand had his SCAR assault rifle raised and was scanning the skies.

She drove the Badger out of the back of the Osprey and skidded to a halt. "The BDUs and web gear are in the back."

He noticed that her adrenaline was starting to kick in and her voice went up. She paced back and forth then stopped and yelled at the trees,

"FUCK! I DO NOT LIKE GETTING SHOT AT! That little bastard put holes in my beautiful black bird! Don your battle rattle darlin' I wanna fuck something up!" Elsie was steaming mad.

Rand let her have some space and went around to the back of the little armoured car. Inside he found the black ops uniforms and the web gear. He tried to put it all on correctly, but got only so far before he needed help from Elsie who was starting to calm down.

"Sorry hon. I'm not used to being shot at. Usually I'm the one pouring bullets on everyone else. The adrenaline rush is really intense." She suddenly sat down, shaking.

Rand sympathised. "I got like that once when I was kayaking in whitewater. I got washed into a huge rapid and nearly drowned. I was so pissed-off when I came out that I tried to swing at the guy who saved me. Lucky I was still half-way in the water and all I managed to do was splash him."

She chuckled at that and stood up.

Rand gave her a hug and said, "Elsie? What's 'battle rattle'?"

She laughed, releasing the last of the tension, "That just means all your combat gear. It rattles around. Now let's see where you're at with this stuff."

She showed him how to get everything on, including the Camelback, a large water pouch that mounts on the back. The water is sucked from a tube that comes over the shoulder. With all the gear on Rand felt much safer, it was like a suit of armour.

She changed out of her red leather suit. "I'm not doing this in heels."

When she was finished they stood and looked at each other.

"Hey, didn't I see you on CNN?" She giggled at him.

"We look like we're under serious threat here, and we're standing in a state park in New Jersey, possibly the only two people left on the planet."

"Someone just shot at us Elsie."

"No Rand, the more I think about it, I believe it was an automated defense system. There's been no human input in the place for almost a year. At a certain point the base defences have to go on alert don't you think? Anything that's not radiating IFF gets targeted."

"That's pretty extreme."

"They do it in case of nuclear war. They don't want the enemy to take the base."

"Ah, good ol' cold war paranoia. Now that I can believe." Rand tutted.

"We need to be careful in there. There may still be automated defense systems in the facility."

"Yes definitely. It's good to have all this stuff on, but I still feel like a ninja SWAT goat farmer."

She dug around in the back of the Badger while Rand checked over his web gear getting everything situated. Suddenly she turned carrying a cake with candles and singing happy birthday.

"Oh my God where did you? Did you make that? You're awesome thank you Elsie!"

They sat eating cake on the hood of the Badger when Elsie said, "Okay, now for your presents."

"Really? You mean the breakfast and massage and adventure wasn't all of it?"

She handed him a rectangular, black leather patch. It had Velcro on one side and was printed in gold block letters on the other; CAPTAIN RAND CARTER, 'PAPA BEAR', NW-1, USAF. Then she handed him a pin, it was a pair of wings made of silver.

"Now you're CAPTAIN ninja SWAT goat farmer."

The God String

Rand was deeply honoured. "What's the NW-1 stand for?"

"New World One. The first Air Force of the new world."

"But, how did you…"

"I found the machine that makes them on the base."

"It's perfect. Thank you." Rand beamed with pride. He had never accomplished anything, but here he was a Captain in the Air Force being decorated by one of the world's best astronauts.

"I didn't even go to college!"

She hugged him. "The things you can do with an airplane…" She drew back and looked at him. "…baby, they don't teach that in school."

"Okay let's open one of these secret cards, whaddaya say?"

Elsie nodded and took out the briefcase. Inside were the six security cards sealed in their brittle, plastic cases.

"We only got about ten seconds remember?"

"Hang on, I have an idea." Rand took out his iPad and shot it all on video. "Okay, ready."

Elsie cracked open the first plastic case. A yellow card shaped wafer came out. It was like a thick paper cookie that had been engraved. She held it where they both could see it. It read:

MATADOR
I 4 9 0 B T 7 0
Access MLH / key under first stair

03:20410 / terminates 0328 of issue year.

Rand looked at Elsie after he finished reading it all out loud.

"Okay. I think I got it. The…"

The yellow card suddenly got very brittle and started crumbling to dust. In a matter of seconds, it was powder.

"Woah, trippy."

"You were saying?" Elsie had already figured it out, but Rand was so excited she wanted to let him explain.

"Right. The first two lines, *matador* and *I49* blah blah are the actual key code for the door. The 'MLH' is the Montauk Lighthouse. There's some kind of computer stuck underneath the first stair in the lighthouse. 3:20 is when you have to put in the code. '4' is the word 'for', and the 10 is ten minutes or seconds not sure which. That's how long from 3:20 A.M. you have to enter the code. The code doesn't work on any other day than March twenty eighth of any given year."

She clapped, "Bravo! You should have worked in cryptography. I bet that once the code is used it will never work again."

"I'm sure your right. It wouldn't be very good if you fired somebody and they could continue to stroll right into your secret base now would it?"

She handed him three of the cards. "You take three of these and I'll keep the remaining two."

"Why?"

The God String

"I think maybe they are for accessing the place on different days. If anything happens we can use these to get back in. But put each one in a different place. If you fall on your butt and they all are together in the same pocket we lose all of them. If we get separated then that's it, your chance at getting back in here is gone."

"So you think they are copies of the same key?"

"Yes, just a guess."

"Makes sense, good thinking."

"So we have to wait until 3:20 this coming morning to try this out?"

The rest of the day, they situated their gear and practiced with their weapons. Rand had the AA-12 shotgun clipped on to his web harness in front with an extra drum magazine. He also carried two extra drum mags in his backpack. He had four magazines for his .45 and he slung the SCAR on his back with the same. In addition to the body armour, NV helmets and EARs they each carried grenades, detcord, plastic explosives, primers and a remote detonator. The backpacks held rations and the explosives along with spare batteries, spare EARs, rope and assorted other necessities. Rand carried his iPhone facing forward in a chest mount on his web gear and had an iPad in a padded leg pouch. Once Elsie had helped Rand into the gear and he put everything where he wanted it, he tested it out by running back and forth on the lawn.

"We are ready for anything, and we can film it all." Rand said bouncing on his toes. "This stuff doesn't weigh as much as I thought it would that's for sure."

They ate more cake and drank water while they waited for night to fall. Elsie got up and stretched.

"We better set watch while the other tries to get some sleep."

Rand could tell she was a bit tired. "You go ahead and sleep, I can't, I'm too wired. I keep thinking there's something in the trees watching us."

"There probably is. This is a top secret base. Even the trees have eyes and ears."

She lay down in the back of the Osprey while Rand took up watch. As he waited for the last of the day's rays to fade, he inspected his NV helmet. He discovered it had a thermal imaging function as well. When it was in thermal mode, everything showed as black and white. Heat sources were displayed in varying shades of yellow and red. By adjusting a control on the edge of the visor by the jaw, he could control how hot something had to be for it to show up in colour. He double checked his harness and made sure he had enough batteries for hours of operation. Finally the sun went down and he was able to switch on the helmet and fine tune the settings of the thermal imager. Then he just watched and waited. He spent most of his time trying to locate secret cameras. He switched to the powerful night scope on the SCAR and learned that the NV helmet could see through the scope's night vision perfectly though, unlike the helmet the image on the scope still appeared green like traditional night vision. He scanned the woods but all he saw was occasional animal life. At two in the morning. he woke Elsie with a fresh cup of coffee from the cooking station in his Osprey.

"You put a camp stove in your plane? This is a multi-million dollar military aircraft Rand, not a Volkswagen Westfalia." She teased him, but changed her mind when he handed her a hot cup of joe.

"I've been thinking Rand. It's March twenty seventh, your birthday. What are the chances that we would be here just over twelve hours before this key worked?"

"Yeah, I've been thinking about that. I'd put the chances at slim to none, but then it happened to Frodo."

"What?"

"The Lord of the Rings. Remember when they were trying to get into Moria? It had to be a full moon that showed the dwarf runes on the door so they could read them, but they happened to be there on the one night that it would work. After discovering you on the space station I have practically come to expect serendipity."

"Lord of the Rings huh? Elsie just looked at him. 'I didn't know you were such a geek."

"Oh yeah," he gave her a cheesy grin, "I'm a major geek. How else could I be so hip?"

Montgomery Thompson

Chapter 10

Down the hatch

*'If you don't know where you're going,
any road will get you there.'*
~Lewis Carroll

They approached the Montauk Point Light with night vision on, scanning carefully. The giant tower pointed at the sky like a white finger with a large red stripe through the center. The old house was a two-story colonial, sided in weathered grey cedar shingles with white trim. The night was cool but clear and, tinged with the smell of the sea. Rand took point while Elsie constantly swept behind them.

"There could be survivors holed up in here, so don't shoot unless you are sure we're in danger."

"You really think so?"

"No, but it's best to be safe."

They passed the main house and went through the closest entrance to the tower, an old oil room was attached to the side. Rand used the shotgun on each of the hinges and the door fell inwards. "It's a museum." Several displays including one of the original lighthouse lenses decorated the room. "Now I feel bad for shooting in the door."

"This lighthouse has been here since seventeen ninety-six. I had no idea."

"Thanks, that makes me feel even worse."

"It might be an historical site, but it's also a front for a heavily guarded secret base. Stay frosty."

They went in cautiously. Elsie first this time, staying low so Rand could fire over her head with the shotgun.

"I know it sounds paranoid, but let's put on gas masks. One of the automatic defences could be to fill the place with nerve gas or something."

"And we would have no way of knowing until it was too late. Good idea."

"The NV helmets seem to be able to filter particulates like smoke and ash but I doubt they function as full gas masks."

They slung their NV helmets over their backs then strapped on gas masks. Turning right, they went through a doorway into the base of the tower. A metal stairway rose from the floor, spiralling up over eighty-six feet to the light at the top.

Rand bent down and looked underneath the first stair.

"Nothing."

"How about stuck to the bottom of it?"

"Nope."

"Hmm."

"Let's keep looking."

The God String

Going right out of the tower doorway took them back through the oil room and into the central hallway of the keepers house, which was now a gift shop. In the middle of the hallway a set of stairs went up to the send floor. A heavy rope was hung across with a sign that read *AUTHORISED PERSONNEL ONLY.*

"That's more like it." Elsie surveyed the staircase.

Rand pulled up on the first step of the carpeted stairs. "Bingo." It opened like a hatch.

Rand turned and looked up at Elsie who suddenly got excited. "I think this is it."

At first, it just looked like an empty box, but in the bottom Rand found a false floor. He searched with his fingers until he found a hole in the corner. The piece came up easily.

"Careful Rand, there's wiring attached to it."

Rand froze. "It looks like computer ribbon cable."

"Try to see what's underneath without turning it over."

Rand bent down, holding the board above him and peeked underneath.

"It's an iPad mini."

"Anything that looks like a level or some mercury in a glass tube or anything like that?"

"Nope, just the little iPad."

She thought for a second then said, "Okay, I think it's safe."

Rand turned it over carefully and switched it on. The screen showed only the keyboard and an old school flashing cursor. "I can't access any of the apps."

"No, it would be completely reprogrammed to do only the one function."

"Dang, I wanted to play Angry Birds." Rand said feigning disappointment. "Hey how is this thing still running?"

"It must be getting power from the ribbon cable. There's undoubtedly a generator somewhere around here."

They waited until 3:22 a.m. just in case their watches were out of sync. Then Rand typed in the first code: MATADOR, the screen prompt came back with, ENTER CODE 2:, Rand typed in I490BT70 and hit Enter. A dull click sounded from underneath the staircase and the screen read *ACCESS GRANTED*.

"Where did that click come from?"

Elsie walked around to the storage door under the staircase.

"From here I think."

She waited for Rand to get into position and opened the little door. Sure enough, there was a set of metal stairs leading down.

Rand couldn't believe his eyes, "I am totally freaking out. This is so exciting!"

The rickety, folding metal stairs took them down to a small landing where an old steel door stood. It was painted army green with patches of rust and had no markings. Rand had to stoop because of the low ceiling. The space at the bottom was cramped for the two of them with all of their gear on. When they opened the old steel door into an elevator the contrast of décor couldn't have been more pronounced. Modern and clean, the small elevator was walled with brushed, stainless steel panels, bright fluorescent lighting and a carpeted floor. Inside there were only two buttons; unmarked, one above the other.

"Going down?" Elsie reached to push the lower button.

"WAIT!"

She froze, her finger hovering over the button. "What?"

"They could have this thing booby trapped. I want to test it first."

"Hon I don't think -"

"Just humour me. Maybe it's just all those years of D&D but I have a funny feeling."

"All right."

They stepped back out of the elevator and Rand reached around with the large front sight of the AA-12 shotgun and tapped the lower button. Two gates closed from the top and bottom of the opening and met in the middle while the steel door swung closed automatically.

Elsie looked at Rand, "See. I told you it was alright."

A clunk sound came from inside the box and a loud, metal rolling sound sped down and away from them with a whine. There was a loud bang when the elevator struck the bottom then a gentle whirr as the motor pulled the car back up. Elsie was wide eyed.

"You were saying?'"

"Jesus Rand. That would have killed us! That's got to be a forty-foot fall and I think it wasn't just falling it was actually pulled down, I could hear the motor! How did you know?"

"I didn't. I just thought about what I would do if I were building a top-secret base."

"Well you just keep thinking about that. And let me know the minute you have any more funny feelings!"

The inside of the elevator showed no signs of damage. They tested the top button as well but it seemed to make the elevator go down nicely. After it returned to the top they got in nervously.

"I love climbing into deathtraps. Yeah. Makes me feel all cozy." Rand muttered to himself.

He winced when Elsie pushed the top button but the elevator descended at a normal rate. At the bottom, they touched down softly and the gate lifted into a small white, solid cement room with two miniguns mounted to the ceiling. On the far wall there was a white, solid steel door with a keypad next to it. To either side of the door were two gun ports, similar to those on an armoured car. They stayed in the elevator looking at the macabre set-up.

"I take it those aren't for making Swiss cheese."

"No. For Swiss I think they use a fifty cal. These are for cheddar."

Elsie turned Rand around and dug into his pack. She came up with an MRE. "Meal, Ready to Eat. An essential part of a Marine's diet." She held it up with a wave then tossed the package into the room and winced back into the elevator. It landed with a smack on the floor.

"Nothing. I think it's safe."

Rand waved his hand into the room but the guns didn't move. "I don't trust em, so I'm gonna have to dust em."

"I agree, no explosives though, we'll get fragged."

"Okay." He brought up the shotgun and emptied twenty rounds into both miniguns. The solid slugs ricocheted around the room but none came back to bite them. After getting pounded by so many twelve-gauge rounds, the miniguns were bent and useless.

"Okay, that should do it." Rand stepped into the room. "All clear."

"Rand, ALWAYS reload before you move from cover."

He became aware that he was standing in the open with an empty clip. "Oops." He reloaded, stashed the empty in his backpack and placed a fresh drum clip in the pouch of his web harness. He joined Elsie at the heavy door and studied the keypad.

"Hon, I think we're gonna need to open another card." She had him shoot video while she pulled out a card from his side pocket.

"Okay we're rolling."

She cracked open the casing. It was formatted just like the first card:

PRESTON
NICHOLS

Access primary TSS control module / unrestricted single use.

Rand stopped filming as the card crumbled away.

"Got it. Where and what is a TSS control module and who the heck is Preston Nichols?"

Elsie was thinking. "I don't think it matters. That's just the code. It could have been someone's kid, or dog, who knows? What's confusing me is the 'unrestricted single use' part."

Rand thought out loud. "Okay, unrestricted. Go anywhere or use it at any time. There's no time stamp on it. That must be it. It's a one-time key to get into the TSS place, whatever that is. Once you use it it's no good after that, but it doesn't matter when you use it."

"Okay, but does that mean this door?"

"No I don't think so. We haven't seen anything of the facility yet, so I don't think we're at any kind of control module."

"That makes sense."

"I guess we pull another card. But give me a second while I write down the information from the last card while it's still fresh. That way we don't have to go through all the video again."

When he was done he got ready to shoot video again and said, "Okay, go for it."

They repeated the procedure. The card read:
P T R M O O N
4 1 0 4 2 0 S A G E

The God String

Disrupter Station 1 / unrestricted single use

"Disrupter? Sounds very sci-fi."

"I dunno, a weapon maybe? There's still no clue as to how to open this door. Maybe this is Disruptor Station 1."

"I don't think so hon." Elsie pointed to a small sign above the door that read *RECEPTION*.

Rand made a stupid face, "I think this is the reception area. Der." He copied the information down in writing then got ready to video again. "Let's go one more time."

"Hang on." Elsie held out her hand. "Let me see all the cards."

She took Rand's cards from him and combined them in a stack with hers. "See how the colours gradually go from yellow to red?"

"Yeah. We just opened two of the dark red ones."

"Right, so maybe those are for the heart of facility. The first card we opened was bright yellow. Let's go with the next colour down from there."

She picked out the most yellow one from the stack.

"Ready?"

Rand nodded and raised the video camera "Go."

The casing cracked open to reveal the fragile card. It read:

F N G S O A P

T H E R E I S A C O W 1 3 3 7

Reception / unrestricted single use

Elsie started laughing, "Oh that's good!"

"What is it?"

"Well I know it's military for sure. FNG stands for 'fucking new guy.'"

"Okay. Well that makes sense. I'm not sure about the soap and the cows but at least we got something to do with the reception area. Maybe we'll find out about the soap and the cows later though I'm not sure I want to."

"Probably not. These things can be as obscure as some geek reference to a video game. But it says 'reception' and that's what we needed to know."

"Well let's give it a try."

Elsie went over to the keypad and typed in the first code: FNGSOAP. She got the prompt to enter the second code, THEREISACOW1337. She hit enter and heard a click from the door. ACCESS GRANTED.

"Ta da, we're in."

"We'd better hurry. That door probably doesn't tolerate being open for long."

"No, probably not. Let's go."

They found themselves at the end of a long, well-lit, hexagonal hallway made of solid cement. It was painted off-white and had a large grey letter 'A' on the right hand wall.

"Remember that, the letter is to identify this hallway. There will be more I'm sure."

"Every D&D geek knows, map as you go." He waggled a pen in the air.

The first room was on the left. It had a reception desk that looked a lot like a doctors office. Elsie smiled. Things were starting to look familiar.

"Standard protocol. Here's where they check-in; get a badge, wait for their POC... I mean point of contact, sorry. Acronyms for everything."

They looked around the office and found no records or paperwork, just an ID card machine and a couple of blank cards.

Rand looked at Elsie. "They really covered their tracks didn't they?"

She nodded slowly, in a way that said she suspected something sinister. Rand was starting to feel like he might be in a little over his head. Then Elsie said,

"C'mon, there's more to see. We have to crack the secret of the Earthworm Project."

"You make it sound like we're in an episode of Scooby-Doo."

"Maybe we are!" She laughed.

Rand chuckled, "You are one crazy cool chick, but can we please take off these gas masks?"

"Oh yeah, if they haven't gassed us by now they probably won't."

They peeled of the masks and rubbed their faces.

"So what's the first weird thing you notice about this place?"

Rand thought a minute, then his eyes went wide. "Power."

'Yeah, lights, ventilation, elevators and everything. I wonder where they get it from?"

They went down the hallway, past a waiting area with chairs and a coffee table. There were unlocked double doors that spanned the hallway. Another hallway stretched to the left and right as far as Rand could see.

"How bout left?" Rand said as he scribbled on his map.

"Sure, one's as good as the other."

After about ten feet, they stopped at a door on their left. Inside was a large area that held a caged armoury. Further down there was an indoor firing range with a raised viewing area behind the firing stations.

"Recognise those?" She pointed to the SCAR rifles hanging on the wall next to M1A1's, M4's, SAW's, P-90's and MP5's. "There were definitely Special Forces stationed here. Most of these are SpecOps weapons."

Rand looked around, but again there wasn't a scrap of paperwork anywhere. "Everything must be on computer."

Out of the armoury they turned left again, continuing down the long passageway. In the right wall a short, wide hallway opened up that lead to double doors. They passed through these and continued to check the length of the hallway they were in. They located the barracks and leisure area for what looked like around forty people. There was a pool table, three TVs and a snack bar, but no papers, pictures or information about the residents. Going back the way they came, they followed the hall labeled '1' back past the double doors they came through and to the far end. They felt like they had been walking forever. When they approached the end of the hall there was another door with

The God String

a keypad station. This one had a blue hued, square blank screen that stuck out from the wall like a small table.

"Here we go again. Next card?"

"Yep. Ready?" Rand started shooting video.

"Go." She cracked the card case and read:

S C H L A G E R

Q f m 6 a X I D Q

Access primary plant/ Imprint for multiple

"Well that's rather arbitrary. I was just starting to think these guys had a sense of humour. Obviously the pass codes were created by separate departments."

"Imprint for multiple?"

"|Look at that pad for me and tell me if it looks like some one has held their finger, thumb, hand or eye up to it."

"How bout' their butt?"

"Funny. I saw that movie, that part was hilarious."

"Looks like a full hand type of scanner."

"Okay, since I'm guessing you haven't done this before, step on up."

Rand went to the keyboard.

"Now type in the code and when it prompts you, put your right hand firmly against the pad and stay as still as you can."

Rand did exactly as she said. The blue screen felt like it had gel underneath a plastic sheet. It whirred but there was no fantastic light show like in the movies.

"Uh oh. It's asking for your name."

"What do I put in?"

"Not your name that's for sure. You aren't anywhere on their system. Crap."

"Wait, what was the name of that kid on the first card? Preston something."

"Yes, put in Preston!"

"But what if he's already in there?"

"I doubt that the names of registered personnel would be used as a password. It's probably the name of some guy's dad or favourite baseball player or something. We don't have an option."

Rand entered PRESTON. The screen went blank for a split second then said: LAST NAME.

"It took it. Now it wants a last name."

"Gimme your notes!"

"Here it is - 'Nichols'."

He entered the name and waited.

The door beeped open. ACCESS GRANTED Preston Nichols

"Whew." They went through the door.

"Thank you Cabair."

"Who?"

"Cabair was the name of the company where I built a home base in England. It's where I learned to fly the Airbus. It was also there that I learned to take copious notes."

"The screen said 'Access granted Preston Nichols'. I think the security system thinks you are Preston Nichols now."

"Maybe this is where you actually register your name for the first time. Usually, I would think they did that at reception. It's possible that the imprint machine was locked away somewhere, we didn't search that area at all."

"Well, if that's the case, then we could have put in any name. What's done is done though. From now on you're Preston Nichols."

They went through the door and stopped dead in their tracks, wide-eyed. The stood on a landing made of steel grate. A cat walk wound it's way down from there in a series of stairs and landings. The room dropped four stories and was the size of half a football field.

"Woah."

"I think we found the power system."

"For what, New York City?"

A throbbing hum filled the room. The small walkway lead to a room on the left. They entered through a heavy door. Large windows looked over the engineering works forty feet below. Inside the control room were two rows of desks lined with a wall of computer screens.

"This is nuclear, it's gotta be."

"Jesus, an underground nuclear power plant right in New Jersey? People would have had a complete fit about this."

"Well they have nuclear reactors on submarines, aircraft carriers and satellites, why not a secret base?"

"I'm guessing there's a lot more to see if they need a power plant this size."

"How the hell do they do construction on a place like this without anyone knowing?"

"I have no idea, but it's really impressive."

Rand laughed, "Well the power is up and running that's for sure. Let's see what else we can find."

They left the control room and went back out the main door. Elsie stopped Rand as the door closed behind them.

"Wait a sec. Try your hand on that pad to see if you can get back in."

He touched his hand to the pad and the door responded with a click.

"Sweet."

They took the right that they had passed up before. It was passageway 'B', Rand noted. It began with double doors and ended with double doors.

"Don't you think they could have come up with something more creative than 'A' and '1' and 'B'? I mean, where are all the huge X-Men doors that look like bank vaults?"

"It's all much more common sense than that. The passageways are labeled like this so that in an emergency people will know where they are at first glance. Not as fun right now, but definitely a better way to go when you're in an emergency and running for your life."

"Yeah, you're probably right."

Down hallway 'B' was the mess hall, the kitchen and the gym. All of these were very modern and had a more welcoming décor. Then there was a meeting room that was all done in wood and leather with a large screen at one end. At the end of the hall were two doors labeled 'Presidential Situation Room'.

Rand looked at Elsie, "Guess what room this is?"

Inside was an immense oval table imprinted with the Presidential Seal. The table was surrounded by high backed black leather chairs and there were an array of phone systems and microphones on the table all neatly arranged. The far wall was covered in flat screens of various sizes.

"What is it with the president and ovals?"

"No kidding, look at the size of this thing." Rand sat in the larger chair at the head of the table. "The President of the United States would sit here in times of world crisis and make decisions about the fate of billions of people and this is the best they could come up with?"

"Kinda sucks doesn't it?"

"No kidding, I mean why didn't they call in a Hollywood designer to do up something super hi-tech and amazing? This is what you get when you let the world be run by stuff-shirt lawyers and pencil pushers. All practicality, no pizzazz."

They ate some sandwiches and looked through the cabinets but found only office supplies and a variety of spare cords for projectors and laptops so they continued on. In the corner of the room was a guard station in the form of a small podium with a barcode scanner, though there was no computer to hook the scanner to. Past the guard station was a stairway that wound down to the right.

"Something tells me not a lot of people got to come down here." Elsie said.

Four flights of steel and concrete stairs, took them further into the heart of the complex. The walls of the staircase were labeled with a giant 'a' in grey and were painted light blue, but the fluorescent light bathed everything in a yellowish haze. It reminded Rand of the morgue at the hospital in Belfast. At the bottom of the stairs the landing turned right into a door. The door opened into small white cement room with miniguns on the ceiling, a duplicate of the one at the entry of the facility. A keyboard and hand scanner station were mounted next to a heavy door across the room from Rand and Elsie.

"I wonder if I'm already in the system now?" Rand started to walk over to the hand scanner.

"Rand NO!" Elsie yelled from behind him. Rand felt himself being yanked from the collar as she drug him back out the door. The whine of the miniguns spooling up was replaced by a rib-shaking roar as the guns poured hundreds of rounds into the stairwell in mere seconds. Elsie had yanked Rand back around the corner. He stumbled backwards on the stairs, falling on her as the first rounds impacted the wall. He could feel bullet fragments and concrete peppering his back and legs. Scrambling to his feet he grabbed Elsie by the harness and threw her up the stairs. She recovered reached down to pull him up. They both ran up a full flight before they turned around. The guns had stopped firing. She whirled on him.

"Rand!"

"I know, I know! I'm sorry!"

"Sorry? Jesus you almost got killed! You have to be careful!"

"I'm sorry Elsie, I really am."

"I know. It's alright. Are you okay?" She turned him around and looked at his back

"Yeah I'm fine, you?"

"I'm okay." She spun around and looked at his legs. "You took some hits from shrapnel. That gel body armour really works thank God."

"Man you reacted fast, thanks for pulling me outta there."

"Me? You threw me up the stairs! I felt like I had a jetpack on."

They sat on the stairs and took a breather.

"We can stop now if you want. We've only been at this for a couple of hours now but it's already been a long day. I mean, we've been shot at twice now."

"No way! I haven't had this much fun ever! That is... I mean... unless you want to. It has been a long day and a little rest probably wouldn't be a bad thing and…"

Elsie walked over to him and planted her lips on his. Then drew back and looked into his smiling face. "C'mon tough guy, let's figure out what to do about those guns."

They decided to go about it methodically. First, Elsie threw out the MRE packet. The guns didn't go off.

"Okay, now we know it's not set off by motion detector."

Next, Rand cracked the heat packet from an MRE and let it get hot. Then he tossed that into the room. The miniguns tore the packet to shreds.

"Whoa! Okay, they don't like heat." Rand's eyes were wide with excitement.

"Okay then. Toss one heat pack out and while the guns are distracted, take them out with the shotgun. I'll have another pack ready to go in case they go through the first one before you're done, okay?"

"Okay.' Rand loaded a clip of explosive rounds and prepared to round the corner. He flipped the facemark on his NV helmet down and used the remote sighting system so he didn't have to poke his head around the corner.

"Remember, just like at the Senator's house. Sight and shoot. Pick one target at a time and don't stop shooting until it's neutralised. If you can only take care of one then ditch back around the corner and we'll go again. We have four more MRE's so there's plenty of time."

"What if there are more of these stations?"

"We'll worry about that when we get there. We've got more MREs in the Ospreys. Worst case, we turn around and go home, so no big deal."

"Right. Okay." Rand's breathing was short, his muscles flexed. The thought of rounding the corner against live fire had him wired.

"Okay." He said again. "Okay, I'm ready!" He said yet again. "Elsie?" He turned and looked at her.

She was sitting with her chin on her hand, staring at him with a look. "We're not doing anything until you calm down."

Rand stared at her for a second then breathed out and said "Right."

She rubbed his shoulders, "Take it easy big guy. You can do this, no problem."

"Yeah, no problem." He took a couple of long, deep breaths and felt much better. Turning to her, he smiled and said, "Thanks."

"Okay, go get em." She tossed the hot pack into the room. Rand peeked his gun sight around just enough that he could see the first minigun then everything went into slow motion. The minigun swivelled to follow the heat pack as it dropped to the ground. The shotgun sight came level with the minigun and Rand squeezed the trigger. Six rounds pounded into the minigun and exploded, shearing off the ammunition track. The gun seized up.

He leaned forward to see further around the corner. The second minigun came into view. It was churning out rounds as it shredded the heat pack into confetti.

The shotgun sight was still coming to bear on the minigun when it finished with the first pack. The spinning barrels began swivelling up towards him. Rand knew he wouldn't make it back around the corner, he was leaning too far forward.

Just then, out of the corner of his eye he saw another heat packet go flying off to his right. The minigun tracked it and started hitting it in the air. Rand knew it was now or never as he brought the shotgun up and unleashed another six rounds. The minigun shattered into spinning pieces of steel.

"Rand!"

The slow motion of Rand's perception returned to normal. Elsie was pulling on the back of his pants.

"Rand, for God's sake stand up!"

He was leaning out, both feet on the stair. Elsie had him by his web gear, straining to hold onto him as he leaned out at an angle. He stepped down and righted himself.

Elsie let go and rubbed her arm. "Jesus! I almost dropped you."

"What happened?"

"You blew the shit out of those miniguns that's what happened!" She laughed. "You were supposed to only put the gun around the corner but you kept trying to look with your head."

"But you were holding on to me. How did you throw the other pack?"

"I, I don't know, I just did. It all happened so fast. Those little bastards really move! For a second there I thought it was gonna get you."

Now the adrenaline kicked in, Rand started shaking a little and sat down on the stairs.

"Man! What a rush!"

The God String

"No kidding baby, look at me I'm shaking too!"

Elsie held out her hands. Rand knew that she didn't get shook up very easily. He reached out and pulled her close. They sat that way until the jitters wore off.

"You know, just when I thought that thing was gonna get a bead on me I saw the packet come flying out of nowhere. If you would have thrown it to the left instead of the right that gun would have tracked right across my face. You totally save my bacon. Again."

"I had no idea what I was doing, I just did it. But your face shouldn't have been out there in the first place!"

"Yeah, apparently these NV helmets take some getting used to. We should train with them to avoid mistakes =like this in the future.. Thanks for saving me."

"No problem hon, you would have done the same for me."

After examining the damage on the guns they made their way over to the hand scanner. Rand got ready to shoot video again and Elsie took out the next card in the stack.

"Ready? Go."

It read:

C B A B B A G E

1 0 2 6 1 7 9 2 E

SAP Level/ Imprint for Isolation access

Rand and Elsie looked at each other and said at the same time,

"Isolation access?"

Rand shook his head, "I don't like the sound of that."

Elsie thought a minute and said, "I think they're using the word isolation to imply an important exclusivity to the access granted. It says: (She made the quote sign in the air with two fingers and talked in a mocked low voice) 'You think you were important before, that ain't nothing, now you're really in deep so don't fuck up.' That's what I think this is."

Rand could see her point. After all she was the military professional and knew how these things worked.

"Okay. So I'll use my hand again?"

Elsie quickly grabbed his hand and then gently held it aside. "Your hand has already been scanned. Maybe I'll go this time."

Rand shrugged. "Fine but what name will you use?"

She thought hard for a minute, "Well, we're pretty sure that doesn't matter but, just in case let me see your notes."

He handed the little book to her.

"Here, PTRMOON. How about Peter Moon?"

Rand looked at her hands, "You don't have the hands of a man. It's going to know you're not male."

"I don't think it makes gender/name distinctions. Hey, Maybe Peter has girly hands. It's worth a shot. Besides, what are they gonna do, shoot at us?"

"Not any more." He grinned.

She entered the code.

The screen came back with 'NUMBER OF PERSONS_____.'

"Oh crap. We've got to say two. There might be floor scales or motion sensors that will count us."

"Just do it hon. The guns are out of commission."

"Okay." Elsie typed '2'.

NAME OF PERSON 1_____.

She entered 'Peter Moon'.

NAME OF PERSON 2_____.

"Oh shit I don't think this is gonna work."

She entered 'Preston Nichols'.

SCAN FOR Peter Moon.

She put her hand in the scanner.

RE-SCAN.

She put her hand on again.

SCAN FOR Preston Nichols.

Rand put his hand on the scanner.

RE-SCAN.

"Your other hand for God's sake!"

"Oh shit, sorry!" Rand put his right hand in this time.

RE-SCAN

"Oh crap! This isn't working!"

"Just put it in there."

ISOLATION ACCESS GRANTED.

The door clicked open. As it opened the small, solid metal door proved to actually be a false front with the real door much larger and over a foot thick.

"Why did it want to scan us so many times?"

"Probably because it hadn't registered Peter Moon yet. I don't know. I have no idea how this whole system works.

I'm sure if there was someone to explain it to us it would make complete sense. The military doesn't do a half-ass job of security."

"Maybe it was just dusty.'"

The massive door opened onto a long cylindrical hallway finished with polished birch wood and a thick linen fabric wainscot. The wide floor was made of a grippy, dark grey rubber material that was soft but gave excellent traction.

"Wow, trippy."

"It looks like something out of Goldfinger."

They worked their way down the corridor keeping an eye out for hidden security systems. A heavy thud shook the floor behind them, making them spin around. The big door had closed. Rand gave Elsie a worried look. She shrugged.

"I have to make sure." He said walking back to the door and putting his hand in the scanner.

ISOLATION ACCESS Preston Nichols.

"Okay that's the same."

ISOLATION DAY 1 OF 300."

'What? Elsie we're stuck down here for three hundred days?"

"No!" Elsie ran over to the screen. "That can't be. Why would they lock people in here for that long? Rand we can't stay down here, we've got to get out!"

"Okay Elsie, take it easy. We'll figure a way out. I remember the power plant went down three stories. We went down four flights of stairs. That means we're not far below it. We have a lot of explosives too, so if push comes to shove we can blast through the ceiling. Before we do that though, let's just see where we are and what is going on with this place. Then we can make a decision on what to do when we have all the information okay?"

"Right. You're right Rand. Sorry I freaked. I'm just not used to being so far below ground."

"Actually we started out on a bluff. I bet we're barely below sea level."

"You're right, I'm being really over reactive."

"It's alright hon, we're just taking turns. After all, we've been shot at twice now. The nerves are a bit on edge."

"Yeah, a bit. I'm good now. Let's move on."

At the end of the cylindrical hall there was a T-junction. The décor continued in the same style of wide cylindrical corridors, wood paneling and cloth wainscot. An opening on the left led into a large living area with white leather retro furniture and a pool table. The place would have made four stars in the hotel business. Four large plasma TV's and a bar provided further amenities. On three walls stood nine doors that lead to private apartments. These were spacious with their own private living room, bedroom, kitchen and bathroom all luxuriously furnished.

They searched the living areas and found a picture of a man with his family.

"This man, he's wearing a shirt that says 'Team Hadron 09'. He's part of the team that set up the Large Hadron Collider."

Rand took a stab at a scenario.

"So these people down here were all scientists working on something to do with particle acceleration and they had to stay isolated for almost a year while they worked and lived down here. That's the picture I'm getting."

She looked at him, "Yeah, I agree. Let's see what else there is. We can come back here when we start to get into the nitty gritty."

They both felt like they were on to something and that this wasn't just an excursion for fun any more. Rand reloaded his shotgun with a full mag of explosive rounds and turned up his earpiece. They left the living quarters and kept walking down the gently winding hallway. After five minutes they stopped.

"How far does this go?" Elsie said.

Rand was looking up at the ceiling. "Do you hear that? Listen."

Elsie strained her ears.

"Turn up your earpiece hon.'

'Oh, right." Then she heard it. "That's the sea."

They looked at each other then took off at a run down the long hallway. After a hundred yards the decor turned from sandy/beige retro to cement industrial. In another fifty yards it turned to a tunnel cut out of raw rock with a cement floor. The rock glistened damply and the smell of salt grew stronger.

"It's definitely the ocean and it's close."

The hallway began to widen significantly, finally stretching to over twenty feet wide and equally as high. The tunnel opened into a massive cave that sprawled out to their left for several hundred feet. In front of them the cement floor went on for roughly seventy five feet then ended abruptly in a drop off into the water.

"It's an underground pier." Rand said, wide-eyed.

Two cranes were frozen mid-motion in the act of picking shipping containers off of something that looked like a dark-grey steel barge.

"I can hear the sound of surf. It's coming from above us." Elsie pointed at the ceiling above the water.

"So we're underwater?"

"Just barely. Maybe twenty feet below."

There were over twelve containers on the pier and four on the barge, which seemed to be at capacity. A forklift on the pier was parked against a wall with a load of what used to be vegetables.

"This is how they supply the place."

"Don't you think people would see that barge?"

"No." She said moving closer to it. "It's submersible."

Sure enough, Rand could see the enclosed heavy glass cockpit. He was thrilled. He held up his arms and turned to Elsie.

"Wow! What a discovery! Look at this place!"

Elsie smiled and just shook her head,

"I know Rand, it's unbelievable. The base has been around since World War II. I wonder if they have been working on this secret part for that long? This pier probably has. It's just big enough to take a small WWII submarine…" She stopped suddenly and raised her assault rifle. "Rand…look."

Along the far wall of the cave was a line of three small, black delta-wing planes. They had no cockpit but two small missiles hung from each wing.

"That's like the little bastard that shot at you." Rand raised the AA-12. "I'll wager they get their targeting from some station above ground."

"The lighthouse. I bet there's a targeting radar up in the light."

"That would do it."

The little black planes sat in a row, each one attached to a kind of cart.

Rand moved closer, "Look, they shift over one at a time and attach to this rail that's recessed into the pier."

Elsie recognised the engineering. "That's the catapult that launches them. It's like an aircraft carrier. See, there's a launch tube with a guide rail." She leaned in to look up the tube. "Yep, there's the door. I bet you can't even tell it's there from the outside."

Rand was surveying the launch mechanism. "And here's why we didn't get attacked by all of them." He pointed at a flat piece of steel that had come off of one of the carts and lodged into the catapult track.

"They got stuck." Rand said with a laugh.

Elsie wasn't laughing. "That means the little fuckers are still live." She said backing away and bringing up her SCAR assault rifle. Rand could hear the whine of servos coming from inside the UAV. Through the smoked canopy he suddenly saw the red glow of a laser optic swivel and point at him. He jumped back and opened up with the AA-12 shotgun. Behind him Elsie's SCAR drew lines of holes in the skin of the first plane then connected with the fuel tank in the wing and exploded. Rand continued backing away as the auto-shotgun chugged explosive rounds into the remaining two aircraft, shredding them into scrap before they too burst into flame. The heat wave washed over the both of them as pieces of metal bounced by their feet with a dull tinkling sound. Rand hefted the shotgun up onto his shoulder and looked over at Elsie. She looked back at him and smiled.

"That'll teach them to put holes in my Osprey."

They walked back the way they had came, reloading as they went. At the entrance Rand noticed another ramp going steeply down and to the left.

Elsie frowned, "But that leads out to sea."

The ramp descended for twenty feet ending in landing area with a hatch that sat only two feet off the floor. Rand knelt down and slowly cranked the wheel. The hatch opened easily, revealing a short, thick-walled plexiglas tube that lead to another hatch attached to a submersible. Rand had to drag himself down the tube, but the floor was padded with a carpet that was easy to slide on.

"Here's our way out of here Els." He said, looking out of a little porthole to the submarine. "This is a little sub designed to pick up the shipping containers off the ocean floor. It's totally obvious. Look at the arms. Maybe they use it for smaller runs." Rand slid back out and closed the hatch. "We can easily get to the surface with this."

A more complete picture was coming to Elsie. "Check this out Rand: A big cargo ship heads into New York for a routine shipping run. As it passes this place by it drops several containers out of the bottom of its hull through a special door. Hell, maybe it just pushes them off the back. Either way the containers hit the bottom of the ocean. It's not very deep here."

"Right. Sounds feasible so far."

"So then the little sub and the barge come out and they load it all up and bring it back. In a couple of runs they're completely stocked."

Rand nodded. "The base is secret, but just in case it's discovered it's still under the disguise of a Presidential fallout shelter. It's double cover. Double top secret just to hide what the real secret is. The only thing that would help disguise it even more is if there were some conspiracy theory about it being a secret base."

She gave him a big smile, "Exactly. So what's the REAL secret? Why are they here? What are they doing?"

Rand was getting excited all over again. "I don't know Elsie but this is the best birthday anyone has ever had EVER!"

She laughed and kissed him. "Now, let's go see what else there is."

"Okay, but please remind me to take that mini-sub for a ride."

They retraced their steps back the way they came. The hallway didn't seem so long now. They passed hallway 'C' then started down past the T junction.

"This is where we chose to go left. Now we're headed right from our original position coming from the reception area."

"Gotcha. Your map is coming in handy."

The décor had returned to the cylindrical passageways and calmly lighted, muted colours of a Bond film.

"The only thing this place is missing is cheesy elevator music."

The came to a door with a small window. Peering in, they could see a sophisticated chemistry lab. The ceiling was over twenty feet high in the thousand square-foot room. Ten-foot high tanks of liquid helium, oxygen and nitrogen stood along the far wall. Storage containers with radioactive symbols were stacked in a locker. Tubes and wires ran everywhere and banks of computer cooling fans filled the room with white noise.

"I have no idea what any of this is." Rand looked at her questioningly.

"Don't look at me." She said, "I just fly the plane."

"There's nothing here that gives any clues. What little I know about chemistry tells me that they are doing something using very cold materials. Maybe for cooling, I don't know. They probably also use this lab for tests involving the reactor. Just a guess though."

They left the lab and ended up at the end of the hall where the sign on an unassuming little door said 'Disrupter Station 1'.

Rand's heart thumped. "We're getting closer."

Elsie suddenly turned ten years old and jumped up and down clapping her hands. Rand took out his notes. "Peter Moon you're up."

He entered the code for the disrupter station 1: PTRMOON. At the next prompt he entered the code: 410420SAGE. Another prompt appeared for a hand scan and Elsie put her hand in. The door open with a heavy click.

DISRUPTER STATION 1 ACCESS GRANTED Peter Moon.

The door was only about four inches thick but they got the impression it was very heavy as whining motors slowly swung it towards them. Another normal door was right behind it.

"I think we're getting the hang of this."

"The vault door looks like it stayed open most of the time, kind of like the vault door at the bank. Look at the marks on the floor, it's on wheels."

"If it was open all the time then I wonder why they would have closed it?"

"Maybe for some kind of special operation?"

"I'm thinking there is some huge gun called a disruptor. Maybe they locked the base down when they test fired it."

She look at him, clearly impressed. "That makes the most sense out of anything we have come up with. An energy weapon. They have been trying to develop them for years."

They opened the normal door and came out on a steel grate landing overlooking a large cave with raw stone walls that had been roughly cut. Large light fixtures on the floor pointed up at the walls reflecting the dim, reddish colour of the rock. The heavy steel grid catwalk system straddled the top of a gigantic forty-foot in diameter blue pipe. The whole thing was built over a rocky bowl about seventy feet deep. A set of wide, steel grate stairs descended from the platform paralleled by an industrial handicapped elevator that landed on the cave floor below. The pipe came out of the wall and exited through the opposite wall, its lower section buried into the rock floor of the cave. Large bundles of wires ran along the cave floor and over and into the huge pipe at intervals.

"What the...? We've gone from double-oh-seven to heavy duty industrial."

"This is definitely more recent than the rest of the facility. Within the last five years at least." Elsie looked down over the railing.

They followed the wide catwalk over the pipe a short distance where it widened into a small glass room with four desks filled with flat screen computer monitors. The only wall that wasn't glass was against the rock wall and lined with computer cabinets. Thick bundles of wiring were all neatly channeled and came right out of the rock. With no lock on the door they entered easily.

"Here's our control station." Rand surmised.

"Okay, let's see if we can find out about the disruptor beam." Elsie started rummaging through the cabinets at the wall while Rand sat down and tried his hand at the computers.

"That was easy. This isn't a weapons control center, it's called 'Cooling Station One'. It says it right here on the desktop graphic."

"Rand I think I found something here." She was looking at a thick technical manual. "If this is cooling station one… hold on, that can't be. It would mean…"

"Elsie you're starting to babble. What is it?"

"That huge tube down there is a particle accelerator." Elsie shook her head in disbelief. "The largest particle accelerator on earth is the Large Hadron Collider and it's the same size of that tube out there. I bet it runs out to sea. It must go for miles. And the other end… I don't even know where that goes. I can't believe what I'm seeing." Elsie's hand was on her forehead. She was completely stunned at the size of the operation.

"So what does it do?"

"It's a particle accelerator. Rand, Hadron is the largest particle accelerator in the world, a project of massive scale not to mention budget. The scientific community watched

The God String

it being built over years and years. When it was finally started up, there were protests around the world from people who thought that it would create a black hole and destroy the earth. The Large Hadron Collider is a big, big deal."

"So you're saying that this thing is the same kind of doohickey."

"Yes."

"Right. No disrespect intended, but if it took the world's scientific community all that to build the Hadron machine, then how the hell did they build this in secret? And more importantly, why?"

"That's why I'm freaking out Rand." She sat down on a chair at one of the workstations. "Wow! I mean, this is WAY bigger than I ever imagined."

Rand handed her the technical manual. "Find out more."

Elsie began to rummage through the information. After a couple of minutes she sucked in a breath and turned to Rand. She had gone completely white.

"Elsie? You okay?"

She just held out the manual and pointed at a spot on the page. Rand took it from her and read. 'Dark Matter Disrupter cooling station', "Okay, I don't know what that is."

Her voice was shaky. "Rand, remember what I just said about the Hadron…"

"Yes."

"…and how big it is…"

"Uh huh."

"Rand, what we're sitting on right now…"

"Yeah?"

"…is only for cooling the collider that's somewhere in this facility."

Rand started to get the picture.

"So if this station is only for cooling, then how big is the main thingy-whatever?"

"I don't know. Big. Really, really big. Like…the biggest thing on earth."

"How the hell could they get budget for all this?"

"Oh God, Rand do you know how many two-hundred dollar hammers the Navy has purchased? They get congressional approval for some really large amounts of money, but only a percentage of it actually gets spent on what they get approval for. The rest gets funnelled into projects like this. This though, has got to be the granddaddy of them all."

"Okay, so where's the rest of this big contraption?"

Elsie loved the way he simplified things. No drama, just a big contraption, which in truth it was. It calmed her.

"Well, if it's some kind of accelerator it's going to be running far underground for stability and for a distance of, I'm guessing, over a hundred miles."

"So we're talking something that would completely encircle New York."

"Uh, yeah."

The God String

"Awesome."

"Yes. For once, the use of the word is justifiable."

Montgomery Thompson

Chapter 11

Between the lines

'The beginning of knowledge is the discovery of something we do not understand.'
~Ironically unknown

"I don't know about you but my brain could use a break." Rand poured out some coffee from his thermos and served up pieces of his birthday cake as they talked about how amazing and exciting the whole things was. They wondered how Spang was doing and laughed and talked about the flock, the garden and the house. It did not escape their attention that the circumstances surrounding their little picnic were most bizarre. But then, Rand reasoned, there had probably been a lot of lunches eaten down there as men worked away in secret. Just average Joes doing their part for national security, having lunch. The thought helped to soothe their nerves and ground their awe.

When they were ready to move on they took the wheelchair elevator from the platform down four stories to the base of the huge cooling tube. As they descended the temperature rose sharply in comparison to the passageways of the main facility. They were obviously no longer in the air-conditioned section. The air was humid and hot, and moisture collected on the surface of the dark, rough hewn rock.

At the bottom of the elevator they found a golf cart attached to a charging station. A small cement road followed alongside the huge cooling pipe for about twenty yards before it passed through a wall. A cable track was bolted to the rock and followed alongside the road.

"This is all fibre optic and power cabling. There must be enough here for a small city." Rand noted.

Lighting burned in the form of huge construction lamps that had been placed at floor level and reflected off the walls. It gave the light a golden quality and revealed just how dense the moisture was that hung in the air. They unplugged the golf cart and climbed in.

"Well this is handy I must say." Rand settled in behind the wheel.

"I take it as an indicator of just how far this road goes."

"Yeah, keep an eye on the meter. We want to make sure we have enough juice to get back."

The road stayed with the pipe in the form of a narrow tunnel. The small entrance only gave them a few feet on either side of the golf cart as they squeezed through.

"I'll bet a day didn't go by down here when someone didn't mention widening this tunnel." Elsie said, reaching out and touching the wall.

The tunnel sloped down at a steep angle and crossed under the massive pipe for several minutes. It was like driving underneath a ship.

"I just don't understand how the pipe got into the rock. It's like they were digging it out, not building it in."

Suddenly, the cavern opened up into an area over mile long.

"Good Lord." The scale of the cavern hit Rand with a mild case of vertigo. The little road was carved into the rock wall along the right hand side. Hundreds of giant industrial lights were scattered on the floor, shining up at the ceiling creating fans of golden light in the misty air. A strong steel safety rail was bolted down the length of its descending course.

"Rand, look!" In the distance, several other cooling pipes of the same size came out of various points in the cave walls. All of them appeared to be straight as an arrow and had their own small roads that accompanied them. Excavation equipment sat rusting in mid-motion, grouped near the walls along the rough floor of the cavern.

Rand stopped the cart, astonished. His eyes struggling to grasp the scale of what he was seeing. Elsie just sat in the cart with her hands to her mouth shaking her head in disbelief.

"What is this place?'

"Elsie, there's no way they built this. This isn't a building site, it's an archeological excavation."

"This is freaking creepy is what it is. Rand I'm seriously spooked here."

'It's okay. I think we've got the place to ourselves. Just think of the guys running the excavators. Just average Joes having lunch right?"

"Yeah, okay, that helps… kind of."

They continued on the paved path. Down and down they went, sometimes in tunnels barely as wide as the cart, sometimes much wider. Rand kept saying, "How did this get here?"

"Even aside from that, how did they do it? I mean, how could they have worked on this without anyone knowing?"

"That's the big question for me. Are they building it, or are the excavating it?"

As the road descended to the ground level of the cavern they passed a row of construction trailers. Over thirty golf carts were lined up, ready for use. Huge junction boxes connected the power, network and communications cabling then sent it on down the line. They continued on to the end of the cavern and entered a tunnel wide enough for three golf carts side-by-side with a ceiling over ten feet high.

"This was obviously a main thoroughfare." Elsie said pointing at the golf carts and various mining vehicles scattered over the road. They picked their way around the maze of vehicles as they worked through the tunnel, and after about twenty minutes they entered a cavern that dwarfed the previous one. Rand estimated the distance at somewhere around five miles in length, two miles in width

The God String

and well over five hundred feet high. He stopped the cart and just stared.

"This has got to be the largest cavern in the world." He mumbled, dumbstruck.

Massive stadium lights shone up to the ceiling that glittered with a spectacular array of crystalline structures. "It looks like the night sky."

"No," Elsie murmured, "it looks like space. The stars are that clear, that colourful…" She reached her hand up like she could touch them.

They stood next to the cart just staring for minutes. Suddenly Elsie grabbed Rand's arm, "Look at that!"

In the distance, across the cavern floor strewn with lifts, cranes, and drilling gear, a section of exposed pipe had been excavated from the rock. It towered over ten stories though most of it was still embedded in the stone.

"Is that…the main pipe? God Rand, just that section alone is the size of a cruise ship, and that's not even all of it."

The whole room hummed loudly with a loping pulse of energy.

Elsie sighed, "I'm getting tired of having my mind blown."

"I know what you mean," Rand chuckled, "the scale of this is just too much. It hurts my head to think about it."

Elsie raised her rifle to look at the structure through the scope. "There's something else. It's up on the wall above the big pipe. It looks human sized."

Rand raised his scope and scanned the far wall in the distance. It was over four miles away but he finally zeroed in on what Elsie was talking about. 'Yeah, I got it. It looks like a big window overlooking the cavern.'

"It's way up there though. Oh wait…"

"Yep I see it, an elevator up the side of the cliff face. Let's go."

As they got closer the little cart felt minuscule next to the looming wall. Neither one could stop looking up. The exposed section of pipe rose ominously above them. It was the same blue colour as the smaller pipes and covered with cabling and tubes. Several of the giant cooling pipes ran parallel to the larger pipe's course, exposed at the top and bottom of the hole in the rock.

'What the heck is it?' Rand's tone was slightly exasperated. "It's totally smooth like they polished it. It looks anodised but…not. I you know what I mean."

"I don't know baby, but I think we're about to find out."

They pulled the cart up to the lift. It was modern and built mostly of stainless steel. The elevator car was a half circle of thick glass that made up the walls and door. The floor was carpeted and the controls were in black touch screen glass that glowed blue. As soon as the door to the elevator closed the air conditioning system immediately cooled the interior.

"Oh that's nice." Rand pulled his shirt neck away from his skin and let the cool air flow in.

"I think we're on the trigger end of this thing now."

The God String

Rand gave Elsie a tentative look, "Do we press up or down?"

"I think the time for booby traps is long gone at this point. We're literally in the belly of the beast."

She touched the *UP* button as Rand held his breath and grimaced.

Gently and quietly the lift rose up the rock face, gaining speed as it went. Rand breathed a sigh of relief. From the rising elevator car they could see the expanse of the cavern spread out before them. The view only added to the awe inspiring size of the project.

"Earthworm. I get now." Rand muttered.

To the left and over mile away they could see the tunnel entrance they had emerged from. To the right was the side of the monolithic blue-grey pipe revealed in the rock that miners had been feverishly chipping away at for who knew how long. At the top, the elevator slowed to a stop and doors behind them opened up. They turned and looked into a small brightly lit, pinewood-panelled landing area with a stainless steel door on the far wall.

"Here we go again." Rand crouched behind the elevator door and scanned the entry for robotic sentries. Elsie touched him on the shoulder.

"It's clear hon. Too dangerous to have live ammo around so many workers. I'm pretty sure we are past the armed checkpoints from here on out."

"Okay, never hurts to be sure."

She gave a giggle and moved across the dark tiled floor to the access panel next to the door. There was no input keyboard, only the blue-lit hand scanner. Rand joined her and held his hand above the scanner then glanced back at Elsie. She shrugged. He pressed his hand into the scanner and was rewarded with the movement of the door, which slipped into the wall sideways.

"Finally! A Star Trek door." Rand said excitedly.

"Happy now?"

"Yes, definitely."

Elsie followed him in to the next room.

The décor continued in the same pine paneling and stainless accents that reflected a subdued light from sconces on the walls. To the left, as they came in the door, a thick glass window overlooked the sprawling cavern. Most of the room was filled with computer desks, laid out in a modern open-office plan. The pine wood panels opened to reveal storage for everything from office supplies to coffee but the majority was technical manuals, data storage and books. They went from desk to desk getting an overview of the contents of the room. As Elsie reached the last desk she turned, her head tilted slightly as she looked past Rand who was rummaging through a desk with his back to the big window.

"This is the main control room for the Dark Matter Disrupter." She Elsie flatly.

Rand looked up, "How do you know that?"

The God String

She stood stock still, staring straight ahead with a blank expression on her face and slowly raised her arm in a robotic motion, pointing behind him. His eyes went wide and he quickly turned, bringing his shotgun to bear.

There above the window was a little sign that read, 'Dark Matter Disrupter Control Room'.

Elsie giggled behind him. "Gotcha."

He sighed and turned back to her, "Not funny. You looked like a pod person."

"Nothing like a little sci-fi humour to keep you on your toes." She teased.

They looked through bookshelves with thick volumes of papers full of calculations and engineering drawings.

"Some of these date back to the sixties." Elsie was fascinated.

They both spent the next hour pouring over the material and saying very little other than the occasional 'wow' and 'no way'.

Finally Rand looked up. "Elsie I think I've got something here. It's some sort of report."

She stopped what she was doing and came over, still carrying the book she had been reading. "I've found something too. Let's see what you have." She took the report and began scanning through it. "It's a report of results. Come over to the big table." She set Rand's book down on the big central conference table and opened the book she had brought over. "Hang on to your socks honey. In this place the truth really is stranger than fiction."

He looked at her apprehensively as she began to explain what they had found.

"This whole thing is like a big particle accelerator, but it's on a scale never seen before. It's actually about six giant particle accelerators in one." She showed Rand plans of the accelerator. The diagram was just a schematic and had no reference for the actual physical size of the thing.

"A regular particle accelerator smashes atoms together at nearly the speed of light to see what comes out of them."

Rand looked at her, "Like breaking something to see what it's made of?"

"Yep. They use huge magnets to pull the particles around which is the same as what they are doing here, but the difference is that here they are swirling them around and around without colliding them. You see dark matter isn't effected by gravity in the same way that matter is."

Rand jumped in, "And dark matter is what they are trying to collide?"

She smiled at him, "You're not just a pretty face are you?"

"Aw."

"Anyway, you're dead on. They're trying to collide dark matter. Actually not trying, they are. They whirl matter around until the 'wind' gets the dark matter to follow. Then they quickly divert the flow of the matter while the dark matter keeps going, smack! Straight into the dark matter coming at it from the opposite direction."

Rand scratched his head, "What happens then?"

The God String

"This is where it really gets interesting. They don't only do this once, they keep doing it over and over. It's like pointing two super highways of opposing traffic into each other and letting a string of cars loose. Eventually there's a massive pile up of compressed dark matter and it reaches a combustion point."

"You mean it explodes?"

"No, not according to this guy." Elsie held up a thick technical manual that was old and very worn.

"Which guy?"

"Meet Reverend Doctor Oskar Remmel. Apparently he's the one who came up with all of this."

"Okay so what's Rommel…"

"Remmel."

"Dremel?"

"Rand."

"Oh okay," Rand made a face, "Dr. Remmel. What's he say?"

"He says you're a sarcastic little shit." She poked him.

"Hey!"

"Are you listening to this?"

"Yes, go ahead."

"Dr. Remmel says that years ago they discovered that matter is only half-here; it disappears and reappears constantly. He theorises that over half of the matter in the universe is shifting back and forth the through the fabric of space and time."

Rand nodded, "Yeah, I heard that too on Cosmos."

"Right, well remember that this guy was doing all of this in the fifties."

"Sounds like he was ahead of his time."

"Funny you should say that. When the Dark Matter is about to explode, it makes a big shift in the fabric of space and time. It creates a very temporary misalignment or pinch. This pinch touches two points of the fabric together creating a time / space bridge. The bigger the pinch, the wider the bridge."

"Wait! You're talking about a time machine?" Rand was incredulous.

"Exactly, and further research has added to his theories. They think they can control it."

"Control time?"

"Kind of, they keep hammering the Dark Matter as it's exploding through the fabric. Each explosion is a pulse, they hit it faster and faster and the pulses set up a harmonic wave. They can control the frequency of the harmonic wave which, if I'm understanding this correctly, allows them to widen the pinch."

"So they can put themselves anywhere in time they want." Rand was shaking his head. "It's a wormhole with a steering wheel."

"Something like that, yeah. There's a lot more he says here. We're in what he calls 'FirstTime'. He calls it FirstTime because humankind is literally the first ones along the time line. Like pioneers.

The God String

"How does he know that? What if there are time travellers who went into the future?"

"He says we can't travel to a future that has never been. Remmel is a Reverend and a Scientist. The guy figures religion into his theories. His philosophy is that science explains God's creation. He says that creation comes along with us as we live. Time doesn't exist outside of our dimension, but for us, it's linear. It starts at point A – the past, and ends at point B – us. He also refers to this linear time path we are on as the 'main string'. We can only go back to what was…"

"Not forward to what has never been." Rand finished her sentence, finally understanding. "But how does he know we're the first?"

"Well the primary evidence is because no one has come back. No one from the future has ever come back in the world."

"That's hardly evidence." Rand snorted. "Maybe they did and we don't know about it."

"We're human beings. What's the first thing we would do if we built a time machine? Go back! We would try to stop world wars or bring back the cure to the plague or a million different things. Man doesn't build things that he doesn't use."

"But what about the theory that you can't screw with the past? Wouldn't it have some far reaching effect that would eventually spell our demise?"

"No."

"Whaddaya mean no? You can't brush off an entire argument about time travel with a simple no."

"Yes I can because I agree with Dr. Remmel. He says that when you intervene in past events by travelling back through time then the possible results appear in parallel universes; alternate 'strings' are created. It's like picking up a drop of water from the ocean and throwing it back into the ocean in a different spot. There are no repercussions."

"Wouldn't there be strange, unexplainable events?"

"Like Bigfoot? Like the Philadelphia experiment? Spare me. This isn't fiction. This is real. Hidden in these pages is the real truth. Look around you. The government doesn't throw this kind of effort into conjecture. At some point Remmel must have proven his theories were right."

She cracked open the book again. "Here. Let's add what you found to what Remmel's book says. It says that the first test created no results, but a noticeable shift occurred. He thinks nothing happened because of a principal he calls the 'God string'.

"Yeah, like you said, he's a priest as well as a scientist. He believes that every human soul is bound to creation."

"Yes but even more specifically, A time. If they are close enough to their time, they will get automatically aligned to it and notice no change at all. What you found seems to document one of their experiments." She scanned the papers that Rand was looking at. "Here it is. The shift that happened was only for a nano second so it effected nothing."

The God String

"Wait a minute. They actually started this thing up?"

Elsie turned through the thick volume for a few minutes "Each one of these sections details the results of experiments for the year."

They both looked up at similar books that lined the shelves. "So each book is a year of research? Wait, how far do they go back?" Rand headed for the nearest shelf and started counting back through the dates. Elsie joined him and after ten minutes they had their answer.

"Looks like they have been trying to replicate what Remmel did since the fifties."

"But did they ever try to actually time shift?"

"Yeah, but it only worked once according to this. They know it worked but there was no result because of the God string principle."

"Okay, run that by me again Els."

"The time shift was too small. If you are even close to the time you came from you bond to that string automatically. A nano second time shift would do nothing."

"Oh my God Elsie, what if that's what happened to us?"

They looked at each other. He could see her mind working furiously. Then the idea formed across her face, she had something.

"Okay, what if everyone got shifted but us?"

"Yes, it's like they got paused for a fraction of a second but we kept on going."

She pulled two grenades, one frag and one smoke, off her harness and set them on the long table.

"I think I understand Els, I don't need an analogy."

"But I do, just to make this all solid to me. Okay, we're this frag grenade and the rest of humanity is this smoke grenade. When they fired this thing off they hiccupped. They stopped. Just for a minuscule amount of time, say a nanosecond. No one would notice, but for some reason you and I…" She scooted the frag grenade up an inch, "…we kept on going."

"But what about this God string principle, wouldn't we just snap back to our correct time? Why wouldn't we be under the same rules as everyone else?"

"Maybe there is something in Remmel's papers that will give us a clue."

Rand got up and paced back and forth rubbing his chin. Elsie watched him. They were both going to need time to think. She went over to a long counter and rummaged through the shelves. Finding what she was looking for she set a pot of coffee to brew then went back to the books she was looking through. Rand went over to the computers at the control desk and started to go through records. After over an hour of pouring through computer entries and documentation, Rand stood up excitedly.

"Ah ha! It says here that the last time they fired this thing up was for something they called 'the main event'. That would explain why they closed the big door. Sounds to me like an actual live test."

The God String

Elsie came over and handed him a fresh cup of coffee. "Definitely."

"Get a load of this, it doesn't mention a test specifically but the last entry was on the day everyone disappeared; October 10th, 10:00 A.M."

"That's it Rand! That's exactly when it must have happened!"

"Okay, what do we know?"

"We know that we were both asleep."

"And therein lies the clue."

"But a lot of people were sleeping."

"Yeah. But I was out like a light Elsie. I slept hard that night."

"So did I, but what does that have to do with anything? And what about all the animals and the cars and houses? Wouldn't they have been left behind too?"

"No, because of the God String. You said, that in Remmel's theory God holds each of us to our place in time and creation comes along with us. Now remember this guy is a believer, like me. We know that God is the source of all goodness and that he cares for every one of us, every breath, thought and molecule."

Elsie nodded, "Okay, I can appreciate your belief system as it applies to this theory. Keep going."

"Have you ever heard of astral-travel? It means you go out of your body when you meditate deeply or sometimes even when you sleep."

"I've heard the theory, yes"

"Well maybe that's where you and I were while we were sleeping. You said you were sleeping very deeply, I was too. Maybe our string was not connected to our time in that moment. When everyone else shifted, we were immune to the effects to the time shift and coasted on forward. A new God string was made for us. God's creation was brought forward with us, like a duplicate, to care for us."

"That's a lot of presumption Rand."

"Well, I call it faith. Listen, God doesn't want us just floating about in empty time and space. Think of it like an automatic, natural reaction to human presence. Creation just comes along with us. It's part of the package, naturally."

Elsie was having a hard time swallowing the religious part of Rand's argument, but she couldn't deny that it was the only solution that made sense so far.

"Okay, let's say God is real. Why would he do that for me? Bring a complete duplicate of the entirety of the universe into existence. You're a believer, I'm not. Wouldn't he pick one of his people?"

"Elsie I don't pretend to know how God works, but I know that he knows all of us, no matter what we believe or don't. The natural systems he sets up operate on their own. Rain falls to the benefit or detriment of believers and non-believers alike just as lightening strikes the just and unjust. We just happened to be out-of-body when somebody decided to press the button on Dr. Freakshow's whizz-bang gizmo here, and it ripped everything we ever cared about from us. If I ever see that son-of-a-bitch I'm gonna hit him so hard he'll feel pain in his past."

Elsie reached up and took his face gently in her hands.

"But you found me didn't you? So there's some good that can come out of the bad. It doesn't make it right, but for me it's one of the most important things that's ever happened in my life. Over all the things I strived for, being a pilot even being an astronaut, none of it compares to you."

Rand held her tight and kissed her, "I feel the same Elsie. Maybe it is a gift. Maybe he chose us. I know that we are supposed to be together. If we weren't, we wouldn't be."

"Well, we've come this far. Let's see where it ends."

At the far end of the room behind the long conference table, the floor steeply sloped away. The carpet ended and the paneling took an odd shape as Rand went down the ramp a little and peeked around the corner. Elsie watched him from the other side of the table.

Rand called back to her, "It's an optical illusion. It looks like the room stops but it doesn't. I think it's just a designer being crafty. This passage was definitely used."

Elsie joined him. The passageway was wide and cut roughly out of the dark rock. The floor was level, smooth cement with soft light emanating from the same stainless steel sconces as the rooms before. They both kept a hand on their weapons as they followed the path that wound down in a gentle left hand bend.

Rand said back to Elsie, "Is it just me or does this whole place seem like it was built for wheelchair access?"

Elsie stopped and thought for a moment. "You're absolutely right Rand. Everything is ramps, paved paths and lifts. Even the small submersible had a ramp leading to it."

"The cooling station was new but all of the older construction in this place has no stairs. I'll betcha Remmel was in a wheelchair."

The slope levelled into a landing area that was blocked by a wall and a door of solid stainless steel.

"Whoa, what's a bank vault doing in here?" Rand raised his AA-12 and backed up.

"Easy tiger, I think we're at the inner sanctum. See, keypad and scanning screen right by the door. Same set-up, different door. You got the notes?"

"Yep."

Rand typed in the last code: PRESTON then NICHOLS.

"Who the heck are Preston Nichols and Peter Moon?"

"Beats me. If the internet still worked I'd look em up on Wikipedia."

TSS CONTROL SCAN FOR ACCESS read the prompt.

Rand put his hand in the scanner.

Preston Nichols WELCOME TRAVELLER.

A series of solid clicks came from inside the door then slowly and silently it swung open.

The God String

Montgomery Thompson

Chapter 12

Operation Nosey

'What's in store for me in the direction I don't take?'
-Jack Kerouac

The room was small and smelled like dust. A single bulb hung above a grey-green control console in the center of the room. In front of them was a cement landing with a steel railing that forced a right hand turn down a small ramp. The yellow paint on the railing was worn from use and the floor was stained from years of traffic.

"More ramps. I think you may be right about old Remmel."

Towards the back of the room, behind the console were several rows of grey computer cabinets. Some had glass doors that held tape reel computers, others were filled with large square buttons with sections of mesh that revealed the guts of the electronics in an array of glowing tubes.

"This place is right out of the fifties." Rand said as he swept the flashlight on the end of his shotgun over the room.

Elsie found the light switch and flipped it on. Bright fluorescent lights fluttered to life revealing a room that looked much like the equipment, old but well serviced.

Rand rolled his eyes. "Is everything in this place a freakin' mystery?"

Elsie examined the equipment, completely absorbed.

"According to the manufacturing plate on the cabinet, this was built in 1952. It's old Air Force stuff. These computers wouldn't even be powerful enough to make a calculator now. Why would they keep these around?"

Rand came over to Elsie. "I'm more interested in why that door scanner read 'welcome traveler'."

Elsie frowned, "It did?"

"Yeah."

"I didn't see it. I just followed you. That's bizarre."

"Par for the course around here."

"I just don't get it. All this hi-tech stuff and at the end is a control room from the fifties. It doesn't make any sense." Elsie went to the console and surveyed the controls while Rand looked around behind the cabinets.

"Here we go. Rand look at this." She was pointing at a small plastic sign on the console.

"Time / Space Shift control." She read the placard. "Well it doesn't leave room for interpretation. T.S.S.. This is definitely it, mission control for this place."

Rand scratched his head. "Weird. Why would they spend so much time and money on building a super high-tech machine just to give it such a low-tech front end?"

The God String

Dominating the control console were two large black plastic knobs that sat side by side. To the left of them was a vertical strip of smaller knobs that was outlined by a thin red line of paint that formed a round-cornered box. The box was labeled 'Test Module'. On the right was a vertical row of four smaller black knobs. Around these and the larger black knobs was painted a thin white line. On top of the panel were two industrial sized buttons, one black, the other red labeled simply 'start' and 'stop'.

Elsie was examining the large knobs on the slanted face of the console.

"Look, you can see how many times these have been twisted over the years. There are wear marks from people's fingers. But the big knobs have barely been touched."

Rand took a stab at a theory. "The big ones are probably the real controls. See, they're labeled 'variation' and 'frequency'. Obviously those are the two variables you have to control to get the shift you want. But there are no pointers or marks on the knobs, so there's not a calibrated range of action like one to ten on a volume knob.

"In other words, you can't just pick a date and go to it."

"Right. I guess you just kind of do it by feel. Which makes sense because time know nothing about hours, days and years. Those are just things that humans use to measure time."

"That would explain why the test module controls are worn but the actual controls aren't."

"But why are there five test controls?"

"They mirror the other bank of five on the other side, but see, the five on the left share the same white border as the big knobs. The ones on the right are bordered in red. The red ones are the test controls, the ones in white are the real ones. Obviously they were trying to learn how to fine tune the shift."

"It's like the X-38 controls, the simulator is built in to the actual working device."

"That would be important with such a dangerous, one-of-a-kind experimental piece of technology."

"But how do the small controls work?"

"I don't know for sure. Without any labels there's no way to tell what they do. My guess is that they are like the trim controls on a plane. They make minor, small moves to fine tune the settings of the main controls."

"Right," Rand said beginning to form a theory, "maybe by working only with the finer controls they could get a reaction out of the machine without initialising an actual time shift." He reached for the main controls.

"Don't Rand!"| Elsie grabbed his arm. "Don't turn that thing on."

"But Elsie we're going to have to at some point. We might be able to make things normal again."

"I know Rand, but I don't want to lose you. Besides, we don't know what it will do. It hasn't been on in over a year."

Rand turned to her and held her shoulders. "Listen." He held her still for a moment. The hum of the massive machine droned through the whole complex. "Elsie this thing has been on since it was built. I'm starting to think that Reverend Doctor Remmel died before he could get it to work and it was this Preston Nichols and Peter Moon who actually headed up the project most recently."

"What do you mean?"

"I think Dr Remmel actually took a stab at testing his theory in the fifties, right here in this room. That's where all this gear came from. He must have been successful in some small way before he died. I think powers who backed the project didn't know how to duplicate his efforts so they kept his stuff here, set up exactly as he left it to try and make it work."

"Rand, that makes a lot of sense."

"Good, because my brain hurts."

"Maybe he figured out how to control it." She turned to Rand excitedly. "He died or something must have happened to him. His experience with the equipm - oh my!" Elsie stopped mid-sentence, her eyes widening.

"What?"

"He did it! He went back in time. He disappeared and they didn't have his knowledge and experience anymore!" She jumped up and down. "I have it Rand! I think I have the whole picture!"

"Good, for God sake please tell me."

"Okay, my working theory. This is a time machine. Doctor Remmel worked for the government at some secret facility like Area 51 or Los Alamos or something in the fifties. Maybe he was working on particle control as part of the program to study nuclear bombs after the war. The reason I say that is because this is Air Force gear and it's state-of-the-art for nineteen fifty-two."

"With ya so far."

"But Remmel wasn't that interested in the bomb, he needed a particle accelerator to do his work. According to some of these papers particle accelerators have been around since the late nineteen thirties. So Remmel breaks away from the bomb study group when he starts making real headway. The government backs him and they begin a new project here, inside this base which has been operating secretly for years. It's everything they need. It's safe, underground and stable, plus they've got the ocean for cooling, etcetera."

"Yep, the evidence backs that up, keep going." Rand nodded, trying to keep up with her.

"So he builds his machine and has success. The problem is, right in the middle of it all, he's gone. He disappeared right from this room. They try to replicate what happened but can't, they need Remmel and his genius to do it."

"Creepy. Okay, go on."

"Through the years they start to realize the enormous potential of his project and funnel all kinds of money into it. They run test after test but can't get it right. Finally they throw enough power at it and something happens, but they don't know what."

"The bigger hammer principle. Typical military. They got more than they bargained for."

The God String

"Right! Dr Remmel's machine was small and efficient. The military's version was a monster. It worked so well it paused the whole world for a nanosecond."

"It all makes sense Elsie. Pop! Oops, we shifted the world. Bastards." Rand looked at the floor and thought about Remmel having stood right there. "I got a bit more than I bargained for on this little trip."

"Sorry baby. This was meant to be a fun adventure. But the good news is that we finally have some answers."

"Yeah, and answers always lead to choices. Elsie let's go home. I mean, back home to New River and think this over. We're under no pressure here, there's no time limit. We'll disable the defences and pry open all the doors so we can come back anytime we want. But no matter what, I've made up my mind. You are mine and I am yours. Through time and space God brought us together and I am going to stay with you."

Elsie held her hands together over her mouth as happy tears broke loose. Then her eyes went wide as Rand fell to his knees and said, "Be my wife Elsie, please. I love you in this time and every time for all time. Will you?"

She fell on her knees and wrapped her arms around his neck, "Yes, yes, God yes Rand."

They held each other for a long time at the foot of the old console.

"I don't know how this will work out, but I know it will." He released her and stood, helping her up as well.

Pushing her hair back he gave her a big, mischievous smile and said, "Let's blow this taco stand baby."

She laughed, wiping away tears. "Where do you get this stuff?"

They headed back the way they came and Rand video recorded the whole route. At every door they wrapped detcord around the exposed hinges on the opposite side and blew them off. The heavy doors fell to the ground with a thump. Finally, they came to the massive isolation access door. Rand had saved most of the detcord for this one. He jammed the looped door charges in the left and right sides, where he knew the big steel bolts were placed, then packed all of the remaining detcord in the seams.

"Okay hon this is gonna be a big one."

He attached the radio detonator to the door charges and the retreated down the hallway to the kitchen.

"Let me. Please?"

Rand handed her the detonator.

Elsie kissed him then she squeezed the detonator with a sarcastic grin and said, "Gimme some sugar baby!"

The massive explosion shook the whole facility. From their hiding place in the kitchen, pots and pans jumped and banged against each other.

Rand looked at Elsie, "Now that's battle rattle."

She laughed, "Thank God for these ear pieces."

They walked over to the twisted hulk of steel that used to be the door.

The God String

"Isolation my butt. I declare this facility permanently open to the public. And by public, I mean us."

They pushed the *UP* button on the wall and the elevator to the lighthouse came down. Rand carefully tore a piece of cardboard from an open MRE box and shaped it with duct tape into a guard that he taped over the *DOWN* button in case they might forget the booby trap.

Rand wiggled his eyebrows at her, "Musicians have duct tape skills."

Then they stepped in and ascended. Day had become night as they exited the keeper's house. The Ospreys sat as they had left them, as did the Badger. They took off their gear and put it in the back of the rig.

"Oh man it's good to get out of this stuff." Rand rubbed his shoulders.

"It's hot bath time as soon as we get home." Elsie stacked the last of her web gear on the pile.

"Oh baby!" Elsie slapped her forehead, "You didn't get your submarine ride."

"I'm too tired for it anyway hon. We can always come back. Maybe I'll put it on a truck and add it to the collection at our dock."

The radios were quiet as they flew their respective planes back to New River, each thoughtful of what they had learned and what they would do next. They touched down just after midnight and drove to the house. Spang was a flurry of excitement at their return and they lavished him with attention. After a hot bath they both went immediately to sleep and didn't wake up for over twelve hours.

One week later, they went to a small chapel outside of New River to marry each other. Rand said the mass then he started the prayer they had written together to say just before their vows.

"God, I know that you do so much for us. You brought this universe here through time for Elsie and I, this we now know. As a symbol of our gratitude, devotion and love for you, we place this simple pine bough on your altar to symbolise…'

Suddenly, both of them went weak. The room around them separated into multi-coloured layers and a thumping wave of sound pulsed deafeningly in their ears. They stood at the altar, reeling and clutching at each other. Through the disorienting vibration and colour they began to see figures in the chapel materialising as people kneeling in the pews. Through the distorted vision and the nauseous waves of shifting hues the congregation stood up and began pointing at the altar. A priest was next to the altar looking at them. The thrumming waves shook them more violently and they were thrown to the ground. The priest reached out his hand to Elsie who tried to take his hand. Just as their finger were about to touch the entire congregation vanished. In a flash of blinding light Rand and Elsie passed out.

The God String

Rand woke looking at the red-carpeted floor of the chapel. He struggled to his feet and staggered over to Elsie.

"Elsie!" She opened her eyes in a daze, then she focused on his face.

"Rand? What the hell was that!"

He held her as they steadied themselves. The dizziness was wearing off.

"I don't know baby. It happened once before." He sat her down by the altar.

She looked at him, "Really? Where? When?"

It only took a minute before they felt completely normal again. Rand told her about the Christmas in England that he had placed a bough on the altar and seen the same thing.

"Have you been to church since then?"

He thought. "No, I haven't."

"Rand I haven't been a believer, but I sure am starting to think these theories about the God string are correct."

"Yes Elsie, I'm sure they are. It must be that in places of worship, He's there. It's such a unifying force that everyone is pulled together even through time. Maybe our string got too close to the string we're from. I…I don't know."

"But this doesn't happen back in the time we came from though and He's there too right?"

"Absolutely. However, there are quite a few unexplained events in the world and quite a few of them coincide with religious activity. I believe it's possible they could be related. Maybe it's because we're the only ones in this creation."

"Or maybe it's like you said, because we are the only other string and it's running so close to the main one, only a nano second away. Oh, it's all too much. Let's just get home." Elsie was deflated. She wanted a beautiful wedding but God had stopped it. "Talk about a sign." She mumbled as they rode home in the Rolls.

That night Rand made every effort to make a romantic evening but Elsie was too much in her head for anything.

"I love you Rand, but right now I need to be alone. There's something knocking on the door of my mind and I need to be silent and alone to hear it."

He told her he understood and let her be. The truth was that he was feeling the same but was too worried about her to give any time to himself.

Elsie sat on the little porch in their room on the second story of the house. Tall pine trees swayed in a gentle breeze and soothed her frazzled nerves.

"I want to marry Rand. He's the last man on earth, but the only man for me." She talked to God out loud, letting her frustration be heard. She had never done anything like this before.

You're married already. She thought she thought.

"But I'm not happy with him. Bob's an asshole and he never loved me. Besides I can never go back there."

Never say never.

"It's too far. I've come too far to go back."

Your children are there.

The God String

"I miss them so much!" She cried now, sobbing in desperation.

They miss you too.

"I want to be with Rand."

Close one door, and another will open.

"Yeah. That's so true."

I love you.

She cried a while longer and thought about the voice that she had just talked with. She knew it was her voice, but it was definitely not her. It was something very familiar, comforting and wise. She got up and blew her nose then went downstairs. Rand was outside sitting on the porch swing. She came and sat with him. He wrapped his arms her and pulled her close. They sat looking in the night, swaying gently in the swing.

"We have to try it Rand. We have to try and go back."

"I know."

"I don't want to lose you."

"You won't."

"Moira doesn't want to lose you either."

"I know. It's one of the most difficult things I've ever had to face. I feel wretched, but I will explain it to her. It's strange. Everything I've been through, the biggest thing I've learned about is love. I love you. Before you I never really understood what love was." He sighed, "It will be hard, but in the end I believe she will know that what we had wasn't real. At the very least she will know that I am in love with someone else. If that makes me the bad guy then so be it."

They talked into the night about Moira and how horrible it would be when one day you wake up and the man your with tells you he doesn't want to be with you any more. It was difficult they knew, but it was survivable. Moira would be okay. Elsie's kids would have to get used to visiting their father and having Rand as a step-dad. It was daunting for Rand to think about. He knew nothing about being a dad, but he already had the answer. Now he knew how to love, and armed with that he knew he could love Elsie's children as much as he loved her. It was clear they had to go back. The next day they set the animals loose on the base with piles of feed in covered areas.

"They should be able to survive for a long time." Rand knew they would be inside the huge fenced parameter of the base, free from predators and with plenty of grass.

"They should be fine." Elsie tried to comfort him.

Concern creased his face. "I made a vow to take care of them."

"And you have Rand. They are probably the healthiest animals in the world. But now we have to leave it to God. He'll take care of them."

Rand turned and looked at Elsie with a smile. "That's a beautiful thing to say."

Elsie changed the subject and switched into commander mode. "We should pack like we're going on a one-way mission; full readiness. We don't know what is going to happen when we use that thing."

The God String

Rand agreed. They could end up anywhere… or when. In the end, they took just about everything they had on Rand's birthday with the exception of the Badger. Satisfied that they had vanquished the threat of the drones, they decided to travel together in just one Osprey. The fear of what they were about to attempt was palpable but neither one mentioned it. They closed up the house and made sure everything was made ready to endure at least one winter without them.

Elsie threw a sheet over the long brocade upholstered couch in the living room. It was the last piece of furniture to be covered. "We might be able to come back. Who knows, maybe the machine won't work."

Rand sighed, "I just don't know baby." He held her close knowing that these might be his last days with her.

The decision of whether or not to take Spang was made quickly.

"But if something goes wrong or anything happens like it did the first time we went into the base, he could get killed Rand." Elsie argued.

"I know hon, but if we leave him here he won't be able to fend for himself at all. He's not a hunter." He reasoned. "Besides, he would chase the chickens and pester the goats. He might get kicked and injured."

"Okay, for better or worse, he comes with us." She conceded.

Rand scoured the base and scrounged up the pieces he needed to make a special backpack that Spang could ride in.

A titanium cage protected him in case Rand landed on his back but let Spang see everything that was going on over his shoulder. The cage was padded and when Spang was clipped in he could still shift about and even curl up and sleep if he wanted. Rand could still pack everything he needed to the sides and underneath Spang's protective cage. Finally everything was done and they loaded the last supplies into the Guardian and headed for the base. When they arrived, they transferred the last of the gear into the Osprey. Rand modelled the pack for Elsie.

"Look hon, its Captain ninja SWAT goat farmer Carter and the strange dog shaped growth on his back, Spang." He tried to lift their spirits with humour but it just didn't work. One consolation was that Spang seemed to enjoy the backpack.

"Okay," Elsie sighed, "it's time to go."

They climbed into the Osprey and once more lifted off for Montauk. The afternoon sky was clear and bright. As they flew along the New Jersey shoreline the spires of New York glittered in the sun. Vegetation had begun to cover the city in a mossy green carpet and the empty buildings swarmed with birds of every description. Fifty minutes later, they set down in the field outside the lighthouse. The lowering sun cast long slanting shadows in the tall grass.

They dressed in black and grey night camouflage with the full body armour pads. It was extra weight but Rand decided to take extra batteries, a solar charger and ammunition. Spang was scooped up and placed securely in the backpack, then they made their way down into the underground facility. Neither one spoke as they travelled the halls of the base and a feeling of anxiety grew.

Spang began to fidget as they entered the door to the cooling platform. "Easy buddy, what's the matter? Something in here you don't like?" Rand stopped and made sure Spang was comfortable, but the little dog was on high alert. Elsie kept her weapon up and she scanned the area as Rand put his pack back on. Bringing the big AA-12 machine-shotgun up to his shoulder he covered the rear and they continued forward cautiously. Spang continued to fuss as they rode the golf cart to the cooling control elevator, but once inside he calmed down.

The control room was exactly the same as they had left it; papers scattered everywhere and two grenades on the table.

"Oops." Elsie said guiltily, "Forgot about those, oh well." As her web gear was already full, she left them there.

"This is going to take some doing."

They set their gear down and let Spang run free. Rand started reading everything about the last experiment and noting what the various controls were set to. Elsie put on some coffee and sat down at another station to do the same as Spang curled up under Rand's chair and went to sleep. Rand brought a manual over to one of the workstations to check the settings on the computer.

"Okay this is the primary magneto monitor… MagSync app is open and running." Rand talked himself through it.

"Elsie, this station is already set up and running from what it looks like."

"Hang on a sec." She got up and went over to another station. "So is this one. All of them are from what I can tell. A lot of these manuals are incomplete like…they don't mention the big collider at all. All of this documentation is for the small TSS or theory studies."

"Wait a sec Els!" Rand slapped himself on the forehead. "The whole system is set exactly to where it was when the nano second shift happened. It never shut off."

"Of course. I bet the knobs are set for that nano second shift too."

"So, we're ready to go?"

"Pioneers again." Elsie sighed.

Rand put Spang back into the backpack and they made their way down the concealed hallway at the back of the room. The large stainless steel door stood open, just as they had left it. Inside was the old nineteen fifties control panel.

"Ready?" Rand looked at her and held back the intense desire to grab her and run from there and never come back no matter what she said.

Elsie saw the look on his face and knew instantly what he was feeling. "Oh baby! I don't want to go!" She threw her arms around him. He kissed her again and again and held her to him as if he was trying to soak her into him.

"I love you Elsie, I always will. Whatever happens I will always try to come to you."

The God String

She cried but her voice stayed steady. "I love you Rand, I will marry you, I will. We will be together one way or the other, in this life or the next, forever."

They kissed again, like it was their last. Then they pulled apart. He placed his hand on the large black start button at the top of the console.

"You know what to do if anything dangerous starts to happen right?"

"Yes, hit the big red stop button."

"Right." He stood tall and squared himself. "I'm just going to make small move to try to go back that one nano second." Whatever happened he had lived well and loved big. He focused on the task at hand believing that this could all turn out really well.

"Ready?"

"If anyone can do this Rand, you can. I believe in you." She held onto the console and nodded. "Ready."

He pushed the button and nothing happened. Elsie looked at him. Rand shrugged, "So yeah, it's already on."

'Right. Okay, try the main knobs.'

Rand turned the left knob slowly to the right. "Right is more, left is less…usually." The hum that continuously permeated the facility began to pulse louder. As he turned the big knob more to the right the pulse quickened, becoming sharper until it was making a quick succession of deep thuds. He continued until it sounded like the rotors of the Osprey on landing; a very rapid drum roll of intense thumps that made his bones vibrate. Then he started on the right knob, turning it slowly to the right.

The depth of the thumps began to rise. The sound went from a deep bass up to a mid-range knocking sound like someone hammering on wood. The pitch continued to rise until it was a high ringing at the edge of hearing. As the sound rose, the room and the console began to separate into colours ever so slightly in his vision.

"More!" Elsie shouted to him over the noise. "It has to go much faster!" Elsie knew all about powerful engines, this thing was just idling. They needed to hit the throttle or it would shake itself and the whole complex apart. She ducked under his arm and put her hands on his and cranked up both knobs until the sharp pounding evened into one solid tone. Then other tones began to emerge, low and high, rising and lowering to join the original one. When the first couple of tones finally matched the original it was like mono had become stereo. The combined tones made the room seem bigger. Then they realised that there were so many more tones that were merging to join in. With each one came a new colour, shimmering over and through the next. Reality was coming unglued. Rand knew that his eyes were working perfectly and that it was not only matter, but space and time itself that were being separated. The sight of it was impossible to comprehend or express yet, he knew what it was.

Elsie had stopped turning the main knobs to the right and was now working on the smaller fine tuning bank of knobs. With each movement the sensation either grew stronger or weaker. Finally the vision and sound coalesced again into one tone. Rand thought it sounded like monks in a monastery chanting 'ohm'. The room became shrouded in a dark grey fog, almost black but closer to the colour of asphalt.

Elsie made one more tweak and suddenly the event seem to stabilise. People suddenly appeared. They were hazy, like looking through a foggy glass shower door. Elsie worked with the smaller dials and they began to get clearer.

They were still in the room but the room looked newer. All around them a maelstrom of light and sound swirled, rumbled, twisted and crackled. They were men, roughly eight of them in military uniforms; a mix of U.S. armed forces. All of them were officers. The men were definitely surprised, some were pointing at them. One man drew a gun and levelled it at Rand.

Rand shook his head at him, 'No.'

"I don't think it would hit us." Elsie's voice cut through the din as if she was inside his head. "Wow, I didn't think I could talk to you!" She said surprised.

"Where did these guys come from?"

"Not where, when. Look at the room, it's practically new."

"So we're back in time?"

"I think we're just passing through. Remember the congregation in the chapel?"

"Yeah, who could forget."

"That's how they see us, just like we see them. We're just a hazy vision that appeared at the controls of the machine."

One of the officer's comrades encouraged him to put the weapon away. Then they stood there looking at each other not knowing what to do.

Suddenly something pushed the military people aside. A man in a wheelchair emerged in the center of the group. He had a semi-ring of white hair around a balding head. His long white smock and pocket full of pens identified him immediately as a scientist. The man was in his mid-fifties. "Remmel!" Rand shouted.

"I see him, no need to shout." Elsie spoke calmly through the swirling cacophony of light and sound. "You were right, he's in a wheelchair."

Remmel approached, leaned in close and, reaching out, passed his hand through them. They flinched but kept their hands on the controls. The man seemed very excited. He pointed at the center of the control panel at a blank area, his hand fluttering through the console. Suddenly Rand understood.

"He's trying to give us instructions."

"Yes I know! Pull the big knob off and put it on that little post there on the left."

Rand looked. There was a small metal post about half an inch tall and at least half that size in a semi-circle diameter poking out of a bare part in the console.

He pulled the left knob straight up, being very careful not to change the setting. It came off easily. He turned it

The God String

over and glanced at the bottom of the knob. It was just as he thought, a brass inset matched the half-moon shape of the post. He tried his best to line it up then pushed it onto the post. The scientist gave him a thumbs up and nodded. Then he twisted his hand left and pointed at his watch, then pointed over his shoulder. He twisted his hand right and pointed toward Rand.

"He says that you go back in time to the left and forward by turning it right." Elsie's voice sounded like she was talking through a fan. Rand was starting to get queasy. The scientist suddenly lurched and looked around him. He gestured at Rand and Elsie with panic on his face.

"Time to go baby!" Elsie had to shout now. The lights danced erratically.

Rand's skin went tingly. Suddenly he was struck by a panicky sensation, like he was in an impending car accident.

"Go Rand! Get us out of here!" Elsie yelled.

The scientist, officers and control room shook violently as the image separated and blurred into an exploding prism of colour.

Rand quickly rolled the knob to the left. The room, the console, light and sound all evaporated into darkness as Elsie screamed 'Raannnn…!' and vanished.

ABOUT THE AUTHOR

Musician, kayak guide, renaissance swashbuckler... Montgomery Thompson like to do fun stuff. Born in Maryland, raised in Colorado, Monte claims Sandpoint, Idaho as his hometown but most of the time he can be found in the hills of Northern Ireland.

Also from Montgomery Thompson

The Second String
The second book in The God String series.

Augmentia
The first book in Augmentia series featuring a subtle but crucial cross-plot- tie-in with The God String series

His works for kids include:

The Christmas Wish Tree
A Celtic faery Christmas tale for middle grade and up.

The Shielding of Mortimer Townes
A middle-grade science fiction adventure!

Online

For more information and links go to:
https://montejthompson.wixsite.com/books

Link to Monte on Facebook at:
https://www.facebook.com/MonteJThompson

The author welcomes exploration of the theories, conspiracy theories and research of people, places and events relating to the accounts in this story.

Printed by Amazon Italia Logistica S.r.l.
Torrazza Piemonte (TO), Italy